A STREAMLINE OF ECHOES

CHAELI SMITH

MILTON & HUGO L.L.C.
4407 Park Ave., Suite 5
Union City, NJ 07087, USA

Website: *www. miltonandhugo.com*
Hotline: *1- 888-778-0033*
Email: *info@miltonandhugo.com*

Ordering Information:
Quantity sales. Special discounts are available on quantity purchases by corporations, associations, and others. For details, contact the publisher at the address above.

Library of Congress Control Number: 2024927158
ISBN-13:   979-8-89285-323-1   [Paperback Edition]
                979-8-89285-322-4   [Digital Edition]

Rev. date: 12/11/2024

Mom and Nana, this one's for you. The depth of this dedication holds a meaning only a few people will begin to understand.

Contents

ACKNOWLEDGMENTS

I would not be where I am today without the light and guidance of God, the support of my family, and many other influences that have impacted my life. Thank you, Jesus, for instilling this gift inside of me to share with the rest of the world. It has been such an honor to write and create such a compelling story to bring to life.

To my beautiful mother, thank you for choosing me. I was meant to be yours, and thank you for keeping all of my secrets, especially this one. To my dad and best friend, thank you for being my partner in crime. You have taught me more than you will ever know. It's because of you that I discovered one of my greatest loves, NC State. More specifically, basketball. To my grandfather, thank you for teaching me everything, especially unwavering love and forgiveness. To my grandmother, thank you for showing me what everlasting kindness looks like. To my uncle Dean, thank you for sharing your love of the ocean with me. Being on the water is something I can't quite describe. You'll always be my personal bodyguard. And lastly, to my Nana, I wish you were here, and I miss you fiercely. I wish I could read it with you, page by page. But I know you already have.

Some of my inspirations include musicians. By reading the lyrics to their songs and listening to their music, I found myself thinking about this project of a lifetime. A few of my favorites include the Zac Brown Band, Luke Combs, Morgan Wallen, Taylor Swift, Post

Malone, Billie Eilish, and Elevation Worship. And when it's time to shift gears, watching NC State basketball brings me infectious joy, fuels my momentum, and inspires my creativity. If you know, you know.

From the very beginning, my close friend Mikayla has supported me every step of the way. Mikayla is one of those once-in-a-lifetime people I am endlessly grateful for! She is the first person I ever told about this project and before I even had the first chapter written. She has listened to all of my ideas and motivated me to where I am today. Her love for reading and writing matches mine, and I will always be thankful for all of her insight and friendship over the past few years. I couldn't have done this without her.

I would also like to say a huge thank you to my publishing team. Emma, Holly, and everyone at Milton & Hugo, thank you for turning my words into a story, something I will be able to look back on forever. Thank you for helping my dreams come true.

Next is a group of young authors, influencers, and speakers who have impacted me throughout the past several years. I enjoy following them and gaining wisdom and knowledge through their work. They are Madison Prewett-Troutt, Sadie Robertson Huff, Jeanine Amapola Ward, and Grace Valentine.

And lastly, I want to acknowledge you, the reader. To whoever is reading this, thank you. Thank you for taking the time to read the first book I have worked tremendously on this past year. If you read it for fun or relate to any of the themes throughout, just know you are not alone and were meant to read it; and in a way, I consider you a friend. These were not the lightest topics to cover yet have been prominent in many people's lives, including mine. They have taught me life lessons and have shown me joys and blessings that I thought were unimaginable. But all of these experiences have shown me that your past doesn't define your future and your life is what you make it. You have one life, so live it to serve others!

DEAR READER

Before you start reading, I just wanted to say thank you for opening the cover and turning the page. Thank you for your support thus far, and what an exciting and wild ride this has been. I wouldn't have believed you a year ago if you told me I would be publishing a book. This is like a pinch-me moment where I am still in complete shock. But when I put pen to paper or in this case when I start to type, everything flows. I love the creative process of bringing your words to life. I've spent hours on end at the computer or even writing on my phone at the beach jotting down all of my ideas and turning them into a captivating story that shows my style as a writer. I'm so grateful for the opportunity to have the chance to be able to share this novel with you.

This book was written to bring awareness to those who were adopted or are thinking about adopting. It is for those who have gone through heartbreak and traumas, those who are finding their way in the world, those who are looking for their person, and those who are trying to start over. Know that you're not alone. And if you remember one thing, know that God is love.

Chapter 1
FLASHBACK

Who am I? I wondered about this all the time. Not just as an adult but as a child too. The question consists of only three words, yet its significance surpasses what most individuals would even attempt to comprehend. When I think of the question, I don't just think about my name or where I live now. I think about all the "what-ifs." I sit and wonder not where I was raised but where I was born and the history that I left behind or maybe something that was waiting for me. I wanted answers, but maybe my past was looking for me too. Maybe moving was a sign or leading me in the right direction. But all I could do was take it day by day, praying that one day I could stop searching.

Is this really my life? Fresh out of graduate school, securing my dream job, moving to Orlando, and buying my first home. What more could a girl dream of, or more importantly I like to say what more could a girl run from or be searching for? Love, stability, happiness, freedom, a fresh start, a place of contentment and comfort. Being twenty-four years old, trying to start over, and moving forward from what I had left behind.

I had exchanged late nights studying for working a nine-to-five, living in a two-bedroom apartment with my best friend for living alone in a three-bedroom house on the beach, and oak trees for palm trees when I moved to Florida. But most importantly I went from being the quiet girl who let everyone walk all over her to an independent woman who makes her own decisions. As much pressure as my job is, nothing is more rewarding than helping those who have gone through similar paths that I have. All I could do was give everything I had, know that God pulled me through, and keep my faith rooted in the foundation I have built my entire life on.

I was adopted from Changsha, China, when I was eleven months old but was raised in Charleston, South Carolina. I loved Charleston, but it was the only place I had ever known and had nothing else to compare it to. My parents always told me that they couldn't envision themselves or me for that matter residing anywhere else. At an early age, I was taught to be focused on my education and to complete my duties as a member of the church we went to. Every Wednesday night and Sunday morning, I was there. When I grew older, I started teaching the younger children and leading Sunday school church, hence one of the reasons I wanted to go into foster care. I love being around kids; they are so intelligent and observe everything. Sometimes they point out details I would have overlooked. They make life more fun and remind us to not take the smaller things for granted.

Charleston was an elegant town with cobblestone streets, pastel-colored houses, and waterfront views. It's every college girl's dream. There were lots of local restaurants that played live music, shops that had the most unique treasures, and views that I would always remember when I came home. I can reminisce about the smell just thinking back to when I was there. And when I close my eyes, my thoughts take me back to the carefree life I once had—from the distinct scent of the beach where the pristine waterway met the sky to the streets packed with people eating every type of food you could imagine.

My parents built our house on the water. It was two stories and a soft pale-gray color that almost looked white. There were white shutters and a wooden door. In the back were a pool, a shed, and the outline of the wooden fort I used to play on but is now covered by a firepit. I remember climbing up the steps of the fort with my stuffed animals. I would sit them in my lap as I slid down the slide or lay them on the ground on top of a beach towel so they could watch me swing. I wish I could go back to not having a worry in the world or having any questions about who I was or where I came from. No stress or responsibilities. I wished I was a kid again.

As much as I loved Charleston, I saw it as my past and present, but not my future. I had lived there my whole life until I moved into college at the University of Miami where I received both my bachelor's and master's degrees. I was pondering on the decision to walk away from all that I had ever known but felt something calling me to do otherwise. I wanted to make a difference to serve Jesus in the way He would have wanted me to. Jesus didn't stay grounded in one place. He traveled all over to serve His people. This was my calling to do the same.

I made this decision because my parents always had me on a short leash. I never did anything bad or misbehaved in high school: no drugs, no boyfriends, and heck, I never to this day have received a speeding ticket. And since I was an only child, I couldn't disappoint them. I went to school, worked, participated in several clubs, and was a youth group leader. Mentoring young adults to love and accept Christ as I have is one of the greatest joys I have ever experienced. I had a 5.0 GPA in high school, had a 4.0 all through college, and always graduated first in my class. My parents were supportive of me but not my dream to go away for college. Just like every other parent, they wanted me to stay close to home. *Close to my roots.* They wanted me to go to college in Charleston like they did and follow in their footsteps. I was being persuaded to become a lawyer like my mother or a dentist like my father.

Even though there is nothing wrong with either of those careers, I wanted something that could be mine. I didn't want to be covered in anyone else's shadow or be compared to others. When I was little, I wanted to be a dentist, a veterinarian, a teacher, or even a business owner. But as I learned about my past, I knew that I wanted to help children who were going to be adopted like me find themselves and let them know that they are not alone. And that there are people out there like *us*.

Being adopted comes with its own pros and cons. One of the upsides is having a unique background and not having the same "my parents brought me home from the hospital" type story and that they were brought home the next day. When I tell people where I was born and that I'm adopted, I get asked more questions than a celebrity trying to run away from the paparazzi. Some of the most common are "What country were you born in?" "How old were you when you were adopted?" "Do you remember anything?" "Have you met or do you know your birth parents?" "Can you speak or write Mandarin?" And the list goes on. I want to crawl into a hole when someone asks me anything. I know it is just natural curiosity, but let a girl breathe. If anyone wants to know these answers, it is me. But I don't. I wish I did. Trust me.

Growing up was difficult at times because the kids in my class would treat me differently. They would tell me my adoptive parents weren't really my parents because we didn't look alike. Some kids even told me my parents don't love me as much because I'm not biologically related to them. I have been asked on more than one occasion how much I cost or if I was traded. I've been told I was adopted because my parents were going to make money. And once in an interview during college, I was asked if I was a communist. I was stunned, to say the least. I have also been discriminated against because of my nationality and skin color. That I wasn't capable of doing certain things or I was expected to exceed at another. Let's just say I have thick skin and don't let those people get to me. It says more about them than it does me. I choose to rise above because I refuse to let people who have no understanding of who I am dictate my identity or determine who they think I should be.

From what my adoptive parents have told me, I am from Changsha, China, and was left at an orphanage. I had a "nanny" who cared and tended after me along with all of the other children. They showed me pictures of the room I used to sleep in. There were cribs lined up across the room until you couldn't fit any more in there. It reminded me of a pet store and how all of the cages are lined up waiting for people to come and tap on the glass thinking about which bird, dog, or cat they want to take home with them. This isn't something you would normally see in America. In one of the pictures, I was sitting in the crib next to another baby. I was grinning from ear to ear, wearing a light-blue coat and navy leggings with flowers on them. In a way, I *remember* that room and everything in it. It's like I could teleport and I would be right back there not knowing any difference. And sometimes I wish I could. I wanted answers. Even if they weren't picture-perfect, at least they would be real and raw and not trying to camouflage themselves from reality.

For the first time in a while, I felt some sense of urgency to want to know the truth, to find if I have any living biological relatives. If so, did they know who I was, or would I just be another stranger they would pass by? I felt again, alone and isolated. Nobody else understood the void I have in my heart trying to comprehend who I am.

China is located in eastern Asia and is one of the highest populated countries in the world. Millions upon millions of people and then there was me. Was I that one in a million? It sure has felt like it at times while other times I ask why? Why me? I am grateful to be in America, but one of my greatest fears is the unknown, and I am the definition of it, so in a way I am afraid of myself. To my knowledge, I have no living biological relatives who could lead me to the right answers. I know my adoptive parents won't have them, and even if they did, there's no guarantee they would tell me. Or the truth anyways. They were supportive when I shared my career decision and goals but also wanted to know why. My mother asked, "Why do you want to do that? Isn't it all sad and depressing?" She sighed. "Don't you want to be close to home?"

My dad questioned, "Addison, we can't prevent her from pursuing what she wants in college, but I'm also curious about what drives your passion to choose that particular career path." He paused. "If that's what you want, you've always gone after your dreams."

I replied, "I want to help children find themselves in this world and to fulfill people's wishes of becoming parents."

My mother interrupted, "James, but she's talked about being a dentist like you for so long."

"But that's the point. I want to do my own thing and walk my own path and not have to be in the shadows of anyone, not even my parents."

They didn't ask me much after that. In fact, I felt it drove a wedge between us. High school graduation came in no time, and then I was moving to Miami. They drove with me to move my stuff in but barely spoke the entire drive. We observed the scenery as palm trees entered in the background, and you could see the ocean for miles. It's like they were avoiding any excitement, which made me reconsider staying in Charleston like they wanted.

But I had to do this for me. I am an adult, and I can't rely on my parents forever. They will always be there for me, and I will be grateful, but I need to have a backbone of my own. I need to prove I can handle living on my own and master the game of survival because not everyone does. I've had countless friends and cousins sacrifice their dreams for their parents or significant other. I have attended several funerals for friends and family who have died from various causes such as illness, car accidents, substance abuse, and suicide. From these experiences, I have come to understand that life is short and can be taken away unexpectedly, but above all, it is a precious gift. It is a gift from God that is irreplaceable, and each person has a unique purpose in His eyes, which should be valued above all else.

Whenever I have a hard day or just need a reminder of my purpose, that my life and impact matter, I refer back to Psalm 23. It is my lifeline. This verse in the Bible is one of the most influential in my opinion. It lets you know that despite your battles or journey to God, He is always with you. And if you obey Him, you will dwell in His house forever.

Chaeli Smith

My birth parents were never mentioned by my adoptive parents. They may not have known them, or maybe they did. From the stories I heard and pictures I saw, I was living at an orphanage until they came to get me. But something never sat right with me. Every time I mentioned going back to visit, they wouldn't be opposed, but they would always change the subject or tell me I should wait until I'm older. Well, how much longer are they going to keep saying that? I'm twenty-four years old after all.

One thing about being adopted is knowing that you will always have questions about who you are, and nobody will ever know your *whole* story. One may know you from birth until you are adopted, and some may know from when you are adopted until you are an adult. But no individual will ever know the full truth, not even you. There are so many questions I have about that gap from when I was born until I turned one. What happened to my birth parents? And most importantly, are they still alive?

Chapter 2
THE BEGINNING OF THE END

It's the middle of May, so it feels like summer in Florida. If you know, you know. It's hot, humid, and impossible not to feel sticky. Most of the time I am wiping sweat off my forehead that later transpires by the breeze of the ocean. I'm not made for the cold, and as much as I love the mountains, I couldn't imagine living anywhere else. When I made the move to Orlando, I bought a house on the beach. It's a modern, charming beach house that overlooks the ocean. It is only one story but has three bedrooms. Even though it came with furniture, I wanted to make the place mine and decorate it with something a little more me. I could tell that the lady before me didn't put any effort into making this a cohesive living space. The furniture was all different colors and textures, the decor on the walls that were left behind looked like she went blindfolded through a thrift store, and whatever she touched, she decorated the house with. It's safe to say I donated it back to where it probably came from.

I spent the first weekend rearranging everything, buying new furniture and decor, and even did some DIY projects. The walls were already an off-white color, so I just added a fresh coat of paint and hung up some pictures and paintings I had done over the years. The walls were the only thing she didn't ruin. I hung some curtains and put a doormat on the front porch along with a wreath and some faux flowers. I can't keep a plant alive, and the Florida heat doesn't help. I had a seasonal kitchen towel draped on the handle of the stove, just like Mother and Grandmother had always done. And I added a vase with tulips sitting in the kitchen next to the blender. There was another vase in the dining room that matched the china that I bought with me from South Carolina. I added new rugs throughout the entire house—one in the living room, one in the dining room, and one in my bedroom. Another thing about me is I hate walking barefoot on cold floors. It feels like walking on glass but ten times worse.

I had bought new bedding, organized all of my belongings, and scrubbed the entire house. There was still a lot to do, but I was content with what I accomplished alone in one weekend. To make the evenings go by, I would either sit on the balcony and paint, curl up on the couch with a good book, go on a beach walk, or bake something new. Now, my house is 97 percent complete. The house is fully furnished, all of my belongings are unpacked, and I even added some outdoor furniture and a swing. And even though it wasn't finished, it was something I am proud of and that was mine. It was home.

Chaeli Smith

As I stare at the ocean, just a few feet from my house, I get an alarming phone call. I answered, and my boss said, "Adaire, we have a 911 case that needs your attention immediately. I will send you the details of where you need to arrive. Get here stat."

I thought to myself, *What type of case is this emergency that I must go to on a Saturday morning?*

I am the assistant director of foster parent recruitment in Orlando. When I was one year into graduate school, I applied for the heck of it. It was more of a "If I get it, I do, or if I don't, I don't" situation. I like the office I work at. It has two stories, has a large parking lot, and is close to where I live. I have my own office on the first floor. It's a good size with a window. I tried to make it feel like home by adding pictures, both of my diplomas, a lamp, a chair, pillows, and even my own minifridge. It is on the same side as all of the other administration. I hear lots of sidebar conversations about someone's date the night before, if someone had died, or just talking about what they did during the weekend. The printer goes off every five minutes, and I can see all of the people who park and wander inside to the front desk. My coworkers are nice, and even though I have lived here since January, it feels like I have been here for ages. Charleston will always be where I grew up, but I want to find my forever home—a place that could be mine with no strings attached. Maybe it is Charleston, or maybe it is here. I just want to live somewhere and feel like I belong.

I raced inside, put on some makeup, changed clothes, and jumped in the car. Even though my gas was about empty, the office was only about a five-minute drive. My mind was swarming with hundreds of possibilities of what it could be. Did it have to do with children whose parents passed away, those who came from a different country, children who were lost? It could also be children who were abused by their parents or those who had just run away. I had no clue but at the same time prepared for the worst. Being involved with children who have no home is always hard because they are so young and have no control of where life takes them, and some of them may even blame it on themselves.

Of course, traffic was backed up. I swore I hit every red light. It's like they were turning red on purpose. Next, there was a traffic jam and a car accident. Then finally I pulled up to the office, and my boss was waiting for me in the parking lot.

Robin Cordell was the director of foster parent recruitment. She was a shorter woman with dirty-blonde hair and always wore red lipstick. She was blunt and said whatever came to mind but was always nice to me, and we would laugh when we were together. She would always end up in my office at some point during the day. She would sit with her legs crossed, talking about everything from the case we were working on to how her husband got on her nerves the night before and how she made him sleep on the couch. She has a daughter my age named Maggie. She lives in Vermont with her boyfriend, Vince. They have been dating for about a year. Every time I ask her about them, she changes the subject. She said she likes them together but knows Maggie could do better. She feels like Maggie is settling for comfort rather than what she deserves.

We always knew how to make the best out of some of these situations. I knew this was a serious matter because one, it was the weekend and two, she was pacing back and forth in the parking lot. She says she does this so her legs don't become numb from the horrible news.

She yelled, "Come on, get in the car! We have to get going! The ambulance is meeting us there," as she hopped in the driver's seat. She drives a silver Honda Pilot, and every time I get in her car, there are always wrappers from Reese's cups and empty Diet Coke bottles rolling on the floor. Sometimes I think to myself, *Is this all she lives off?* But I would understand why with some of the things we see on a daily basis.

I sat in the passenger seat next to her, moving trash out of the way, and asked, "Do you have any details about this case? How urgent is it?"

"I know about as much as you do," she said as she took a swig of Diet Coke and left a lipstick stain around the rim of the bottle.

She always drove with candy in her left hand while her right hand was on top of the wheel. She would always fly through yellow lights so we wouldn't be stuck longer than we had to. She told me once that yellow is her least favorite color because of this, and every time she sees someone wearing yellow, it makes her feel rushed. She also hates bees and yellow jackets; this proves her point. So I've learned three things about

Robin since working with her this year: (1) She hates the color yellow. (2) She hates being rushed even though we are half the time. (3) She lives off Diet Coke and Reese's peanut butter cups. And to throw another thing in there, she truly is a good boss, even if she is tough and hard to get through sometimes. She cares about her employees and the people that we serve. We had gone the back way, so traffic wasn't bad, and pulled up to the airport as an ambulance and another social worker were waiting for us.

We jumped out of the car, and Robin called out, "What in the world is going on?"

The social worker on this case, Sam Lloyd, said, "There was a plane crash coming from China, and the parents didn't make it. They had two daughters. One was three, and the other was eleven months old. We don't know much else."

"Happy Saturday to us." Robin let out a big sigh.

All I heard was "from China" and "eleven months old." Once again there was another sign, trying to tell me something. Is this déjà vu?

I heard the dispatcher through the walkie-talkie say, "We have both children in our custody and are bringing them to CPS. Both parents are confirmed dead. Both children are fine. They were on a separate plane, and it just landed. Copy, over."

Oh gosh, those poor children. Their parents were gone in just a matter of minutes. I was told that they were moving to the States due to the husband's career and to make a better life for their family. Sacrifice. Due to spacing, their parents hired a nanny to fly with them. That's all she was hired for; she took the next flight out to China. It's daunting to think that their parents packed and moved across the world for them to just end up in a plane crash. The only thing good to come out of this is that their children are alive and healthy.

I stood there on the cement with flashbacks of every memory I tried to forget but remembered anyways of my days in China at the orphanage. My mind traveled back to when I was a baby. It was like lights flashing but instead of bright lights, pieces of my memory coming back. In the back of my mind, I saw a crib and a woman in her late thirties. I couldn't make her face out, just a blurry image trying to come clear. The last memory that faded out was coming home from the airport. The next thing I knew, I was in America.

I was trying to piece together what had happened to me. I remember the orphanage but had no recollection of my birth parents, but I knew one thing. There was a reason why they gave me up, and maybe they were still living. Maybe when I remember something, it's a sign to not stop until I have all the pieces together.

We were waiting for the security guards to bring the children to us so they could be evaluated and placed in a temporary home. I couldn't help but want to cry. I thought to myself they are only three and almost one (I was eleven months old when I was adopted from China). They flew to a strange country on an airplane without their parents and now are never going to see either one of them again. I know when they get older, they will have so many questions. And I will be one of the only people to know most of their story, or at least the beginning. Unlike me, who knows pieces of my story, but am sure part of it is a lie. At this point, I don't know what pieces are even included.

The security guards approached us with both children. One was carrying the three-year-old. She had gorgeous black hair, piercing black eyes, and warm golden skin. She was wrapped in a light-pink blanket with her head resting on his shoulder. The other guard had a baby carrier that was covered because the baby was asleep. She was asleep, knowing that when she woke up little did she know her whole world had changed for the worse. The three-year-old's name was Lucy, and the other baby's name was Isla.

Lucy was shy but walked over to me and let me pick her up. She was as sweet as you could imagine and had fallen back asleep with her head on my shoulder while grasping my hair with her fingers. A medic approached to make sure she was okay. She squeezed onto me, so I went with her, just like she once did to her mother. She still had muscle memory. As she was sitting on the stretcher, a tall (and handsome, I might add) gentleman approached. He was around 6'3", was tan, had dark hair, and had a piercing smile. He had on a collared button-down shirt, dress pants, loafers, and a badge that had the hospital logo.

"Hi, I'm Michael Bennett. I'm a pediatrician and international recruiter." He nodded and shook my hand.

"Pleasure to meet you. I'm Adaire Carter, the assistant director of foster parent recruitment." I paused, not knowing what to say next, but was also avoiding eye contact.

"This case is sad, isn't it? I mean, how these girls are never going to understand the sacrifice their parents made for them?"

"But they will know one day when they are older. I pray that they find the perfect adoptive parents."

"Me too. Were you on call today?"

"I normally am off on weekends except for emergent cases that Robin needs my help on."

Our conversation continued as the medics were doing what they needed to do. We waited for Lucy to get evaluated, and then she clung to me once again as if she knew me in another universe. I felt in a way she was just like me coming to a new country and clinging to one person. Dr. Bennett proceeded to walk beside me as I was carrying Lucy back to where Isla and Robin were waiting. Next, Dr. Bennett checked on Isla to make sure she was okay. He woke her up, but she was a pleasant baby and didn't cry.

I hadn't had a nice conversation with a guy since college. He wasn't my boyfriend, but we had a fling. We talked for about seven months and met through mutual friends. At first, things were going well. We saw each other often but never went on official dates. He never asked, and neither did I. I didn't want to sound desperate or needy, as he would say. We mainly talked on the phone or texted. I would ask how his day was, and all I received was one- or two-word answers. He forgot about Valentine's Day and was too drunk to come to my birthday dinner in January. He had more important things to do but tried to make it up to me like always and buy me flowers and write me a note—a note that held nothing but failed promises and expectations. All of the flowers he gave me died within a few days. Probably due to the lack of water or he would buy them three days in advance. He would leave them in his car as he chugged down a bottle of whiskey.

The girls I went to college with asked why I put up with it. I didn't really give an answer, but I also didn't defend him because I knew they were telling the truth. He was sweet one day telling me I deserved everything this world had to offer, that he wanted to build a house and start our lives together, that he wanted to marry me and have children. Then he would pause after he nursed his third glass of liquor and tell me how horrible I was, that I was spoiled and didn't deserve anything good to happen to me, that I ruined his life and how selfish I was for interfering with his career. It was me—I was the root of everything. He had to blame anyone but himself for self-sabotage.

He would get angry if I didn't answer the phone some days. Then the next day he would tell me to paint and to call him when I could because I deserved happiness. He wanted to control me like a robot. If I was grocery shopping, he would threaten me to grab his liquor of choice that week or else. Sometimes it was whiskey; maybe it was beer? Whatever would

Chaeli Smith

satisfy his misery in the moment. He shoved me against the wall in my dorm while screaming at me, saying I was the worst thing to come into his life. Once he had me in a chokehold, and the only reason I didn't lose consciousness was because my roommate and best friend, Ellie, walked in, hit him with a lamp, and called the cops. After that, I never saw him again. I had a restraining order, but that didn't mean he was going to listen. Even though I never physically saw him, I could hear his voice. I had nightmares for weeks and couldn't sleep alone. Ellie made every night a sleepover after that. Sometimes I could feel him standing over me and watching me, that he would tease or grab me, call me names and threaten to choke me. I could smell the booze and cologne all in one. I spent the following week going to therapy sessions and still go once a month just to catch up.

' Since then, I haven't been able to make eye contact with any man. I couldn't be *that* girl again. The girl who fell for the guy who sweet-talked her back into an abusive relationship. Even though it wasn't official, it felt like I was living in a horror movie that wouldn't end no matter how many times I wanted to press the pause or off button. He broke his restraining order trying to follow me on campus. The cops later found out that he had a gun and pocketknife on him. He was also taking drugs and had prior convictions that resurfaced. He is now in jail. And for good. The nightmares slowly turned into hopes of finding something *new*.

My focus cleared, and my shoulders relaxed. "You seem really good with kids. I know they must love you."

"And I love them back. Being around children is such a gift and the main reason I love what I do. Being around sick children isn't easy. But once you get them up and running, it is the most rewarding thing I get to experience. I can see Lucy really likes you."

"She is just the sweetest but has no idea how her world has changed in just a matter of moments. I love kids. They are such a joy to work with even though a lot of their stories are sad and traumatic. Kids are resilient. They are stronger than we think and give them credit for."

We loaded up both girls in Robin's car and drove them to their placement for the next few days. Dr. Bennett followed us the whole way. The drive was about thirty minutes west, and I noticed that we got farther and farther away from the ocean, and the smell of salt air slowly faded right behind it.

Of course, Robin noticed that I was talking to Michael, so she had to add, "I saw you hitting it off with Dr. Bennett. He's really attractive. You should go for it."

"We were just making small talk about the case. I'm sure he has a girlfriend or is married."

Rolling her eyes, she replied, "You won't know until you ask, girl, and I didn't see a ring!"

"I am not asking him out. We are working on this case together, which will probably end within a few days, and then I'll never see him again."

In a sarcastic voice, she said, "Well, if I were you, I would want to see him after just a few days. Girl, he's handsome. Are you blind? And he was *so* into you."

"I don't know if making small talk with someone means you're into them. Besides, we are both busy with our careers."

I found Michael to be quite handsome, and I noticed that we share similar interests and lifestyles and enjoy working with children. But that doesn't mean that we are soulmates. Am I right? Part of me wanted to ask him to grab coffee or walk on the beach one morning, but at the same time, I feared starting something new and getting hurt soon after. I was running away from love, not running into it.

I thought to myself, *Here comes someone else into my life that will eventually leave.* I've never had that constant person in my life that I feel is here to stay and for the right reasons. So therefore, I have all four walls up and several barriers guarding those walls so that nobody can ever hurt me again, or it will seem less painful when they leave.

Upon our arrival and as we pulled in, a woman stood on the front porch, waving and pacing back and forth. Eventually, she came to meet us in the driveway. She seemed welcoming and excited to help out. She greeted us and introduced herself by saying, "Hello, I'm LeeAnna Price. I guess I will be fostering these two girls for a few days." She smiled and shook all of our hands before calling her husband, Richard. He was about a head taller than her, had an easy demeanor and smile, and introduced himself. Robin, Michael, and I introduced ourselves and proceeded to thank them for taking in the girls until we could sort some things out. Robin mentioned that they were interested in adoption but wanted to foster first.

Their house was a two-story modern-style home that was a light-blue color with a two-car garage. There was a swing on the front porch with all of the flowers blooming to their peak. You could see the pink roses from the mailbox. It was very comforting riding up to it, and I could definitely see the girls living here, part-time anyways. And as for LeeAnna and Richard, they seemed like a great couple. They had full-time jobs, lived in a nice neighborhood, and were as friendly as you could ever hope for—just a few qualities all parents should have. They were probably in their early forties or so, and Robin had said that she had interviewed them a few months ago and would give them a call when she needed them.

They walked with us toward the car with the girls in the back asleep. We opened the trunk and retrieved the two suitcases that they had with them when they left from China. One of the suitcases was a light pink and the other a butter yellow. There was a floral sticker that said *Lucy* on the pink one and a rainbow sticker that said *Isla* on the yellow one. We were all trying to be as quiet as possible to not wake them.

LeeAnna said, "Well, they are beautiful, and we will do everything we can to make this their home for the time being."

Richard proceeded with saying, "We've always loved children but got married a few years ago and felt it was too late to have our own children but would love to foster or adopt."

Who would have thought that all the belongings that these two girls owned were in their small suitcases? In each of the suitcases, there were several changes of clothes, toys, bottles, snacks, medicine, copies of their birth certificates and other documentation, and some books that were written in Mandarin. You could tell that their mother really thought this trip through and packed the necessities. The foster parent recruitment center provided cribs and car seats for each of them.

Michael and I walked the girls in with Robin. I rocked Lucy after we fed them dinner, and Michael did the same to Isla. I read Lucy some books, and we played with dolls, maybe just like her mother once did. She hugged me tight, and I was doing everything I could to hold back tears. She then hugged Michael, and he swooped her up and gave her a bear hug. Lastly, Robin said her goodbyes. I've never seen her soft side, and she claims she doesn't have one. I wish I could take them both with me. We talked about how sad everything was about the parents, but I knew that God had a bigger plan—one much bigger than the eye could see, a plan that only He could see. Once we got them settled in, it was time to head out. It was hard leaving them knowing I may never see either one of them again. I thought about where they will be next year, in five years, in ten years, and so on.

Robin, Michael, and I all walked out and waved to LeeAnna and Richard. I knew that the girls were in good hands.

"It was great meeting and working with you today. You're the real deal," Michael said as he shook my hand, walking back to his car.

"Same to you. Best of luck with everything. I hope that these girls get all of the love they deserve."

"Me too. You were great with them. Lucy didn't want you to leave."

"It was great to see you again, Michael," Robin said.

"You too, Miss Robin, take care." He nodded as he closed the door to his truck.

I thought to myself, *Robin and Michael knew each other prior to this case? Did she call him on purpose to try to set me up with him? Does Robin know about my past too? What about Michael? Are they working together? What is going on? Should I brush it off or be scared?* Once again, my guard was up. And this is exactly why I can't trust anyone, not even my own boss.

When we got in the car, I looked at Robin and asked, "So how long have you known Michael?"

"I've known of him for a few years. He's only twenty-eight years old, you know? But I've only worked with him twice prior to this. And at first, I didn't even think about setting you up, if that's what you are referring to."

"At first? What do you mean?"

"Well, until I saw you two together and having a conversation, I didn't think much of it. I knew he was good at what he does, so I gave him a call. But after seeing you two today, I can tell he's into you. And he's single, FYI," she said with smirk.

"How on earth do you know that? Did you ask him?"

Trying not to give herself away, she said, "Well, right before you started here, I was working with him on another case, and we were talking, and I asked if he was married. He said he hadn't dated since early college. He was too focused on school and his career to settle down. Sounds like someone else I know." She gave me a hard stare. She knew what she was doing; she couldn't fool me. I did think it was intriguing how many similarities we had from just two conversations.

When we were riding back to the office, I remembered that I too was just handed to some lady at an orphanage with only the clothes on my back and nothing more. But who handed me to the lady at the orphanage? I then realized I needed to know who dropped me off and who met this person at the door. Was it planned, or did some stranger find me off the street and decide what to do with me? Or did one of my birth parents drop me off? If so, they either wanted me to be safe or did not want me at all. In the end, they handed me off to some stranger to hopefully take care of me. And that's all I ever wanted, to feel *safe* and that I belonged.

Chapter 3
SHE'S ONLY THREE

The next day, I received a follow-up email regarding the case about Lucy and Isla. This is routine, so I didn't think anything of it. It contained information about them and all of the information regarding their parents. The names of their parents who died in the plane crash were Luis and Sonia Le-Guin. They were from Changsha, China. I had to do a double take. *Changsha?* That's where I am from, or so what my adopted parents told me. I was going to brush this case under the rug, but something in my gut told me that this case is far from over. There is more to this story than anyone is going to be able to come to terms with. I felt in a way that I was also connected to it. I also felt that Dr. Bennett wasn't finished with his role either.

I spent the rest of my Sunday going to church, doing some household chores, and spending time walking on the beach. A few of the ladies I work with go to the same church, and we sit together. On occasion, we will grab lunch afterward, but most of the time I am ready to get home. I enjoy spending Sunday afternoons on the beach or curled up with a good book. I guess it is because I have social anxiety, but another part of me fears that *he* is watching, that out of nowhere he will come and grab me and take me with him. That was one of my biggest fears. I couldn't control him, and I didn't want to. I just wanted him to forget about me.

As I was walking on the beach hearing the ocean talk to me, I couldn't help but think about Lucy and Isla. Are they happy? Did they get enough sleep? Are they eating? How are they adjusting to this new American culture and lifestyle? I know I'm thinking like a parent.

When I think back on my own life and how I grew up, I was born in China but raised with American customs, so that's all I knew. Isla would be just like me, not knowing any better. Lucy might have some memories of their mom and dad and how she was raised. I know she's only three but is old enough to talk and even speaks some Mandarin. How much did she remember? Does she remember her home in China? Did she remember her parents? This was another thing about dealing with cases with young children; you can't go based off their memory. There are some things in life that just can't come to mind no matter how hard you search for them in your brain. And then there are certain memories or details that you will never forget and that every time you think about it, it feels like you are there living it all over, whether you want to or not.

LeeAnna had reached out to me later in the day to let me know that the girls were doing great but still adjusting and that Lucy was asking for me and Michael. I couldn't help but feel comfort in knowing that she remembered me or if I wanted to start crying knowing everything that had happened. It's like *she knew.* Part of me wanted to drive to see them, but I don't know what Robin would think. I didn't want to cross any boundaries or get into any legal trouble.

I told LeeAnna that I was so thankful for her and Richard and all they had done and I would hopefully get to see them all again. She ended the conversation with "Please come and visit anytime and bring Michael." I couldn't help but think, did she think we were a couple? I had literally met this man yesterday. She sounded just like Robin but in a good way.

I called Robin, and she answered, "Is this about Michael? Do you want his contact information? I would be more than happy to provide it." I wanted to smack her through the phone.

"Well, not exactly, but LeeAnna called and said that Lucy asked for us. I am honored, but at the same time, I know we probably aren't allowed to see them again."

"Well, technically no. But if she is wanting you both, since you gave her comfort, I would allow y'all to go see them, but I would need to go with you."

"Oh gosh, really?" I said, trying not to sound too excited—over the girls, not Michael.

"I will give Michael a call and set up a time that we can all go by for a follow-up."

"Okay, just let me know. Thank you, Robin."

I couldn't fall asleep. I was lying in bed and couldn't help but think about Lucy and Isla and if they felt alone, comforted, or even just scared. I also thought this was God's way of connecting us together for a reason. I mean, how big of a coincidence is it that I'm from the *same* part of China they are? I know China is a huge country but specifically *Changsha* and how Isla is eleven months old, just like I was when I first came to America with my adoptive parents. I feel that our stories are parallel in another lifetime trying to connect, trying to reveal the truth.

I know our situations are different, and I wouldn't wish losing your parents in the way they did. But I still didn't know anything about my birth parents, and I may never know at this point. My life is like a puzzle; not all of the pieces are there but completed enough for me to see what it is going to turn out like. But at other times, I feel like someone takes it and drops it from the top of the stairs and I have to put it back together again. The thing is, once I pick up a puzzle, I don't like to put it down until it is finished.

Monday mornings always drag. Don't you just hate the feeling when your alarm goes off in the morning and you hit snooze and it just keeps going off until you make yourself get up? Once that stage passes, I'm awake. I was in an okay mood, and then I received a text from a number I didn't recognize. One name came to mind, Michael. I thought to myself, *I am going to kill Robin*, but I love her at the same time. The text read,

> Hey Adaire! It's Michael, Happy Monday! Robin gave me your number and she mentioned that LeeAnna called you about Lucy wanting to see us. She said for us to pick out a day this week to go there to see the girls. Just let me know your thoughts, I hope you don't think that this is creepy or weird. Maybe I should just stop typing, anyway I hope you have a great day!

I could believe that he just sent that or that I read it. I wondered what Robin told him. Did she call or text him? Did she tell him to text me? Did she tell him what to say? I mean, I wasn't mad about it. After thinking about what to write back and thank goodness I have my read receipts off, I texted back,

> Hey Michael! It was great meeting you the other day. Any day this week works for me, did Robin give you any more details regarding the time? I hope you are having a great start to the week!

Did I really just send that? Oh well, maybe he won't respond or read it and forget to respond. I don't even know why I am freaking out. I mean, we are working on a case together, and I hardly know this person. For all I know he hates children. We may just see each other once more and part ways. Robin knows that I have never had an official boyfriend. Yep, I said it, never. Not even in college. I was too busy studying, working, and traveling to do anything else. I would hang out with my group of friends, go to basketball games, or go out to dinner; but there was no dating. I didn't have time to, and I wouldn't count my fling as anything. Now that I am settled down, I am more open to dating than I was a few years ago. I just want a person who loves Jesus more than anything, understands me, has a curiosity and love for life, and serves others. I also have another list, but that is all I'm sharing for now. Easy to find, right? Wrong.

As I was about to get ready, my phone rang. I was about to jump out of my skull. It was Robin. I am thankful it was her but also hoped it was Michael. I wouldn't have known what to say if it was him or if I would be awkward or just acted casually like we work together. I mean, we technically do.

When I picked up the phone, Robin said, "So did you and Michael pick a day yet?"

"I told him it didn't matter to me, and do you have any idea regarding the time?"

"Well, LeeAnna said any day, even the weekend, and since she works from home, we could stop by anytime and to just give her a heads-up."

"I'll let you know if I hear from Michael."

And then he called. "Hey, Robin, Michael is calling me."

She said in a sarcastic voice, "Well, I'll leave you to it. Call me with the details." She hung up before I can even answer.

Should I answer or let it go to voicemail? Without knowing I did, I pressed the answer button.

"Hello."

"Hey! How are you?"

"I'm good for a Monday. What about you? Are you working today?"

"I'm good. I'm about to head in and work until six. Monday through Wednesday is the longest part of my week."

"Same here. I normally work late the first part of the week and get off early on Friday and have the weekend."

"So about Lucy and Isla . . ."

"Yeah, so Robin called and said that LeeAnna works from home, and we can go anytime."

"Okay great, what about Friday? Since we both get off early? We can stop and see the girls, and afterwards, would you want to go grab a drink and talk?"

A date? I've never been on a real date. I know I'm twenty-four and graduated college, and I've never been on a real date. Sure, I've talked to a few guys here and there, but I lose interest and put my guard up. I also wouldn't say I went on dates when I talked to my ex-situationship, because he never asked me to go on dates. But I wouldn't count this as one? Does he think it is one? I want to say yes, but I'm so used to saying no. So I responded, "That sounds great. I'll let you know when I get off."

"So is that a yes to drinks too?"

"It's a yes to both." I felt the sensation of blushing on my cheeks—something I thought I would never experience again. It brought me back to the times I would feel tingling after he would hit me.

"Great, I'll call you later. I know we both have to go to work. Have a great day."

"Definitely! Have a good day. I will talk to you later."

"Bye. See you soon!"

So I guess I'm going on a date Friday? Well, this is news to me. I didn't want to tell anyone to get their hopes up, especially my best friend, Ellie. Ellie and I have been friends since kindergarten. We went through elementary, middle, and high school together. We were even roommates in college during undergrad. She moved to New York to pursue her dream job in marketing. We still talk every week and FaceTime, but it's not the same. She's been dating a guy named Tyler for three years and always tries to set me up with his friends. But I'm either not interested or too busy with life to go out.

When we were in elementary school, we would ride bikes up and down the street and had no concept of time. We were inseparable—sleepovers every weekend, vacations. Her family became mine. We've traveled all over together from Hawaii to the Bahamas. She is my biggest fan, and I am hers. We always want each other to win in life. She was one of those once-in-a-lifetime friends that you just can't replace. And no matter how much time has passed, we pick right up where we left off.

As I pulled up to the office, I had to remember to not give anything away. I thought about something else to make the redness on my cheeks vanish. I can't let Robin know I'm going out with Michael Friday night, unless he's already told her. I guess I'll know when I see her this morning.

When I got out of my car, I saw Sam Lloyd. He's the social worker from Lucy and Isla's case. Something told me that he was here for a reason, and it wasn't good.

Sam waved at me as I was getting my bags out of the car. I responded, doing the same as I went over to say hello.

He then approached me by asking, "So what are your thoughts on the case? I saw you and Michael talking to each other about it. He seems to be into you."

Trying to play it off, I replied, "I think that this is a sad case I will never be able to forget. And as far as Dr. Bennett goes, he was asking me about the case and nothing more."

"Chill, Michael is a good friend of mine. He asked me for your number, and I told him Robin would have it. So did he text you?"

"Yes, but only about the time we were going to meet at LeeAnna's house to visit the girls." I took a deep breath, trying to think of what to say next.

Thank goodness Robin pulled up and interrupted the conversation. She got out of the car, and as usual, Diet Coke in one hand and her briefcase and bag in the other. She hollered good morning to Sam and me as we walked toward her.

She yelled, "What are you two waiting for? We have work to do!"

Sam asked, "What do you mean?"

"The pilot thinks that the plane crash wasn't an accident, and the FBI is meeting us at the airport. We need to be there in half an hour."

There was a lot of information to be prepared. All of the paperwork was packed along with our laptops and briefcases. As I was collecting my things, all I could think about was what type of person calculated such a plan to make a plane crash, and what was their motive? Was this person or group of people out for revenge or felt absolutely nothing inside them for them to be okay with killing one hundred people? Whoever did this was a criminal mastermind and had the ability to know or learn the mechanics of how to fuse out an aircraft—all while not getting caught.

As we loaded up the trunk, there were candy wrappers trying to fly out. Robin drove, and Sam insisted that I sit in the front beside her. Little did he know how Robin drives. I hope he had breakfast or didn't get motion sickness. Robin needs to have barf bags sitting beside all of the seats. We didn't even leave the parking lot before Robin hit the curb. And not lightly. She treated it as if it was just a small rock you could barely see.

Sam yelled, "What in the heck, Robin! I about flew out through the windshield."

"Just hold on and we'll be there in ten minutes."

This was probably Sam's first and last time riding in the car with Robin. He looked terrified the rest of the way, and I couldn't help but giggle.

After what felt like an eternity, we pulled up to the airport. We went through security and were escorted toward the back. There was a tram waiting to take us to the location where the FBI was. Officers and detectives were everywhere doing research and collecting any evidence they could harvest from the plane crash. Or what was left of it. I was told that there was a rescue team out looking for any survivors and to gather what they could of any remains of the plane or the passengers' belongings. They had brought in all they could find. There were sections of the room taped off with evidence organized and lying on the ground. There was everything from parts of the plane, suitcases, and even remnants of power lines.

One thing in particular caught my eye as I was walking past everything, in utter disbelief and heartbreak for these people and their loved ones. In the corner, there was a vintage book written in Mandarin. The book was nearly destroyed, and the pages were so delicate I felt the need to hold my breath just standing there. I went over to one of the officers and asked if there was a name in the book, telling us who it belonged to. He then gave me a pair of latex gloves and walked over with me. Then he gently picked up the book and told me to flip through the pages to see if anything jumped out at me. Even though I didn't know how to read Mandarin, it looked like a journal of some sort. Then on the last page there was a photo of a young couple, about sixteen years old or maybe a little older. The picture was torn in half but just clear enough to make out their faces. At the bottom right corner, the name *Le-Guin* was written.

It's like time froze, and my world was spinning. That journal belonged to Lucy and Isla's mother. Since it was written in Mandarin, no one could translate it. Part of me felt like it was speaking to me, trying to tell me something about the girls and also about who I was. I called Sam over, who then contacted a translator to type out what each page said and confirmed that we would have it by Friday. Today is Monday. My thoughts will be lingering on what was written on those pages. The pages aren't going to change if we get them today or a week from now. I am just aching to know, and this may be the key to unlocking an alarming mystery.

One of the detectives found a pill bottle. There was no name on it, and the label was faint, so we couldn't decipher what the medication was or who it was prescribed to.

I asked, "Is there a way to see what pharmacy this was from since the bottle is a unique color?" The officer nodded in agreement. They took photos of the bottle and swabbed the inside but left everything as it was so further evidence wouldn't be erased. They were meticulous in their movements to avoid breaking or altering any of the remains of the plane crash. Picture after picture and swab after swab, and after what felt like an eternity, we were released.

I felt like I learned so much but was still stuck on the first page. We were waiting for the book to be translated into English and for the results of the pill bottle. What if? What if the book comes back to just be a diary of a young woman or couple and the pill bottle was just a standard drugstore medication for allergies or headaches? The possibilities are endless, but there is only one answer. No matter how long it takes, I am willing to risk everything. These girls deserve better. I want to advocate for them and their story. I just wish someone did the same for me.

Chapter 4
THE DAYS ARE LONG, BUT THE YEARS ARE SHORT

It's been over two decades since I was adopted. Two decades of wondering who I am. I've accepted who my parents raised me to be, but there is still a void in my head, a feeling that there is more to my story. It is too simple and good to be true. My mind always goes back to those boxes I have in the attic that store the paperwork from my adoption along with other items my birth parents have kept in their original condition— from my framed birth certificate to the toys they bought me. I haven't messed with anything, mainly because I know that if I find something, I will not put it down.

What are you thinking, Adaire? You're not going to find anything. You overthink 99 percent of the time. But something in my gut was telling me that I should open the boxes. So Thursday night I crept in the attic; and underneath the Christmas decorations, there they were, in a storage bin covered with a thin layer of dust, looking at me, knowing I couldn't resist. They held the answers that could help me unlock the truth.

There were three clear storage bins that were labeled *China.* I opened the first box, and it was nothing but files upon files of paperwork. The next one had more files and a binder of the itinerary my adoptive parents used the three weeks they were in China. The last box had the outfit they first saw me in, my baby gown, and more sentimental items most parents would keep in a box, and one day you might go through it. For most people, this is a collection of memories that they will hold on to and pass down for generations to come; but for me, it was evidence—memories intertwined with the unknown truth.

I started with the first box, which had nothing but boring files. I am thankful they are in folders and most of them are written in English. I made three piles: one that could be a lead, the second with papers I might use, and the third is basically useless and tells me nothing. However, I will not throw anything away. Keep the memories, right? I mean, if my parents held on to them this long, they must have some significance.

I set aside papers on my adoptive parents, the orphanage I was staying at, and the adoption agency. I didn't want to write on the original copies, so I took notes on a legal pad and stuck sticky notes everywhere. I am so skeptical that everything could be a clue. But at the same time, what if this is all for nothing? After reading until my eyes were about to pop out of my skull, I had a few main points written out. My adoptive parents had been trying to adopt for a few years, I knew that I had a nanny who looked after me, and according to my parents, I was left on the steps of my orphanage. There were a few things I needed to discover first:

1. Contact the orphanage I was supposedly left at.

2. See if the nanny in all of the pictures is still alive.

3. Complete a DNA test to see if I have any living biological relatives.

As I lay in bed, I thought about my past and what I needed to do to uncover the truth. But my girl brain was about to throw up thinking about my "date" tomorrow with Michael. I didn't know if Michael asked to go out to talk about work, to get information about the plane crash, or to get to know *me*. The real me. I mean, the truth that I knew. I feel like if I let him all the way in, he might run away. I was scared of what could be and all of the judgment.

I texted Robin to ask if I could buy and bring anything for the girls. She told me I could donate or contribute any clothing, toys, food, or essentials that they could possibly need during this transition period. There was a list of their sizes for clothing and shoes, groceries for dietary needs, and even their allergies.

In most cases, I don't ask about this because we only do the drop-offs, and then the children are placed in a permanent situation, or I have little to no interaction with them. But this case was near and dear to my heart.

And something that made me rediscover my yearning to know my own story.

I went ahead and ordered a DNA test to send away, hoping I will get some sort of information back to track down any relatives I may have. At this point, I may not even be from China. I spit in the tube and completed the paperwork. *So close yet so far*, I thought to myself. I walked to the mailbox in my bare feet and pajamas knowing that I was leaning on these answers for temporary support.

The next morning I got a text from Robin stating that I didn't need to be at work until ten and that we would leave from there and head to the airport so the FBI and detectives could go over their findings. So I spent the morning at the grocery store and running errands. I paced the aisles, taking my time and putting in the effort to find the girls "comfort food." I bought the items that were on the list Robin gave me—everything from special formulas to snacks and some over-the-counter medicine. I picked up necessities like diapers and wipes, clothing, shoes, and socks. I even went over to the toy aisle and grabbed a few things that I would have liked as a little girl. I'm so grateful I could do this, but I also had to remember the situation these children were in.

As much as I enjoyed shopping, part of me was also filling a small void in my heart of wanting my own children one day. I have a hope chest with baby clothes, blankets, and shoes. Most of it was mine from when I was a baby. But every time I go somewhere and find something that I can't pass up, I buy it and put it in the chest for *one day.*

I pulled into the parking lot and saw Robin sitting in the car. She rolled down the window and waved me over. She told me to get in but was in a hurry because she wanted to get McDonald's before going to the airport.

Robin was perkier than usual as she said, "Good morning, sunshine! Are you ready for the day?"

I was so confused. "Good morning. Why are you all giggly this early?"

"Well, I got the news that both of the girls are going to be staying with LeeAnna and Richard until they are adopted. I also talked to Michael and agreed it would be a great idea for you two to go and see them whenever you want. LeeAnna was also on board."

"That's great. I would love to. I have food, clothing, and toys in the back of my car to bring them when we go and see them later today!"

"Oh, that's wonderful! How thoughtful of you. I know they will love it. They seem to really like you guys. You should try and visit them together some."

"Michael told us that he was going to meet us there today when we get off."

"Oh, great! You should tell him to meet us at the office, and we can all go together."

"Sure, I'll send him a text."

It was kinda awkward the rest of the way. I didn't want to give anything away, but I also didn't want to act like I didn't want to work with him. We pulled into the McDonald's parking lot, and thank goodness the line was short. While waiting, I texted Michael,

> Hey! Robin told me to text you about you possibly riding with us to LeeAnna and Richard's house when we go and visit the girls? Either way just let me know.

Two minutes later . . .

> Good Morning! Happy Friday, I would be more than happy to. Just let me know what time. Are we still on for tonight? And don't worry, I haven't said anything to anyone about us going out later.

> Great, we should be getting back around noon but I'll let you know for sure when it gets closer. And yes, we are still on for this evening. When we get done visiting the girls we can go from there!

> Sure thing! I have something fun planned, you'll just have to wait and see!

What just happened? Is he setting up a date? I thought this was just quick drinks for an hour or so and I can go on about my weekend. Finally, Robin got her food and then sped to the airport. She's driving with a large latte in one hand and the steering wheel on the other, trying to eat a biscuit and hash browns from her lap. I thought for sure that she was going to spill something. After a few red lights, we turned into the parking lot of the airport. They gave us directions to go around back so we didn't have to walk. We parked and got all of the stuff out the back and, most importantly, Robin's McDonald's. I noticed that there were police cars and a large black sedan that had the FBI logo on it. I was anxious. I was more than ready to find out about everything that happened or what was left to tell.

They guided us to a conference room. There was a projector along with the actual evidence laid out on a table. In the meeting, besides Robin and me, there were two FBI agents, a police officer, a forensic scientist, and a medical examiner.

The medical examiner stated that the parents' bodies were never found and were most likely destroyed from the impact and severity of the crash. There were some body parts retrieved from the crash, but none of them were the parents'. They gathered what they could over the weekend and were able to see all they had collected on Monday. If anything else was brought in, they would let us know. The medical examiner also informed us that the pill bottle was nothing and was traced back to allergy medicine. Welp, so much for cracking this case. The one thing I was most anxious about was the journal. The forensic scientist and translator presented their findings next. They had a binder with each of the pages typed in English. For the most part, it was your typical "Dear Diary" journal entries, but one page read,

October 15th, 1999

There are a lot of things happening in my life this year. I turn 23 next month. This is also the year that I get to meet my first niece. My sister is pregnant and is due at the first of the year. It's a girl and I've dreamed of having two daughters of my own. I want children but there are laws regarding the amount of children we are allowed to have. My sister is also in a difficult situation without the father in the picture. She either has to raise the child alone or give her up for adoption. There are lots of decisions to be made between now and then. But as for me I either have to end things with my love or move to be with him. He is the love of my life but at the same time I want to go off to school. But another part of me wants to help my sister raise her daughter.

One of my life long dreams is to have a family and to raise them in the states to give them a better life. I want to have a good, established career even though I have inheritance money from my mother and grandmother. They left my sister and I a combined 100 million dollars so we can build our dream lives. But even with all of this money, I want to attend college like my older sister. So maybe one day I'll have answers sooner rather than later.

What did I just read? Could this really be what I think it is? Is Sonia my biological aunt? But this is also really stretching it. I mean, I was born in January of 2000, but that's such a reach. I couldn't be that one in a million, could I? But as I sat at the table looking down, holding back the tears, I can only imagine. The last journal entry was dated in 2003 when she got married. The journal was written in hopes of falling in love, and now that she was married, there was no need to keep writing.

But I think you should never stop writing. Write about the days when you were young and carefree to the stage of life where you become a mother, and eventually finish out your career. Write about the day you lay outside and watched the birds fly above the sand dunes, write about the days where you didn't think you would make it to dinner on time, and write about what makes you happy. Find your happiness and go from there.

I felt that I learned so much, but at the same time, there were all of the unknowns that were scratching the surface. The conclusion of the meeting was that the airplane that crashed was working, passed all of the inspections, and ran perfectly the following day. So why out of the blue did it just crash? They were able to save some of the plane along with some luggage. There were no survivors or full bodies, just pieces of some. I know, it's awful and one of my greatest fears. What were those passengers thinking? They knew what was going to happen as they were crashing. But did someone on that plane know this was going to happen? If so, they also knew that they were going to die. So was this a suicide along with a mass murder?

I requested a list of every passenger and staff member who was on the plane along with everyone who was working that week. I gave the list to the forensic science team and FBI. I told them I had a gut feeling that one of the staff members could have potentially done something. The camera footage was also being retrieved. They were going to watch every second of footage from when that plane returned that night and until it boarded. I instructed them to write down every staff member who went near it. Everyone who was working that week would also be called in for questioning. This is the toughest I've ever been on anyone about a case, but I wasn't going to let anything slip through the cracks of my fingers if I had a say. They had their work cut out for them, trust me. I was not going to settle for just "Oh, it was just a plane crash."

Robin and I headed back to the car, and she told me to call Michael to meet us at the office. On the way to see the girls, we were going to stop and pick up a few more things. It was about one o'clock, and I was starving.

I sent Michael a text.

Hey, we are on the way back from the airport. Robin said for you to meet us at the office.

Hey! How was today? I will be there in 10!

Chaeli Smith

It was interesting to say the least, how did it go with you today?

I had a fun morning but glad I am off, see you shortly.

Robin also said something about us shopping for the girls on the way and eating lunch at some point. I don't know if she mentioned that to you or not!

She hinted about it, but either way that sounds fun. We will have to make a game plan when I get there!

Since we were about five minutes from the office, Robin said, "You and Michael go ahead, and I will meet you there. I have a meeting, and then I will meet you both at the house."

"Robin, are you sure? I mean, is the meeting urgent?"

"Yes, I have to make some phone calls. There's Michael's truck. You two have fun." She winked and smiled.

I wanted to back out, but at the same time, I think it would be fun. Maybe? As Michael parked, we pulled in beside him, and Robin rolled down the window.

"Hey, Michael, I told Adaire you two are going ahead without me, and I'll meet you at the house."

"Okay, that sounds good." He waved to Robin as she walked inside. He turned to me. "We could just take my truck and load everything in the back."

"I have some stuff in my car I need to grab." I took a short breath. "Were you busy?"

"I was up until lunch. It's always like that." He paused as we made eye contact, and he looked away. "How was your weekend?"

"Relaxing. I walked on the beach and baked." I smiled, remembering what the waves felt like coming up to partially cover my feet.

Michael helped me unload my car and load the back of his truck, then proceeded to open the passenger door and gave me his hand. It was a touch of false hope. The truck was shiny black just like my car, was high off the ground, had a leather interior, and had that new car smell.

"Michael, I like your truck! Is it new?"

"Thank you. I bought it a few months ago. We're matching with our black vehicles. You have a sick car!"

"Thanks! I was finally able to buy my dream car after college."

"That's impressive! Where did you graduate from?"

"I received my bachelor's and master's from the University of Miami and then moved here. How did you end up in Florida?"

"Well, after high school, I graduated from undergrad in two and a half years and went to Harvard Medical School. I matched here for residency, and I've been here for three years and have about two years left until I become official. Did you take your job because it's next to the beach? I'm joking!"

"That's so awesome. What is your goal after residency? And I took this job so I could start over. I wanted something new for myself, and getting to wake up next to the beach is an added bonus."

We had an easy conversation the entire ride to town. It felt like I was talking to an old friend. We laughed and got to know each other. For the first time in a while, I had lost track of time. He listened to my every word and really paid attention to what I was saying. I was at ease. *What are you doing, Adaire? He is a colleague, maybe a friend, but nothing more. Don't be that girl again. You just can't.*

After we pulled into the parking lot and parked, he came around and opened the door for me. He walked on the side where there was traffic and remained beside me the entire time. It was the small gestures I had seen from afar but never experienced. He grabbed the cart and said, "I'm following you. Lead the way."

"I've already been in here once today but was in a time crunch."

"Oh, really? Well, shop away."

"Let's get the boring stuff out of the way. Let's go find some more toiletries, food, and medicine. I had bought some things earlier but couldn't find anything."

He walked beside me with the cart. I can see him staring at me. As much as I wanted to turn around, I just kept walking like I was alone. Before we put anything in the cart, we always asked the other just to ensure we weren't getting the same thing. We picked up shampoo, bodywash, vitamins, medicine, and some more grocery staples.

I was walking up and down the aisles and knew where everything was from memory. Michael was following me the whole time and would occasionally ask me if he was picking out the right things. He admitted that even though he was a pediatrician, he had never shopped for little girls. He was holding up everything that was pink but also making sure it had all of the best ingredients and nutrients. It's the doctor in him, I thought. But I couldn't help but see his intentions were pure. He wanted the best for the girls.

"Michael, now here's the fun part, the clothes and toys."

"This is actually really fun, and I'm glad I get to do it with you. The last time I was shopping for children was for a work event. Who would have guessed?"

"Who knew you would like shopping for little girls?'

"Now that looks pretty cool. I even want to play with that," he said as he pointed toward a set of blocks.

"I mean, it says two years old and up, so let's get it. Oh, and they have it in different shades of pink."

"Cool. Toss it here."

As we went up and down the aisles of toys and clothes, our car was full, and we had to start hanging stuff from the sides and put the bigger items on the bottom. I tried to carry something, but Michael insisted I put it in the cart as he pushed it. It was about 2:30 p.m. when we headed to check out.

"So where do you want to grab some late lunch? But remember we are going out afterwards."

"Totally up to you. You're the driver."

"I've planned what we are doing later, so it is your turn."

"Okay, I have an idea, but I'll tell you in the truck."

When we were checking out, Michael and I started separating everything by category so it was easier to sort through later. The total was around five hundred dollars, and he insisted on paying. I told him I was paying him half later, but he kept arguing with me. As we walked to the truck, I noticed that Michael switched sides so I would be farthest away from any type of traffic. I mean, he is such a gentleman. I've never been treated like this by any guy before. I just kept thinking to myself, *What if?*

He got to the bed of the truck and started unloading everything. Again, he wouldn't let me touch anything. I literally stood there holding the cart so it didn't roll away. A lady who was walking in offered to take it. He then opened the passenger door for me, again. When he got in, he asked me, "So are you going to tell me where we are going?"

"Since you are making me pick, let's go somewhere quick so we can spend as much time with the girls as possible."

"So where to?"

"Let's go to this coffee shop up the street. They have a ton of stuff to choose from, and we can order it to go."

"That sounds great! I love getting coffee from time to time there."

"Oh really? I get smoothies there on the weekend."

"Well, we should meet here this weekend, if you want to?"

"Sure, that sounds fun. Do you want to walk on the beach afterwards? It's literally my backyard."

"That sounds like a great plan. I promise to not soak you in the ocean."

"Try me, I dare you." We laughed. "So does this mean we are going to be hanging out again?"

"You're stuck with me for another day."

Once again, he helped me out of the truck. I felt weird, but I was trying not to blush over something that doesn't mean anything. It was an unusual feeling I had gotten used to but slowly went away.

The coffee shop wasn't as busy as some days. Normally the line is out the door, and you can hardly see the menu. The cashier took our order, and Michael paid for it. He told me I could pay him back *one day*. He got a sandwich with their famous Parmesan cheese fries, and I got a wrap with sweet potato fries. We ordered different sides so we could share. I know, how romantic. There were a few extra minutes to spare, so he drove to a park on the way. Our view was nothing but the dunes and ocean. Heaven on earth. Even though it was the most simple thing in the world, I couldn't imagine anything else.

We poured the fries in the same box so we could share. Our conversation picked up about where we grew up, our families, and our lifelong dreams. I learned that he is also from South Carolina. He used to play football and basketball in high school and undergrad in college. He said as much as he loved playing, he needed to devote his time more to his dream career. His parents are from Singapore and moved to the States five years before he was born. They wanted to start over and build a foundation for their future family.

He said he was grateful for all of his family's sacrifices and wouldn't be where he was today without them. But also, he didn't want his parents to ever feel disappointed or that they moved to the States for their son to be average. His father, Matthew, is a cardiologist; and his mother, Catherine, is a professor at Harvard. He had felt the pressure as soon as he was able to comprehend all that his parents had given up and all they had accomplished. In high school, he wanted to be a professor like his mother; but toward the end, he changed his mind and wanted to study pediatrics. He was mentored by his father and his colleagues. Since he graduated high school early and went straight into college, his timeline was accelerated for his age. He had a lot of credit going into undergrad and graduated when he was only twenty. Then he attended medical school at Harvard, where his mother taught. Even though he grew up in South Carolina, he moved to Connecticut during middle school. He had been guided his entire life by his parents until he accepted the residency job in Orlando. In a lot of ways we were similar, both wanting to uphold our family standards while also wanting more than what our hometowns had to offer. We knew that we were destined for more.

Like me, he wanted a fresh start, something that we would make our own and do something for ourselves for once and not have the pressure or high expectations of our parents lingering in our ears every time we make a decision for ourselves. I felt that our lives were mirrors of each other, and that conversation was like standing before a reflection, reasoning with ourselves.

I told him about my life growing up and that I was *adopted*. He just looked at me and asked if I knew anything about my birth parents. I said I didn't but that I wanted to know more about my story and I wanted to uncover the truth. He told me he would do anything to help me and threw the idea of going back to China with me if that was something I was considering. I didn't really give an answer and changed the subject. It was time to head to the house, meet Robin, and see the girls.

I texted Robin and let her know we were about twenty minutes away, and she said she should get there the same time we would. Robin also told me that Lucy wanted us, and my eyes couldn't help but sparkle and fill with tears. The rest of the way, Michael and I were talking about how excited we were to see them and how he wanted to open the block set and play as he helped them build a castle. That was really sweet. He mentioned that he loved children and was the reason he specialized in pediatrics.

Chaeli Smith

LeeAnna was outside to greet us as we pulled in. I told her we had a lot of stuff to bring in. She was so grateful and let us know how excited they were for us all to be together. While Michael and Richard unloaded the bags (Michael insisted), LeeAnna took me inside to see the girls. Lucy ran into my arms like she had known me for years, and I scooped up Isla. They were just beautiful. LeeAnna told us to make ourselves at home. Michael walked in from the kitchen and sat beside me on the couch, and Lucy jumped and ran over to him as Isla fell asleep in my arms. Michael gave Lucy the toys we bought for them and opened the blocks he had picked out, and they started to build a castle and small tower. I thought to myself, *He is so good with kids, and I can tell he genuinely loves it by the look on his face.* He watched closely as Lucy would stack blocks on top of each other or hand him one to help her build.

Michael was gentle, patient, and kind toward her and let her do as much of the work as she could. He would pass her a pink block and then a purple one to stack. She was locked in and copying everything he did. It was like he was the left side of the brain, and Lucy was the right.

"You guys are naturals. They really love you guys," LeeAnna stated as she came to sit down in the recliner.

"I've always loved children. They are so resilient, and we don't give them enough credit," Michael replied as he continued to hand Lucy the blocks, one after the other.

"I love all kids but especially Lucy and Isla. I just can't get over their story."

Robin walked in, set a folder of paperwork on the table, and sat down. "I have some things to go over with them, so we will leave you guys alone."

I moved to sit on the floor and played as we watched TV, fixed a few snacks, and showed Lucy the clothes and shoes we bought. She wanted to try them all on and gave us a fashion show. I helped her put on the pink dress and white sandals we picked out at Target.

"Wow, you look like a princess," Michael exclaimed as he was changing Isla. Lucy was grinning and grabbed everything until she had tried everything on. The living room was covered in clothing and toys. But knowing that Lucy was happy was all that mattered. Michael read them a book, colored with them, and played with dolls.

He read them *Goodnight Moon* and pointed to the mouse on every page. Lucy would do the same, mimicking his motions. My want-to-be-mama heart was a puddle watching this. We colored Disney princesses, and Lucy insisted we did one too.

Lucy was very smart for a three-year-old. She knew all of her shapes and colors. She was picking out the colors and coloring between the lines. Michael and I were following behind her, coloring their dresses. Well, he's trying at least. He had the baby in one arm and a blue crayon in his other hand. She then noticed that we bought her the plush Disney dolls and laid the ones we colored next to them. She pointed, and we told her their names. She knew a few words of Mandarin but was mostly fluent in English.

Around six o'clock, I made Lucy dinner while Michael fed Isla a warm bottle. I mean, it is kind of a turn-on when a guy is not only good with kids but also knows how to feed them a bottle. It's like we were role-playing as parents, and in a way, we were. By this time, Robin, LeeAnna, and Richard were just hanging out and talking. LeeAnna showed Robin each of the girls' rooms and put the things we bought them away. You could tell that they put time and effort in making this feel like home. The walls of Lucy's room were light pink with curtains and butterfly night-light. Her clothes were hung and folded so you could find everything. There were toys but looked like they hadn't been touched.

The nursery was white with pink floral canvases hanging on the wall. It gives it some color like how women put blush on their cheeks. There was a pink rug and a soft gray rocking chair with a lamp beside it. There was also a changing table with more of Isla's clothing and diapers. Their home was warm, inviting, and any little girl's dream. I knew they were safe— something they deserved yet didn't know any different.

After dinner, Robin said she would clean the kitchen, so I could help give the girls a bath. Michael and I went into the bathroom and bathed them at the same time. He did Isla in the bathroom sink while I filled the tub for Lucy. We used the tear-free shampoo that all the moms buy and put baby powder on them like my mother once did for me. I remember that special scent. There is nothing like a clean baby smell. Once we finished bathing them, we ended the evening by reading one more book to them. Lucy picked a book about animals. It was pretty funny watching and listening to Michael make all of the noises while she repeated after him. We said our goodbyes as we kissed them good night—even though for us, it was just the beginning.

Chapter 5

IS IT REALLY THE BEGINNING?

I missed the girls already as we headed outside. LeeAnna and Richard told us to come by as often as we could. That was something I could promise. They are seriously the best, and I couldn't have picked better parents for the girls. I wondered what Robin was talking to them about. I got to the truck, and once again Michael never failed to open the door for me. Robin waved us bye and said she would see me next week. Little did she know I was going on this mystery dinner date with Michael. Michael said he would drop me off at my car, and either he could meet at this surprise location or he would pick me up. Whichever I was the most comfortable with.

I told him he could follow me to my house. I know it sounds creepy, but I don't think he's a serial killer or anything. He helped me get out of his truck and into my car. I told him to let me know if I got too far ahead or if he lost me. As soon as I pulled out of the parking lot, he called me.

He said, "Just in case, I have you on speaker."

"I mean, you do have a point, but my house is not even five minutes away, so not too bad."

"Well, I was hoping to stay on the phone longer. But I guess it means we can talk in person sooner."

"So where are we going? You haven't given me any hints all week."

"Well, it is still a surprise. Trust me, you will find out sooner than later."

We joked on the phone the whole way there about how we hit every red light, and then we finally got on the road where I live. As you turn in, you can see the ocean from the driveway.

"I'm kinda jealous you live on the beach. I wouldn't want to leave my house."

"I'm a homebody on the weekend. I just love waking up to this view. I feel like I'm on vacation."

"Well, maybe you can show me around this weekend."

"I have this spot I love to walk to and take pictures of. I might just have to show you."

Once we parked, I invited him to come in as I proceeded to carry the boxes in from the back of my trunk. He was wearing a light-blue button-down, dress pants, and leather loafers. He looks like an Abercrombie model. His hair was perfect, the sleeves on his shirt were cuffed just right, and I caught a whiff of his cologne. I could melt.

I went and changed out of my work clothes. I wanted to wear something that was classy and casual but didn't scream "I know we are going on a date" type of look. So I opted for a black maxi dress, nothing too fancy but also put together. I walked out, and he was standing in the living room with a gorgeous bouquet of pastel flowers.

"Wow, you look great! I love your dress. You know, you didn't have to change."

"Well, I did want to get out of my work clothes and into something more comfortable. And those are beautiful flowers. What are they for?"

"They are for you, silly, and just because. Are you ready?"

"Well, they are stunning, and yes! Just let me grab my keys."

How and where did Michael get a bouquet of flowers? And when did he have time to get them? They must have been in the cooler in the back of his truck from earlier. It was a mix of peonies, baby's breath, carnations, and eucalyptus. They made me think of springtime. How my mother and I would spend endless hours in our garden planting all that our hearts desire—bushes of hydrangeas, roses, and even tulips. They had a sweet smell to them, like I could smell *home* again. Flowers are one of the things that bring me comfort. Nothing screams a clean living space like fresh flowers. Even though I had always bought them myself, I pretended someone sent them to me. It was an old feeling that disappeared and was far gone.

As we backed out of the driveway, I thought about how I hadn't touched a door handle. How weird is that to say? I can't believe this is happening. I mean, we haven't even known each other for a whole week and we're going on a "date." I haven't told anyone about this, not even my parents or best friend. But it's not a date, right? Just two colleagues talking over dinner and drinks. I was confused and wondered what we were doing when he pulled into the grocery store parking lot.

"So I placed an order to pick up. Do you want to come in?"

"Sure. I can't let you have all of the fun. What are we doing here anyways?"

He smiled. "You are going to have to wait and see."

We walked over to the pickup counter, grabbed the two brown paper bags, and headed back out. He put them in the back of the truck, and we headed toward the beach. I had no clue what was in them or where we were going. It sounded like I was in a horror movie at this point.

"We've arrived. I have to walk across the street to get to the beach, but it's close enough."

"Well, Michael, your house is beautiful and not too far from me."

"What a small world. I know this may sound creepy, but I've been planning this for a few days."

He unloaded the groceries and walked in the side door, motioning me to follow. His house was two stories and gave off a modern beach house vibe. Everything was

Chaeli Smith

clean and put together, but I could tell it was missing a woman's touch. There was no seasonal towel hanging on the stove or fresh flowers on the dining room table. I sighed with relief, knowing he was single and not cheating on his girlfriend or wife. I would hate to be the other woman. He led me to the backyard, and there were beautiful string lights and a table sitting directly under them. I could tell he put a lot of thought and effort into this. *Effort.* Something that is foreign to me.

Michael sat the bags on the table and took out a bottle of wine, a huge bowl of pasta, salad, and sourdough bread. As I was unpacking everything, he brought out a tray with two wineglasses, napkins, and dinner and silverware.

"Nicely done, Michael! It really is gorgeous out here." I paused and took in the scenery mixed with the twinkling lights.

"I had to plan something special for our first dinner, and I didn't want it to be awkward if I planned reservations anywhere, so I may have faked you out."

"You did get me. I thought we were going to a bar or something."

"I have a friend who works at the grocery store who is an amazing chef, so I had him make his favorite dish. I'm just trying to make a good first impression."

"Well, you have. Nobody ever has done anything like this."

As I was focusing on Michael, my mind just kept going back to *him*. How he would text me horrible things when we weren't together or how he would threaten to harm me if things didn't go his way. We never had a normal conversation, and he couldn't even hold one unless he was half drunk. And even then, he changed the subject. This was what I thought normal was or the best it was going to get for me. It was a routine feeling that had left my soul a long time ago. Just like memories, trying to resurface.

As we ate dinner and drank wine, we continued talking about life. No work-related anything other than the girls. We mentioned our families, what we did growing up, our favorite hobbies, and our dreams in life. We even touched on past relationships. I was very brief and said I had a fling in college and it didn't work out because I needed to move on. I didn't want to be defined by him or let him have an edge on who I am becoming. I didn't want the judgment or questions that come with it. I established that we share a love of the ocean and traveling the world. I felt that we were the only two people left on earth. Just two souls that have been longing to meet each other. I traced the rim on the wineglass, mimicking the motion I once did outlining the scars *he* left.

The concept of time escaped, and when I looked at my watch, I realized we had ended up sitting outside for over two hours. The bottle of wine was half gone, but I wasn't buzzed. I was more lucid than I had ever been. At one point, the wind was blowing, and he tucked my hair behind my ear. Eight o'clock came, then it was nine, and neither of us wanted to get up; but Michael insisted I didn't touch a single dish. He cleaned up from dinner while I started on dessert. There were the ingredients to make brownies laid out on the counter. And he said that I would know what to do with them.

Fun fact: I love to bake, and that was something I had told him earlier today. So he listens. He really listens. I whipped up some brownie batter in no time. I felt weird invading someone else's kitchen, but it's like something was missing when I cooked alone.

"Wow, I didn't know you could bake like that. No recipe, just from memory." He walked over to me. "Can I help you with anything?"

"I've done it so much my brain remembers automatically. I love to cook, bake, and paint." I looked up at him and saw the twinkle in his eyes, knowing I needed to redirect my attention. "Everything is done for now!"

"Oh wait, really, was that painting in your living room something you did?'

"The one with the flowers I made a few years ago."

"That's really impressive. You should teach me how to paint."

"That sounds really fun actually. Tomorrow after we get breakfast, do you want to come over and paint? Later we could cook dinner together?"

"That sounds perfect. Let's do it. I still can't believe you've never had a boyfriend before. I mean, you're so accomplished for your age, have your life together, know what you want in life, and you're stunning to look at." He looked out the window as he continued, "You are talented and excel in your career."

"Aww, well, you're too sweet. You're not so bad yourself. I mean, you're a doctor and a really great one from what I can see. You love your patients, and I can see that they love you too." I paused for a few seconds. "And as far as my past with men, I'm just picky. I want so much in life, and I look for someone who desires the same things. Like an established career, a home, a family, and a love for traveling the world."

"It's scary how compatible we are. It's like we're the same person. My last relationship was in undergrad, and we argued about the future. I wanted to get my education before committing to her, and she wanted the commitment and for me to follow her across the country to be with her, and I just wasn't willing to sacrifice my dreams for hers, so I broke up with her."

I was taken aback that he was sharing about his past. I've never been around a guy who is open, honest, and authentic. He wasn't trying to hide anything. Sometimes you just need someone to listen.

"I'm sorry to hear about that. Did you date all four years?" I thought, *Maybe I shouldn't have asked that.*

"We only dated for about a year and a half. Her name was Jenna and was a business major. We got along great the first few months, but the honeymoon phase wore off, and we had to come to terms with reality. We weren't going to be the perfect romance couple you see on the screens or read about. She wanted to move to Los

Angeles and wanted me to follow her. She said I could go to medical school there while she worked. I loved her, but I was never in love with her. If you know what I mean?" He took a deep breath and continued, "After six months, we still went out, but it wasn't because I wanted to date her. I just didn't know how to end things. She is not a bad person, but I wasn't willing to put my dreams on hold for her to not support mine. She claimed she did but discouraged me from applying to Harvard because she didn't want to do long distance. But I broke up with her during our junior year, and we haven't spoken since. Our relationship didn't end on bad terms but not good ones either. I wish her the best of luck but have no desire to cross paths with her."

"I'm sorry things didn't work out. I push everyone away because I look for certain qualities and will never settle for less."

"Well, you should be picky. You should never settle for someone that doesn't align with your lifestyle."

"That's what I tell myself when my friends and parents encourage me to go out with whomever." I glanced at the oven. "I can see they are about done."

"That is why I never dated the rest of undergrad or in medical school. I wanted to finish growing on my own before I try to grow with someone else." He glanced at the oven. "They smell amazing. Are they ready? I am dying to try one."

"I think they are. Let's taste them."

Michael pulled out a pair of oven mitts, opened the oven door, and placed the brownies on a cooling rack on top of the stove. They looked perfect, if I do say so myself, since this is my recipe. I mean, who am I? Baking brownies with a guy I met a week ago at midnight. And I'm seeing him in the morning. It has been fun, but I'm holding back because I do not want to get my hopes up that this really could be it. He got a butter knife and cut off a corner piece.

"These are amazing, like I'm serious. This is the best dessert I've ever had. The flavor and texture turned out perfect. Where have you been my whole life?" he added in a serious but joking manner.

"Lots of trial and error along with a lot of experience." I took another bite. "I also baked a lot with my mother."

"I have ice cream. Do you want some?" He walked toward the freezer and pulled out a tub of cookie dough–flavored ice cream.

"Sure! Wait, I have an idea. Give me the scooper."

"That's genius—a brownie ice cream sandwich. That is so good, seriously. But I have had a lot of fun today. From shopping to playing with the girls to eating lunch and dinner, now eating brownies and ice cream."

"Today has been such a dream. I mean, who knew a week ago we would be eating dessert at midnight?"

"So what time do you want to meet up tomorrow? I can come and pick you up, but again, it is whatever you want."

"You can pick me up around nine, if that works for you?"

"Perfect! But seriously I don't remember a night where I was this relaxed and had so much fun."

"Same here. Thank you again for everything. We better get some rest for tomorrow's beach walk."

"Of course, it is my pleasure. I'm just thankful we are getting to know each other. It's a good thing you only live a few minutes away." He started to laugh. "Now you can come and bake for me every night."

As we cleaned up the kitchen, I noticed we were having fun doing simple household tasks. Michael was just comfortable to be around. We danced to "Everywhere" by Fleetwood Mac. I let my guard down with ease and didn't have to think twice. And if I have to add anything, he's a pretty good dancer. As he twirled me around the entire kitchen and living room, I could feel his hand on my back, but nothing further. He was respectful while also trying to win me over.

I grabbed my sweater and purse and headed to the truck. We continued sharing about our evening the entire ride to my house even though it was only five minutes. Like a gentleman, he walked me up to my door and told me good night. The only thought that was keeping me calm was knowing I would get to see him in the morning. He gave me a good, long hug. He didn't know I needed that, but I did. I thought I knew what it felt like to receive a genuine hug from a guy. But I didn't until then. You could hear crickets as we stood on the porch for a minute, hugging each other without saying a word. We didn't need to see or speak to each other; we just understood. That feeling of holding someone else triggered a sensitive sensation that we both recognized and yearned for but also tried to forget.

Chapter 6
THE WAVES LEAD ME TO YOU

I woke up around seven thirty the next morning. It was a great way to start a Saturday, the birds chirping and waves crashing up against the shore. And my favorite part—the smell of being on the ocean. I can't describe it. It's a mixture of salt water and palm trees; there is nothing else like it. Paradise. As I crawled out of bed and headed to the bathroom to get ready, the cold tile pierced the bottom of my feet. I knew sooner than later I would exchange this feeling for warm sand.

I had butterflies in my stomach for the first time but knew immediately what it felt like. I couldn't conceal my feelings. Michael helped embrace the real me. I hinted about my past, and he didn't judge me. He just stared into my eyes and listened. It's like our souls were intertwined and trying to fuse into one. It's like he understood me even though there were no words exchanged. He was the only guy who had gone out of his way to schedule and execute any date. He's a great person, and now I can officially say I really like him.

My head was flooded with a million thoughts. Once again, I always have my guard up. Four walls made of steel that are guarded by another barrier. I never let anyone all the way in, not even my parents or best friend. I don't know why. I guess I'm just afraid that someone else will walk out of my life without an answer. And it would create a bigger wound and leave with more questions than answers. But I am also feeling tingly inside because I do want things to move forward. I keep telling myself, *Just have faith, and you never know if you don't try.*

Michael texted to let me know that he was on the way, meaning I only had five minutes before he arrived. I paced back and forth as I waited for him to pull in. I heard a vehicle approaching, and then the door closed moments later. As I heard footsteps coming up the porch, I grabbed my bag and heard a knock on the door.

Michael stood in the doorway. I noticed this the first time I ever saw him; but he was so handsome, had a good tan, was athletically built, and looked great in athletic apparel. We didn't plan this, but we ended up color coordinating. I was wearing black running shorts, a dark-teal workout tank top with a matching zip-up sweatshirt. He had on dark-teal athletic shorts and a black short-sleeved workout shirt.

"Hey! Good morning! It's great to see you. Are you ready?" He leaned in for a hug, and I stood there and smelled him. I couldn't help but want to hold on for longer.

"Yep, let me lock the door, and we can head out!" I reached for my keys and purse.

"I'm starving and have already looked at the menu this morning. The options are endless!"

"I love McCullen's. They have the best food, staff, and ambiance. We get lunch catered from there during the week."

"I hear it is really beautiful at night and that they have live music and twinkly lights."

"They do. It is such a great atmosphere I feel like I am on vacation. It is really nice once it cools down."

"I think we should go one night to see if it can become a regular tradition for us." He made a face but avoided eye contact.

"Is that another way of asking me out on another date?"

"Did you like how I threw that in there?" He gave off a soft smile as I sat in the passenger seat.

"You're pretty sneaky. But that sounds like a great idea!"

Once again, I did not touch a door handle, and the ride to the restaurant was nice and peaceful. He was playing '70s and '80s music. I told him briefly I loved old-school music, and as soon as he backed out of the driveway, I could hear Billy Joel playing in the background. It was a perfect day to walk on the beach. There was very little wind, not too hot, and it was an off time, so there weren't as many people out. I could hear the waves making that slush sound, kids playing, dogs barking, and tourists asking for directions.

The sun was out, and there wasn't a cloud in the sky as it mirrored the crystal-clear ocean water. These are the rare days you could see all the way to the bottom, seeing schools of fish pace back and forth dodging every human they would encounter. This beach in particular was known for its soft sand near the dunes, but when the waves broke at your feet, you could see every shell imaginable. I had a collection on my back porch. I would rinse them free from any sand and salt water. I had a few clear jars full of them. I mainly sorted them by type but had a few stacks of ones I wanted to paint. Just like us, shells are unique and have their own story. I love painting their markings and scars on canvases just like you would if you were sketching a portrait.

The gravel parking lot to McCullen's wasn't empty but not as packed as I have seen it some mornings. Indoor and outdoor seating was available. Anywhere you sat, you could see the ocean. McCullen's was a locally owned restaurant that had been in business for more than twenty years. They were open from eight in the morning until ten at night and close from two to four in the afternoon to prepare for the dinner rush. They offered dine-in and takeout. Their menu had comfort food ranging from pancakes for breakfast to fried chicken and seafood for lunch and dinner. The owner, Andrea, was a supersweet lady. She was in her sixties and had run the place with her husband, Ted. Andrea had gray-blonde hair about to her shoulders and always wore her hair in a clip. Her cheeks were always sun-kissed from working outside, and she was always friendly and spoke to me. Ted was a bald-headed gentleman but made up for it with his medium-length beard. Andrea said she's tempted to make him shave it. They had lived in Orlando their whole lives, so everyone knew them. And they owned a house on the beach, not too far from mine, and I saw them walk often.

It is normally the same people working the same shifts every week, and I know who is working. When I call, they know my order and that I want it to go. Julia was standing at the front like normal. She was in high school and had long curly brown hair. She hosted during the weekends and had a surprised but confused look on her face when I walked in with Michael. She took us to a table underneath the patio so we could have a close view of the pristine blue water. There were lots of boat traffic, people kayaking, and people riding Jet Skis. The breeze was nice, and the covered patio was an added bonus of not having to squint the entire time.

As Michael pulled out my chair for me, he asked, "So do you have any idea what you're going to get?"

"I always get a smoothie. They are the best, and I normally let Julia surprise me with whatever she thinks I will like." I was taken aback by the fact he pulled out my chair. I thought Hudson, my ex-situationship, never did that.

"That actually sounds fun. We should let her decide." He waved Julia back over. "So we are going to let you order for us. Whatever you think is the best. The only rule is they can't be the same!"

She nodded in agreement. "I'll put the order in. Adaire, I know you want a smoothie, and for your friend?"

"I'll do the same. Thank you, Julia." He smiled as he turned to face me.

Julia handed the ticket to our waitress who was bringing glasses of iced-cold water. She placed the cups with iced water on the table along with some straws. "I'll be right back with your smoothies. Is there anything else I can bring you in the meantime?"

I replied with relief, knowing I could speak up, "I believe I'm good for now. Thank you!"

"Not that I know of. Thank you so much!" Michael added. He then looked at me and asked, "So what do you have planned for us today?"

"Just like you made me wait, you will just have to be patient."

"Sounds fair, but I'm really excited about whatever you have planned. I'm sure it'll be fun no matter what."

The birds sang as they stared below at the water, hoping a school of fish would come just below the surface so they could swoop down and prey on them. As I bent down to pick up the napkin that flew off the table, Michael reached over and put his hand on the corner of the table so I wouldn't bump my head. Once again, another small gesture that existed yet was unfamiliar. I smiled so much around Michael my face would start to hurt. He reciprocated by staring into my eyes and listening like it was music to his ears. He not only listened to every word I said but also apologized and said he wished he could have been there to support me. My mind crossed back to where I would be sitting across the table eating dinner with *him*. In a way, I felt if I chewed my food wrong or looked sad or miserable, it would provoke him. He ordered for me and would hardly let me talk to the waitstaff, especially if they were guys. I felt like a hostage. But I felt comfortable with Michael. He was warm and kind and knew what to say without saying too much. I could feel my shoulders relax and the walls around my heart start to dissolve. He was *different*.

I toyed with the black onyx ring on my finger, wishing it was something else. But it also reminded me of everything I was once promised. The food was finally ready. Julia and our waitress, Avery, brought us our entrees. They placed French toast, chocolate chip waffles, bacon, sausage, grits, hash browns, fruit, and extra condiments in the middle of the table along with two extra plates. It looked heavenly.

"Thank you. It looks phenomenal." Michael nodded.

"Everything is perfect. Thank you both so much." I was starving and excited to dig in.

"Let us know if you need anything," Avery said before she refilled our glasses with water and walked toward her other table.

"I don't know where to start." Michael paused. "You're going to help me finish this, I hope."

"I've never seen so much food in my entire life. But it all looks amazing. Everything here is to die for."

We took the empty plates and put as much food as we could fit. I tried to eat like a lady and could tell he was trying to use proper etiquette. We wanted to impress each other, even though we were comfortable. I felt I could lean back in my chair with ease and didn't have to think about my every move and just enjoy the moment.

Michael combined the French toast with waffles on his fork. "Here, taste it." He paused until there was nothing left on the fork. "Isn't it good?"

"I'm not going to lie—it was delicious. Look at us, a brownie ice cream sandwich and now waffles with French toast."

"I mean, we are geniuses. They should hire us."

We savored every bite more than the previous one until we couldn't eat anymore. This was the first time I had been to a restaurant with a guy since undergrad. I went from being tense and feeling like I wanted to disappear to relaxing my shoulders, letting my guard down, and wondering if I ever knew I would be this happy.

Avery brought us the check. I tried to tell her I was paying, but he insisted. She told me he was more convincing. Since yesterday, I hadn't paid for anything or carried any bags. He's a gentleman and a gentle man.

We headed back to my house afterward to grab a few things before hitting the beach. I had gathered sunscreen, beach towels, containers for shells, and art supplies. I loaded a cooler with ice, bottled water, fruit, other snacks, and some sandwiches in case we got hungry. Michael went into the guest bathroom and changed into swim trunks, a T-shirt that was from a local surf shop, and flip-flops. I slipped on a black one-shoulder one-piece that had a white bow on the right shoulder and a white cover-up.

I normally threw my sandals in the beach bag so my feet could adjust to the hot sand until I met the waves as they thanked me for cooling them off. I wanted to be comfortable but elegant, not something that screams *Jersey Shore*. Michael followed behind me as I ran down the stairs from the back porch. Living steps away from the ocean makes up for the loss of not having a backyard. Michael rolled the cooler while carrying the beach bag and follows me through the sand.

"Let's go down towards the water. It will be easier to roll. Can I help you?" I tried to take something, but he insisted.

"You just lead the way." He stared at the water. "It's beautiful. No wonder you wanted to live here."

"I feel that I'm in another universe. It's just me and the ocean." I took a long pause. "And sometimes that is all I need."

He just stared at me without saying a word. I could tell that he also felt the same, wishing for some everlasting paradise that doesn't exist. He wanted to find peace, just like me. It's like we shared the same thoughts.

After walking for about ten minutes, we arrived at the spot I always settled at to paint. It's out of the way, and not a lot of people wandered down here. Maybe a few fishermen or tourists that scavenged through the shells like they were mining for gold.

We set up the beach towel, and I tossed him a bottle of water. Then I got up and started taking pictures of the ocean and dunes so we could reference them later. He called me over to take a selfie. "Perfect. You're a natural." He relaxed as he put both of his arms around me. I didn't feel afraid for once in my life.

"I normally like to take pictures of everything else but myself. I just feel awkward in photos."

"You should take more pictures of yourself." He looked up from his phone. "Or I can be your photographer?" He nodded as I handed him a blank canvas.

One of the reasons I love painting is because in my book, there are no rules. Just me, a paintbrush, and a blank canvas. It represents starting over and only adding details that you want and make sense to you. If it brings you joy, add it; or if it doesn't, paint over it or make it into something better. It's soothing and peaceful, and just being on the ocean is just the icing on the cake. Who could ever get sick of this view?

"So I normally begin by marking where the landscapes begin. And then I just add details and keep going until I'm satisfied." I picked up a paintbrush and dipped it in water then in light-blue paint and touched it to the canvas. "Here, you try."

"You make it look easy. I hope I don't mess it up." His hand touched mine as I handed him the brush, and I felt an electric shock race up my veins.

"You won't, trust me. These paintings are impossible not to love in the end." I just admired how concentrated he was. He was trying and making an effort. I think back to how Hudson would just sit there and watch something on his phone, not paying me any attention. Or better yet, downing a six-pack of beer then demanding we leave because it's too hot and he's drunk and can't walk to the water to cool off.

He looked at my every move and mimicked me. It's the doctor in him. I could tell he was detail-oriented and had lots of manual dexterity just like myself. We sat and painted for about an hour. Our canvases were different but looked like they belonged *together*. Side by side on the wall. Even though they weren't mirror images of each other, I couldn't imagine them being separated. They tell a story. The same story.

When I was done, I signed my initials and dated *AWC 2024*. He followed my lead and did the same and painted *MEB 2024*. As he studied my painting, he asked, "What does the *W* stand for?

"It's Wren. My middle name is Wren. What about you? What does the *E* represent?"

"That's beautiful, Adaire Wren," he said as he looked into my eyes. "My middle name is Elliot, after my father."

"I love it. Very handsome, I might add." I gave him a nudge.

"Thanks. Our pictures look different, but they need to be kept together."

We were taking it all in—the view, the sun, and each other's company. It was sunny but not too hot to the point we were sweating. The breeze was like air-conditioning mixed with the ocean. The last person who called me by my first and middle name was *him*. And he only did this when he had been drinking and wanted me to bring him something. Normally all I could hear was his voice, but for the first time, I just heard Michael's. It's like I didn't have to be afraid to look up or worry if I was making him angry to the point of being hit or screamed at. Finally a weight lifted off me, and I was no longer afraid.

Our paintings were finished, and we even collected some shells as we wandered up and down the shoreline. I had gotten to the point where I took my cover-up off. Once again, I didn't want to seem like I'm throwing myself at him. But at the same time, I knew these were different circumstances, and his thoughts wouldn't be the same. I wouldn't be called a show-off or slut. I would just be a young woman wanting to enjoy the sunshine as it pierces her skin.

"Wow, I like the black and white. It's very timeless, I might add." He reached into the bag and grabbed the sunscreen. "I thought you might reach for this."

"Thanks. It's one of my favorites!" I took the sunscreen and sprayed it everywhere. "You might want to put some on too. The sun can be violent this time of day."

He took off his shirt, and I gave him the bottle. He already had a good tan, but I couldn't help but notice muscular body and athletic figure. Once we're both slathered in sunscreen, we sat beside each other and enjoyed lunch. I removed the sandwiches, fruit salad, and chips and salsa from the cooler. Even though it was simple, everything always tasted better at the beach. After lunch, we made our way back to the house. The traffic of people picked up even though I could tell it was about to rain.

We washed our feet with the water hose in the back and soaked the shells in fresh water, making every mark more visible. I grabbed the canvases we painted on the beach and handed them to Michael. "Here, these are for you."

"Are you sure you don't want them?" He turned toward me. "They are very nice, but are you sure you don't want at least one of them?"

"I'm sure. You even said they go better together, and besides, they would look great in your kitchen."

"That's a perfect idea, thank you," he said with a soft smile. "Anyways, today was awesome! Who knew I would enjoy painting?"

"You never know until you try, right?" I wanted to say something else but remained silent.

Since he knew we were going to the beach, he brought a change of clothes with him. He washed up in the guest bathroom while I did the same in the other. It was refreshing knowing how easy it was to communicate and get along. Communication is a key in a healthy relationship, but it was one of the things that remained absent when I tried to have any communication with Hudson.

I changed into a floral maxi dress. It was one of my comfort outfits in the summer, no thinking or hesitating, just slip it on and go. I let my hair dry naturally and put on very minimal makeup so that my sun-kissed skin and freckles would peek through. He had walked out in khaki shorts and a light-purple button-down. I could smell his cologne as he passed through the living room and into the driveway to put his bag in the back of his truck. I was sitting on the couch, putting my sandals on. "Make yourself at home. Please sit wherever you want." I continued putting the other sandal on.

"You look stunning. By the way, I love the dress. It brings out your tan features." As he was looking me up and down, he said, "Do a twirl. That dress looks like a good dancing dress." He looked away, trying not to stare.

"Thank you, and so do you. How did you know purple was my favorite color?" I paused. "You smell good too. Is that a new cologne?"

"I thought you might like it."

As the clear blue sky faded into the sunset, we started on dinner. We had gone to the grocery store and local market to pick up the ingredients to make dinner. Neither of us knew what we were in the mood to eat, so we just got in the car and headed into town. Michael said that we could just wing it. As we were browsing the aisles, seeing if anything spoke to us, I told Michael, "I know one thing you have to try." I walked toward the refrigerated section. "We have to make smoothies tonight. Even though we just had them this morning, you just have to trust me."

"I do, and I'm excited. What about Mexican food?"

"That sounds so good. It's one of my favorites."

Our cart had every ingredient imaginable to make tacos, quesadillas, salsa, queso, and nachos. It looked like we were feeding a small army. Michael asked if we could make dessert. I had a lot of baking ingredients at home but picked up the remaining items to make chocolate chip cookies.

As he put some snacks in the cart, he commented, "I guess we should never come to the grocery store hungry again."

I nodded in agreement and proceeded to add more. Everything from fresh produce to junk food, there was every category. Once everything was checked off the list, we headed to the cash register. It was busy, but we passed the time with more small talk. Michael and I enjoyed trying and making new foods but also had our favorites, our special comfort foods. As the cashier was reaching the end of the groceries on the conveyor belt, I reached for my wallet. It's like we were in sync, and Michael did the same. He insisted on paying. I tried to argue, but he just kept saying, "You can pay me in cookies."

The cashier was an older lady. She tittered and said, "Girl, if he offers to pay, let him."

Michael looked at me while saying, "That's great advice." He then tapped his credit card against the machine. The sun was still out even though the clouds were trying to take over. It was hot and humid and the worst time of day, right before sunset. Michael turned the AC on and opened the door. "It's hot out here. I can finish this."

"If you're out here, then I am too." I proceeded to hand him the bags. "You know that before I met you, I always did these things alone. It's nice grocery shopping with you even though you tempt me to buy everything I shouldn't."

"Same. We are both independent, but every now and then, it's nice to have company."

I didn't take any moment for granted. On the drive back to my house, I could feel something inside me start to spark. I followed behind him as we unloaded all of the groceries. I could tell he wanted to do everything for me, but he knew that I would insist on helping, so he remained silent. We started by cooking the hamburger and chicken, then set all of the toppings on the bar in separate bowls. I threw the rice in a pot and mixed up the queso over the stove and chopped up everything for the salsa. He noticed that I put the flowers he gave me on the bar. He stared and observed them as he proceeded to set up everything.

Once everything was done, we made our plates and sat outside on the patio overlooking the water. The sun was just about to fall, and it was the perfect time of day. We ate and held conversation for over an hour before coming in to make dessert. I showed him what I did to make cookies even though it isn't rocket science, but he was interested in me and how I did it. He studied my hands as I was measuring and mixing everything.

"You should open a restaurant. You are a really good cook and know a lot about food." He continued to study my every move.

"It came to mind one time, but it's just a lot of work that goes into opening a restaurant. I would have to curate a menu, pay for a building, hire employees, and so much more. That's one of my dreams, but I know it isn't realistic. I want a life outside of work, not something that would invade all of my time and sanity. I may go crazy!"

"I can tell you've thought a lot about it. I would support you 110 percent, if you decide to go through with it."

"Do you want to help me scoop out some cookie dough? I promise to let you taste it."

"Sounds like a fair trade." He got up and stood next to me. I hadn't realized until now how tall he was. I was tempted to just hug him and bury my head into his chest. That's the type of week I have had, but I resisted. "Like this?"

"Perfect. You are a pro. If I need help, I know who to call."

"I'm in as long as I get to taste test everything. Seriously, if the cookie dough is that delicious, I can only imagine how good they will be once they are baked." We continued until everything was scooped out and placed on a cookie sheet.

Just like every time we were in the kitchen, we danced in the kitchen to whatever played. I felt like we were in a dream. Who knew that I would be dancing with a new guy in the kitchen as we cooked and baked all evening? It was a feeling I had longed for one day, but the hopes left my soul and never resurfaced. I just stopped having expectations so I could never get hurt again.

As the cookies were baking, we cleaned up the kitchen. Michael loaded the dishwasher as I put away the ingredients and wiped off the countertops. I couldn't help but think, *We make a good team.* I went to the freezer and pulled out the ingredients to make smoothies. After everything we have eaten today, we might as well end it on a good note with something healthy. I removed the blender from the cabinet along with two larger glasses. I made the smoothies as he finished washing the dishes.

"Here, try it." I held some in a spoon. "Do you like it?"

"That is out-of-this-world good! I could eat this every day and be satisfied. I'm going to need to start working out more," he joked as he finished the rest of the smoothie.

I could smell the aroma of the cookies filling the house as I walked closer to the oven. I removed the first two pans and put in the last two. I let them rest and cool before touching them. I filled two glasses with milk and put some cookies on a plate. We wiped them out as if we hadn't eaten all day. I pulled the remaining cookies out of the oven and put them all in a container. "I have an idea—let's go sit on the beach. It finally cooled off, and everyone is practically gone."

"It sounds like a perfect ending to the perfect day." He grabbed the container along with some milk as I followed behind him with a blanket and shut the door. All I could think about was *Is this really what* it *feels like?*

Chapter 7
GHOSTS

The sunset turned into dusk, and soon the darkness of the night took over with the exception of the moon and the lights from the fireflies. *Just right*, everything was perfect. It was cooler than before, and a small breeze came, just enough to run through my hair. We sat without saying a word, eating cookies and drinking milk. All I could think about was that I needed to tell him eventually. He couldn't see my face turning ghost white at the thought of finally letting him know about my past and why I always have my guard up.

I was so numb I talked without a filter. "So as you know, we touched on past relationships but never said any details." I took a deep breath. "Well, I want you to know that I have never had an official boyfriend, but I had a fling." He could see the look in my eyes as I couldn't control the tears coming down my face, making a puddle in the sand. He grabbed my hand and let me continue. "I had met him during my senior year in undergrad, and everything was fine until it wasn't.

He had gone from caring and sweet to manipulative and abusive in a matter of days . . . weeks even. The mask finally wore off, and I saw his true colors. They were dark and screamed pure evil."

I paused and realized he was listening to every word I said, taking it to heart. "I felt trapped and suffocated and that there was nobody to save me. That nobody would ever want to love or be with me. He made it seem like he had *won*. I knew that I had to fight but made sure it would be a fight I would be proud of and would be able to learn and grow from. I didn't want to hurt anyone, not even him. I just wanted to move on. I wanted to start over."

Michael couldn't even say anything. He was at a loss for words and started rubbing my back as I continued telling my story, staring at the ocean that disappeared into the reflection of the moon. He listened.

"He made me feel that he was the only person out there for me and I didn't deserve to find happiness. He was nice and had a loose smile when he was deep in a bottle of whiskey. He would get so drunk he couldn't remember what he ate the night before. We didn't live together, but he would come over to my dorm and harass me and apologize in the same breath. He would slap me and tell me I better be at his game *or else*. If I was just one minute late, he would scream at me afterwards or call me during halftime. I was the reason he was having an off night. It was me. It was always me."

I could see him breathing heavily as I spoke, but it was nice that he was being protective of me. There's a difference between protecting and preventing. Michael was protective of my heart, and Hudson was preventing me from my well-being. Just now in this moment, I learned there was a difference, and not every man was Hudson. But at the same time, not every man was like Michael. I learned the difference.

"One day he would call me beautiful and say he would want to spend the rest of his life making me happy and give me everything I wanted because I deserve everything in the world that was good and made me happy. He wanted to build me my dream house and travel all around the world because I was his best friend. Then once he flipped a switch, he would pin me against the wall, choke me, or threaten to kill me. My roommate and best friend walked in on him choking me and called 911 after she threw a lamp at his head. The hand imprints around my throat finally went away, and I filed a restraining order against him. I never saw him until he broke the order, and now he is in prison for good. They dug up his record and found several other disturbing things that he had been reported for—stalking, harassment, and even a DUI. I was not shocked since he drinks enough to keep the ABC store and bars in business. The day he broke his restraining order, he had a gun, pocketknife, and drugs. I could have died that day along with several classmates. The cops who were friends of my dad's said he would never mess with me again. And he hasn't."

I cried until the sand sank and caved in. I couldn't even look Michael in the face. I didn't want to see his reaction. Not just of the story I had told him but also of me crying. I didn't want him to think I was broken or unfixable. I wanted to be heard and seen.

Without saying a word, he scooped me up and placed me on his lap. He hugged me so tight and let me know that I am *safe*. He held me with caution and delicacy. "I couldn't imagine what you were going through." His voice cracked. "I wish I had known you so I could have protected you, been there to talk you through it. I wish I could have been that guy for you." He paused, trying to catch his breath. "Why would he ever do that to you let alone any woman?"

"He was just vile, violent, crazy, and easily provoked. And when you mix that together, he was like a ticking bomb that could go off at any time, and I didn't want to be the one to do it." I started to rub my eyes.

"How long were you with him?" He wiped my face with his shirt. "You deserve better than that."

"About seven months. Even though I broke it off several times, he knew what to say and when to say it. He was a master manipulator."

"I'm so sorry. I don't even have the words. I wish I could take your pain and every thought you have about him." I could hear the strength in his voice, trying not to sound angry at him. "He doesn't deserve you, and he never did. You did the right thing. It takes a lot of strength to just walk away, and you did just that and then some." He continued rubbing his hand along my back, comforting me. I almost fell asleep. "I'm here for you," he whispered. "He will never hurt you again. I promise."

I saw the fury in his eyes start to fade as he was trying to reassure me.

"Out of all the promises you'll make me, this is the one I wish you could keep. He's dangerous. Evil. And a piece of paper or ankle monitor isn't going to stop him."

That was a big promise, I thought to myself, but Michael was unlike anyone I had ever met. Even though I'd known him for a week, it felt like a lifetime since he's on my mind constantly. For once, I'd experienced what it was like to be treated properly and not have anyone scream at me to the point I want to get in my car and never stop. After I left *him* and Miami, I wanted to stay in Florida but go somewhere else. Some place I could be on the ocean but also make my own way in the world.

I continued, "I know if he ever gets released, he will hunt me down. And he's the type that will kill anything in his way to get what he wants."

"Try me."

And out of nowhere, I heard someone in the distance whisper, "I'm sorry." It wasn't Michael. It was the ghost of him.

His eyes twinkled against the moonlight, and fireflies flew around us as fireworks went off in my chest. For the first time, I felt seen and understood. His concern was something that touched me. We watched the waves glow like they were beaming in response to all that had just happened. We stood up and walked into the house. How was it already ten o'clock? I followed him to the door and gave him a hug.

He turned around and said, "I'll see you in the morning."

I went to bed knowing that when I woke up, he would be on his way over to drive us to church, and I couldn't help but fall asleep smiling.

Chapter 8
LET THE DEAD BURY THE DEAD

Hudson Fisher was every college girl's dream boyfriend. He was good-looking, stood at 6'2", had blue eyes and brown hair, and was a D-1 football player. Off the field, he was a senior who would start medical school next fall. Smart, charming, and sweet. What's not to love? Not only that but he asked for my number one night when I was out with my friends. Flattered was an understatement. Why would this college athlete and soon-to-be doctor want anything to do with a small-town girl like me? I'm just ordinary.

He asked me to go to dinner the following weekend, and of course I said yes. I mean, it was just one dinner. He picked me up from my dorm and made a good first impression with Ellie. He made reservations at a fancy steak house, and we had a deep conversation about our future plans. He told me he could see us building one together after he finished medical school and that he could see us living somewhere on the water with a boat. He was on his fourth glass of whiskey before he began to slur his speech as he was telling me how he wanted us to go out the next night too.

Hudson would never have any recollection of the night before, so in his mind, it didn't happen. For three more weeks, it was fancy dinners and clubs. I would let him take me out until early morning on the weekends. When I put my foot down and told him I wanted to study, he would get provoked and demand I wear a skintight dress and go out because I would be good arm candy. So I did. I still managed to be first in my class, but it was with no support from him. I would help him study and complete miscellaneous projects but would be nowhere in sight when I needed him. He was too busy with practice, studying, or partying to pay attention to me. I had given him nothing but time and an endless supply of chances without ever receiving anything in return. But I gave into his behavior because I was too scared to break things off or even worse to be *alone*, even though I already felt that way long before—isolated.

One night was different. We did our normal go out to dinner and have drinks, but he was so drunk I had to drive home. He tried to control the wheel and almost made me wreck into a ditch. Finally he dozed off, and I was able to drive the rest of the way to his apartment. I eventually got him inside, and when I tried to leave, he said under his breath, "Where are you going? Don't you want to be with me?" He was aroused and placed his hand on my arm, squeezing it to ground me.

"I do. I was just grabbing you some water." He eased his hand and let go but watched as I walked in the kitchen. He watched my every move. I knew just what to say and to soften my tone to make it seem I *loved* him. That I liked the way he treated and spoke to me. Because he is as good as it gets. Because I'm not going to find anyone better than him. And at the time my mind said it was him, but reality set me free.

"I don't deserve you. You know I care about you, right? I'm just feeling tired." He kissed me on the neck, and I could feel the whiskey beneath his breath, dripping off his lips as it pierced my skin. Wet. Hot. Reeking of odor. I could feel the moisture seep through my chest and into my heart, making me lovesick.

"You just need to get some rest, and we can talk in the morning." I had to maintain my soft, sweet, and innocent voice. I couldn't sound angry or startled because it would just add fuel to the fire. I had figured him out.

He grabbed my legs and wrist so I was unable to move. I tried to stand up, but he just pinned me to the couch. He would grab my hair or both my wrists. I quit fighting him. I surrendered. But I was reminded of him whenever my body started to ache. I felt and saw the bruises and imprints he left. He started saying how everything was my fault and how I was the reason he got angry. How it was my fault he drank so much because I stressed him out, not football or school but *me*. It was always me and never him. He's Mr. Perfect, remember?

"Please, can we talk about this in the morning when you are feeling better?"

"You're right." He closed his eyes, and I was able to sneak out. I took my shoes off so they wouldn't clack on the floor and wake him. It felt like I was escaping a lion's den. I felt trapped. I felt like I was in prison and nobody would save me. Smothered. Yet this was the routine I went through every time we went out. On the way back to my dorm, I couldn't help but cry and think, *Is this the best it's going to get for me? Maybe I'm not worthy of love.* His intentions needed to be black or white, but they were gray. I wish he would just let me go all the way.

That was just one of the numerous instances where he would grab me hard enough to leave a mark or want to kiss me as his way of apologizing. I had his handprints reminding me of what he did and was capable of. There were outlines of his hands on my arms, waist, and back. He told me he cared about me too much to kill me, right now anyway. At one point, he held a knife up to me and pinned me against the wall as I was doing everything to remain calm so he wouldn't cut or choke me. But when he would sober up, he claimed he would never do such a thing and bring me flowers in hopes I would forget. He would cry to rub away the memories he left and pierce my skin with his lips, hoping everything would fade away.

Just like a creature of habit. Or how mosquitoes bite humans and how scorpions are known as being poisonous. It's their DNA or what they are notorious for; they have to do it in order to survive. I kept telling myself he loved me and that maybe he needed to take his actions out on me in order to get better. Or maybe it was because we both knew I had never been in love and he was trying to persuade me into thinking it was what he wanted it to be. I didn't know any different. I was naive. Stupid. Clueless. Just a dumb girl, as he would say.

Weeks turned into months, and I found myself trapped and lost. I hated myself. I was depressed and felt more lonely than I had ever been. I wanted a way out but was scared. I was scared of him. I didn't want him to drag me out of my dorm one night and beat me or hurt anyone I cared about. I wanted to disappear and become a different person. I wish I could erase everything that happened. I just wanted it to stop.

The last night I had ever seen him was near the end of our senior year (I graduated in two and a half years). He came to my dorm with flowers and brought revenge instead. He thought I was alone, but Ellie and I were about to go to dinner with some friends to celebrate graduation. He insisted I went with him, and I told him *no*. He didn't take that as my answer and started choking me. He pressed me up against the wall, and I was too in shock to react until Ellie ran out of the room because she heard a thump. She screamed, trying to get him to let go of my neck.

"Quit! She can't breathe!" she yelled in panic. He slapped her and continued strangling me. I thought I was going to die and the last thing I would see would be him. She eventually got up and hit him over the head with a lamp. He didn't lose consciousness, but it was enough to make him let go of me. He then went after her, and I ran to my purse and grabbed pepper spray. When he turned around, I sprayed like my life depended on it. And in this case, it did. He buckled to his knees, holding his eyes.

Without even realizing it, I started kicking him while Ellie dialed 911. We were not going to let him escape. I wanted him to feel like I did all these months—a prisoner and nowhere to go. I wanted to know he was in custody with the police and that I could go to bed feeling at ease. I kicked him until he threw up. Finally the cops arrived. Ellie and I could relax for the first time in minutes. I felt this nightmare was ending, but it wasn't the last page. I knew he wasn't going to be done; he had to beat me. The thought of me getting away made him angry.

The next day, the police called to inform me Hudson was to leave me alone and stay away from me if I sign a restraining order. Ellie drove me the next hour so we could sign the paperwork and give our final statements. This was the end. In my mind, the water was still. I thought it was over. Peace was peeking through the window as a rainbow appeared in the sky. It was a sign that he didn't win after all. He didn't get his way.

A week had gone by, and there was no sign of him at school. I didn't even receive a phone call or text message. Normally I would wake up to endless calls, voicemails, and texts. They would be asking me where I was and why I was so awful for not responding and that he had the right to know where I was 24/7 because he wanted to *protect* me. Even though all I ever wanted was to be saved—not from him but because of him. He would get upset if I wanted to hang out with Ellie, go to dinner with friends, or do anything he couldn't control. I felt like a prisoner with an ankle monitor, but now the roles were reversed. I didn't feel hatred, guilt, or sadness. It was an emotion drained from me long ago—freedom.

Despite being watched by the police, he couldn't let me go. He had to get the last laugh and be the one to pull the trigger. Going against the restraining order, he decided to not only come on campus, but came like a hunter searching for deer. He had a gun in his sweatshirt pocket with a pocketknife lying on top of it. Just like anyone wanting revenge would do, he rubbed them with his hands just waiting for the perfect moment to use them. He couldn't do it in the middle of campus. He's the football player everyone knew and loved. He was waiting for me to be walking alone or for me to get into my car. But ever since that night occurred and I filed a restraining order, I was never alone even though my soul left my body at that same moment. He was angry, confused, and getting impatient. He wanted everything to go his way. Because that's what he was used to. Because he was perfect and everything was always my fault and he was the victim.

A few girls spotted him and asked for a picture. Of course he said yes, and he drew a crowd. Ellie called me from across campus letting me know *he* was *here*. My mind went blank, my stomach dropped, and I fell to the ground. In my mind, he was here and here for one thing. He wanted to be the one to write the last page, to kill me. Thankfully, Trevor, a good family friend of mine whom I had known since middle school, was with me. He caught me before I hit my head and called the cops. He walked me to the closest building he could find, which happened to be the gymnasium. We saw a coach walking the hall and told him what was going on and that we had already called the police. He locked the doors to the gym and announced that nobody was allowed to leave or enter the building.

I called Ellie back and told her everything that was going on and to get somewhere safe. She knew he was flighty and saw before her own eyes the monster he transformed into. The police came discreetly without setting off their sirens. They searched the whole campus, every inch until they found him walking toward the gymnasium. That was the last place he was going to search. They had him in custody along with the weapons he was carrying. A friend of my father's was the deputy and told me he will never bother me again. And that was a promise he kept.

"It's over," that was the only thing I could say. My leash was cut, and I was finally able to live for me and not us. I could walk to my car, go to class, and even go out to a restaurant without having the fear he might come behind me demanding that I follow him. That was the first night I could see light at the end of the tunnel. No more storms, just the sun peeking through the clouds. He turned my world of color vague, while our memories remained a rainbow in his head.

Chapter 9
SUNDAY MORNINGS

The dolphins were doing flips in the ocean as the sun took over and rose above the clouds. Just like the clouds, I felt a weight lifted off my shoulders. God works in mysterious ways, one mankind will never be able to comprehend. If He handed everything to us, we would never gain the strength to walk without Him. I've learned over the years that God always has a plan, but He just gives it to us in pieces at a time. He knows we're craving the missing pieces but knows it is just simply not time yet. I give glory to God in every situation I face, because time and time again, He has pulled me through. He helped me overcome the darkness I felt as a child and the trials and tribulations I faced during school, and he certainly brought everything to light with Hudson. I begged God at times to give me the answers so I could escape, so I knew He was there. But I also told God I didn't need easy, just possible.

And most recently I couldn't thank Him enough for sending Michael. When I first moved to Orlando, I was focused on nothing but work and making my own way in the world. I shifted my attention away from relationships. I would avoid contact with any male when I went to the grocery store, to the gym, and even at drive-throughs. I used to be afraid of what could have been if I didn't walk away or if Ellie didn't save me that night. I cried due to the night terrors. I would wake up in a sweat, or some nights I couldn't close my eyes because his image would arise in my dreams or, in this case, nightmares. I remember one conversation Ellie and I had during our late nights studying.

"Ellie, why is it so hard? I don't think he's an evil person. I just think he needs help. I cared for him once, and I still do. I just wasn't the right person for him." We sat in the living space and ate ice cream as she gave me all the advice she could.

"It's not that you didn't love him. He just didn't know how to love you. You love with everything in you. You don't know how to love someone halfway. That's why it ends up hurting you more than them. And not just with Hudson—it could be anyone."

We sobbed as she squeezed my hand. "Adaire, I've known you my whole life. You're the sister I never had. And just know the right person is out there for you. You deserve someone who doesn't even make you think twice of their intentions. You deserve someone who makes you smile without even trying. Someone who you can do the little things with like eating dinner or grocery shopping to having hard conversations with.

But either way, you both come out on top. And it was worth it because you did it together."

Ellie and I had endless conversations about guys. When we were little, we fantasized about our Prince Charming, what color hair he had, the pets we were going to adopt, and what color house we would live in. But all of those things turned into high standards we set for ourselves and to never settle for anything less.

Now all of the night terrors are done, and Hudson is dead to me. I hope he finds peace one day, but he doesn't deserve to know anything about me. Michael is like a breath of fresh air. I was living my day-to-day life, and one day out of the blue I met him. I knew the second I met him there was something different about him—his easy and comforting demeanor, the way he listens and holds a conversation, and the way he is passionate about his career. After getting to know him, I realized there is so much more to him than just being a shy doctor. He is caring, kind, and something I thought I didn't deserve.

He makes me feel like I am the only person left on this planet and that he is content with it. He has gone out of his way to not only ask me on a date but execute it with so much thought and effort. He asked me questions about my past and listened as I talked like he could feel my heart break telling him. He was compassionate, loved to serve others, and was incredibly kind to all those he encountered. He would stop and pet any dog that walked by us on the beach, smile at strangers, wave to children, and be always polite to service workers. He made time for conversation.

I heard his truck pull in the driveway, and a moment later, I heard a knock on the door. There he was once again, standing in my doorway with a smile that melted my heart. He was wearing a white button-up shirt with a blue tie, dress pants, and leather loafers. We coordinated like he read my mind. I had on a blue-and-white dress, heels, and a cardigan draped over my shoulders. I grabbed my Bible and headed toward the door.

"You look amazing. I love the colors in your dress. It's like we don't even need to plan our outfits. They just go together, like you and me," he said as he held back his flirting and leaned in for a hug.

I smiled lightly. "It's like we just knew in some way. You look great. I love the tie!"

"You know, I'm still trying to win you over."

Our conversation continued as he helped me in the truck. "Let me move these to the back seat." He grabbed his Bible and jacket. He always made sure my dress wouldn't get caught in the door and proceeded to close it.

Just a few miles up the road, there was a community church where I would join my work friends and some people I had met since moving here. It was a smaller, more intimate church, which I liked. It was out of the way but still close enough to the ocean you could take in the view and hear the waves singing. There wasn't a designated parking lot, just a field with dirt and the remaining gravel the wind decided to leave behind. Families were walking on the side of the street, and people of all ages came. There were children's church and youth group activities in the back. I had volunteered at a few events as it reminded me of being back home, something I knew I missed but wanted to incorporate back into my life.

"Hey! Miss Adaire," a few of the little girls I had gotten to know said as they waved from across the street.

I waved back. "It's good seeing you guys again. I'll see you inside." There's just something about kids that I love but also made me miss Lucy and Isla. I know it has been two days but has felt like two years.

Michael followed me and didn't leave my side. I introduced him to all of my coworkers and friends I had met since attending this church. Like always, he was pleasant and welcoming to everyone. We sat on a pew next to Leah. Leah was the person I was closest to other than Robin. She was in her early forties and had a son who was in high school. Her husband traveled for work, so we would always sit together. She told me she liked Michael and thought he was good for me, but that's all she said. She knew that I was new to all of this and didn't want to say anything that would trigger me.

The service was always good, but during the sermon, I would always refer to my Bible and would jot down notes on the side column. I noticed Michael doing the same. I also observed that almost every page in his Bible had notes on it, and verses were highlighted, mirroring mine.

In a way, God made me wait all these years so that when the right person and time came, *I knew.* Even though I had only known him a week, I just felt something that was indescribable. A feeling that God gave me for a reason. In my heart, I just knew.

When church was over, I introduced Michael to Lilly. She was the little girl who waved at me as we were walking in. She was five years old and had just started kindergarten. She had dark-brown hair and blue eyes and looked like an American girl doll. She was as sweet as a pie, and for a moment, I wondered what it would like to have children of my own someday—a familiar thought that pulled at my heartstrings. I had gotten close to her this winter when I would help out during children's church on Wednesday nights. She would always sit in my lap and let me braid her hair and read the Bible with her. Her elder sister also waved at me earlier, and her name was Oakley. She had light-brown hair and dark eyes. They looked like twins. She was nine years old and loved to talk to me about what she was learning in school or read to me her favorite verse of the week.

"Girls, this is my friend Michael." They smiled and waved, and he did the same. "He works with me, and I thought I would bring him to church."

"Hi, girls, it is nice to meet you both," Michael said as he bent down to shake their hands. "Isn't Miss Adaire the best?"

"Hi, and yes, she is," Lilly said as she came over for me to pick her up. "She plays with me too!"

"She is my favorite teacher," Oakley said, coming over toward me. They asked Michael, "Are you coming on Wednesday?"

"I have to work, but I will try and make it."

They smiled as they walked beside us along with their mother, Martha. Martha was in her thirties, and her husband was in the military, so when I met them, we instantly became friends. Her husband comes home maybe twice a year, so she relies on her family and friends a lot. I have gotten to know and love her girls, and maybe Michael would too. We said our goodbyes as they hugged each of us. Lilly had given Michael a sticker, and he wore it on his shirt with pride. When we got in the car, he took it off and stuck it on the mirror above his head.

"There, now I can keep it forever. I didn't want it to blow off."

The crowd dwindled down, and the lot grew empty as we sat and people-watched. After pulling out, we headed to grab lunch in town and wanted something that was quick and easy so we could walk on the beach before Michael left to get ready for work tomorrow. We decided on one of the local cafes and grabbed sandwiches, and I had snacks at the house.

"I planned ahead and bought my bathing suit just in case," he adjusted his head just enough to make eye contact.

"You always think of everything. Anyways, the girls seemed to like you. So are you gonna keep your promise?"

"About coming on Wednesday? Of course, I'll have to see what I can work out. What time does it start?"

"I normally leave around four thirty to help set before it starts at five."

"I'll be there. That's a promise."

Once again, he promised. The only thing left to do is to see if he upholds this one along with a few others he has made me. I have high hopes but no expectations. The feeling of someone keeping their promises was drained from me years ago.

The last stop was to swing by my house to change and grab some snacks, drinks, and towels. Then it was time to hit the beach. I never brought a lot, just a beach bag with sunscreen, towels, a container for shells, and a cooler with food and drinks. I didn't own a beach chair. I just didn't like the hassle of having to carry or clean it. They rusted by the end of the season anyway. To me, they were just another thing that was temporary. That word took over my life sooner than I realized.

Our spot was once again free, like it was waiting for us. There were birds flying around us, hoping we would throw them some food as they waited for schools of fish to come in the shallow waters. Before we ate lunch, we set up beach towels and laid the cooler and bags on the edges so they wouldn't blow away. I removed my cover-up, and he did the same with his shirt before he followed me to the water as the waves crashed at our feet and fiddler crabs scoured the wet sand before burying themselves.

Our hands touched. My hand connected to his like they were magnets. We held hands as we walked through shallow waters no deeper than our knees. He pulled me closer to him like he was protecting me, keeping me safe. Safe from the ocean and from anyone or anything, including Hudson. As we walked back toward our spot, he squatted down, so I got on his back. He walked out farther into the ocean as the water began to take over our bodies. When he put me down, it was to my chest. We swam, talked, and looked at the clouds as the sun continued to beat down on us. I was in a trance, not wanting this day to end. I felt like we were on our own island. Even in a room full of people, I feel like the only girl. He makes me feel a certain type of way—special.

We made our way back to the beach to sit and have lunch together. I had left the sandwiches out so they would bake in the sun while our drinks cooled on ice. "So when are we going to see the girls again?" He took a swig of water and unwrapped his sandwich. "I think we should go together this week."

"What about Thursday or even Friday, since it is the start of the weekend? I couldn't think of anything I would rather be doing!"

"That sounds great, even though it seems like a year from now. Being away from them is hard. They are all I think about."

"I miss them so much. I know they are in good hands. So if they're happy, I am too."

"You know, this weekend has been amazing thanks to you. I can't recall the last time I was so relaxed and having this much fun."

"Same here." I paused to take a bite. "I don't remember the last time I was this content with life. I just want to thank you for listening and being here for me."

"Anytime. You know you can talk to me about anything, and it stays between us."

"Most people would run for the hills once I told them about my past and especially about him. But you didn't. You just sat and comforted me and let me say what I needed without judgment."

"You didn't have to ask. And the fact that you told me everything that happened with such composure shows how strong you are to overcome it."

"A lot of people see me as someone who was a victim to violence and relationship abuse."

"I don't. I see the strongest person I have ever laid my eyes on. You walk with such grace in everything you do. Any person would have just run away, but you walked away learning, knowing you deserve better. You not only beat him at his own game, you survived."

At this point, he had grabbed my hand, showing me comfort without saying anything. Actions speak louder than words, and his did just that. He massaged my hand as we sat there in silence. It's like his heart hugged mine, telling me everything was going to be okay. He reassured me. He *showed* it.

A few hours had passed, so we packed up and started to head in. Neither of us wanted to and agreed we could sit there until sunset but knew that our careers lay ahead, and another workweek started tomorrow. He had to meet with patients and complete another rotation, while I would be slammed in meetings with Robin about the ongoing investigation about the plane crash. We understood the importance of our work and the pride each of us takes in it. That was just another thing that made us click.

Michael helped me unload and put away everything as we snacked on the cookies from the night before. It was cool and refreshing to get out of the sun for a bit. We called it a day and agreed to call each other later. I would have to see him at some point because I had a few of his T-shirts in the washing machine. Once again, that role slipped my mind—I'm doing another man's laundry. But instead of everything wreaking from the scent of alcohol and sweat, it was salt water and sand. I thought to myself, *I could get used to this.*

Chapter 10
COULD IT BE?

Mondays suck. I could just tell it was going to be one of those days. The ones that never end and go by so slow. I was prepared but didn't want to face it. A thunderstorm scattered across the sky, crashing down all at once. The rain was falling as if the clouds were crying out their sadness as lightning took the place of their anger. The ocean was a dark blue. White caps were the only thing you could see for miles. There was no sight of birds in the sky or fish in the ocean, as if they had just vanished into thin air. The only thing that felt like sunshine was a good-morning text from Michael. Every day since we had met, he texts me "Good morning," "Good night," and "I'll see you tomorrow." Those texts are simple yet mean so much. They let you know that they are thinking about you without saying it. It is something that should be normalized in today's society but is rare to find. But somehow I found it.

I felt like I was walking through the ocean just to get to my car. I had on my tall rain boots, and even that was a struggle. Driving through hurricane-like winds was an obstacle. Not only could I hardly see, I felt that the wind was blowing my car from one side of the road to the other. This was another way of saying, "You should have just stayed home." I pulled into the parking lot, and Robin parked beside me. I ran inside while Robin was following behind me. It looked like the carpet was drowning. We had a few people call out, but all of the administrators were there. We had to be. Meeting after meeting and a few phone calls before we could work from home the rest of the week. I had three things to look forward to: Michael, church on Wednesday, and going to see the girls.

"Can we go home now?" Robin said while wiping her face. "I think we should work half a day and then work from home."

"That sounds like a plan to me. Is there anything further about investigation or camera footage?" I dropped my umbrella and took my rain boots off and followed Robin into her office.

"Not that I know of. You know how slow those detectives work. It's like watching paint dry." She gulped down her coffee, wiped her face, and threw her stuff on the floor, creating yet another puddle.

"So how was your weekend?" I tried to change the subject but knew this would lead to another tangent.

"Good but hot. I was about to have a heatstroke on Saturday. So I stayed inside and caught up on some TV shows, read a book, and cleaned. The stuff my husband won't do so I have to." She smirked as she rolled her eyes. "It's like he's allergic to it."

"That's a man for you." I nodded in agreement. "My dad is the same way."

"So what did you do?"

"I stayed at home, walked on the beach, ran errands, the usual."

"Mhmm, I saw you leave church with Michael yesterday. What did I tell you?" She gave me that look and continued downing her coffee. It was all she could do to keep from falling asleep.

"We're just friends, that's all. Besides, I've known him for a week." I didn't know what to say because I was with him all weekend. But I also didn't want to lie because Robin would know before I finished my sentence.

"See, he's not so bad!" She gave her grin, the one that says, "I'm always right" and "I told you so."

"He's great! But we're still just getting to know each other. I would be content with just having him as a good friend." That's the truth, but I know I'm wishing for something more. But that's the thing, I don't know what it's like to be truly in love because I haven't. If what I had with Hudson was considered "real love," then I don't want it. Ever. But it also reassured me that I haven't experienced the best days of my life or met all the people I'm going to love.

The first meeting today was about the weather, the schedule for the rest of the week, and what to do about working remotely. The conclusion was if you feel safe, come in; and if you don't, stay home and log in to the computer. All meetings can be done over Zoom or the phone. For the most part, we are all paid on a salary, so we don't have to clock in or out; we just do what we can. One of the things I like about this company is that their motto is "family first." Our families, our friends, and ourselves come before work. Work can wait, well, sometimes. But there might not be another day with a loved one; or if you have an appointment, go. The same thing goes for vacations. Take off; we all deserve a mental health break.

Soon after that, Robin and I met with Sam via Google Meet to discuss Lucy and Isla and what the status of everything was. For starters, it's only been a week, and there are pending discoveries to be made. So there wasn't much to discuss. We did go over everything that was reported back to the detectives, even though we have all heard it before. We gave Sam a walk-through of our first visit with the girls. Just talking about them gave me that same feeling all mothers must get when they talk about their children. He told us that it was good that we went to see them and should continue doing as much as we could. Sam said that one of the things these girls need more than anything is stability—something I was trying to give to these girls yet can't describe the feeling myself. Even though I lack stability through a person, it doesn't mean it's hard to give.

Stability is the layout for one's life and home, literally. Everyone should be able to endure day-to-day tasks and face tribulations while still standing firm.

Chaeli Smith

With God, all things are stable. With Him, all things are possible.

I told Sam about the journal and emailed him a copy of it. Even though we studied the pages, I felt like we were trying to decipher a code from another universe. We took notes and flagged the pages we thought could be a lead, but nothing. My eyes were starting to cross the more I read over the reports and findings about the plane crash. At one point, I found myself blinking just to keep my eyes from closing. I daydreamed about Michael holding me on the beach that night. How he was sweet and reassuring and told me everything was going to be okay. He let me know he was on *my* side no matter what. He told me he would fight for and with me. He let me know that it was over and I never had to worry again. I did though, but not just about Hudson. I worried for the girls. I worried about the results coming in from the DNA test I took to learn about my ancestors. I worried about the future.

I voiced my thoughts about the security cameras. I told Sam and Robin that there was more to the story than what they were able to dig up. Something wasn't right. Once I gave them my reasoning, they agreed. We were going to contact them every day until they found something. Anything. Anything is better than nothing at all. The meeting concluded with the normal keep in touch as our next one was scheduled for later in the week. As we ended the meeting, Robin shut down her computer.

"That was the longest hour of my entire life." She opened a bottle of Diet Coke and chugged it until it was gone.

"This whole week is going to feel like a month. Waiting on results is the worst feeling, because nothing we do or say will make the results come any faster."

"Those detectives are useless. We might as well have gone through everything ourselves." She paused and grabbed her notes. "We have found more in an hour than they have all week. You can't rely on them for much."

"Maybe they won't disappoint us. I am still hoping that they can find something. Someone."

"Anyways, tell me about you and Michael. I know you didn't just accidentally just run into him at church." She gave me a long, hard stare, one of those "you better not lie to me" looks.

"We started messaging each other and decided to ride together. I mean, it is that simple."

Robin could tell I was getting aggravated and changed the subject to talk about the weather. She said that after lunch, I could work from home until I feel it is safe to drive. I know my house is only five minutes away, but still, five minutes can feel like a long time in these situations. I'm right on the ocean, and if I leave my house, I want to be able to get back to it.

Around noon, we all packed up and left for the week. I had my laptop, a box with some files, and a notebook with all of the information about Lucy and Isla's case.

I trekked to the car, with my rain boots on. The water was about six inches deep by the time I put everything in my trunk. I felt like I was about to drown. I knew that if Michael was here, I wouldn't have to lift a finger. But at the same time, I knew that I had done everything myself for over two decades without relying on anyone else, especially another man. I had lost interest in the idea until I met Michael.

I pulled out of the parking lot, and it looked like a drowned ghost town. There were hardly any cars, just those of us who had to come and go from work. The fog was coming down heavy, steam-like almost. I felt like I was on another planet. I saw no signs of wildlife. No birds or stray dogs, just water. I felt wet and gross, just like I went swimming in the ocean and put on dry clothes without drying off. I mean, ugh. Before I went home, I stopped at the grocery store just like every other person who lived in Orlando who prepared for unpredictable weather.

The parking lot was full; everyone had the same idea. There were people coming and going like we were going into self-preservation mode. Everyone was grabbing bottles of water, pantry staples like soups and canned vegetables, and junk food like cookies and chips. Thankfully, I had a generator, so I stocked up on everything. I bought produce, meats, dairy, frozen products, household paper products, and snacks; and everything I touched I threw in the cart. Once again, my mind went to Michael. The last time I was here was a few days ago, and I was with him.

I picked up baking ingredients to make a few different desserts in hopes of seeing him this week. By the time I got to the register, my cart was full; it looked like I was feeding a few dozen people. But nothing was worse than being stuck in the house with nothing to eat. It's better to be safe than sorry. I loaded the groceries in my car. I could hardly fit anything else in my trunk and back seat.

The drive home was short but seemed longer because I was driving slower than molasses due to the flooded roads. After I unpacked my car, I organized and put all of the groceries away. I wouldn't have to go grocery shopping for another month. I had bought so much food, but my mind went into panic mode at the store. I had bought plastic bags and containers for extra storage. Even with all this food, I was still wondering what I was going to have for dinner. I was nauseated at the idea.

In the meantime, I made a smoothie to chill my thoughts and loosen my nerves. I opened my computer and worked from home for a few hours, answering emails, taking phone calls, and going through files. I had my work cut out for me. Robin even called. We didn't say a whole lot but just kept each other on the phone as we worked. She would make comments about how certain people were aggravating her already and how she wanted to throw her computer into the ocean and never look back. I told her there was always tomorrow and that things like this just take time and that sometimes rushing gets you nowhere but back to the beginning. I wanted to make sure we had all of our facts in order and enough evidence to proceed.

Five o'clock hit, and we called it a day. Even though it was still blowing, at least the rain had stopped. This didn't mean it wasn't going to pour later though; it just needed a break. My phone went off, and it was Michael calling me. My cheeks turned red when his contact came across my screen. It's like I was a teenager in high school blushing about her first boyfriend. I know, I'm lame.

"Hey! How was your day? I was busy, and this is the first break I've had all day."

"My day just got better! I am working from home the rest of the week. What about you? How have you been?"

"Great, now that I am talking to you. I've been swamped, but I'm leaving work now."

"Drive carefully. There is water everywhere. The grocery store was packed. I would be surprised if there was anything left." "I'm about to head there now. Do you need anything else?"

"I think I'm good! I bought the entire store."

"I guess I'll have to come and shop at your house."

"Anytime! So if you want to stop by, you can."

"After I leave the grocery store, I'll swing by. I can pick up some wine if you would like?"

"That sounds perfect. I can start on dinner and dessert."

"I can't wait. I will see you soon."

I went into the kitchen and pulled out the ingredients to make grilled chicken and steak over jasmine rice with sauteed vegetables. First, I marinated the chicken, covered it with plastic wrap, and put it in the refrigerator. Next, I seasoned the steak and let it sit on the counter covered with foil. Lastly, I chopped and seasoned the vegetables before adding them to a pan: first the carrots, then the onion, and lastly the zucchini. I let them rest without cooking them just yet. Once I prepped everything, I pulled the chicken out and began cooking it. Then I started the vegetables and boiling water for the rice. Everything was coming together, and Michael knocked and then opened the door.

"Hey! There was a box on the porch. I'm surprised it wasn't soaked." He let off a smile and set the wine along with a few other bags on the counter before coming over to hug me as I was standing over the stove.

"Thanks. I think I know what it is. You said you were just bringing wine? Either way, it is great to see you." We stood there and looked at each other before I leaned in for another hug. It was just what I needed after a long day.

"These are for you." He pulled a bouquet of flowers from one of the brown grocery bags.

"Well, those are beautiful. Thank you. Do you mind putting them in a vase? I don't want them to go without water for too long."

"Of course," he replied as he was filling up the glass vase I had pointed to. "They're going to look great. I can tell you love flowers."

"I do. They bring me such joy!" Everything was ready to eat, so I handed Michael a bowl, and we dug in. We were starving. I also took a knife and opened the box. Lying inside were a smaller box and an envelope. I knew that maybe some answers were inside, and I couldn't wait to finish dinner, so I opened them both. The envelope was some cheesy thank-you note and was a waste of my time. The box had a card and a piece of paper with a family tree on it. It had my nationality, a list of dead famous people I was related to, etc. All of the boring "this is where you came from" crap on it. I discovered that I was 95 percent Chinese and 5 percent Vietnamese. It also told me I had two relatives still alive in China, in Changsha. For living relatives, it read,

"Lee Gua Wu-Shong, age 65, female, and Sui Li Wu-Shong Le, age 50, female."

My mind froze, and I couldn't even process what I had just read. Could it be? Am I reading this right? Someone pinch me. I couldn't even look at Michael long enough to form a sentence. He just sat there staring at me, waiting for me to say something. Then he stood up and walked over to me and massaged my shoulders.

"It's going to be okay. I'm here for you. Take all of the time you need."

"I just can't process anything right now." I handed him the letter, and he looked back at me.

"Are you okay?" He grabbed my hand and then proceeded to rub my back.

"I'm fine. I'm just trying to take it all in, I guess. Thank you for being here."

He squeezed my hand tighter. "I'm all in. I mean, if you want to dig into this some more, I will support you 100 percent the rest of the way. Whatever you need."

"Part of me wants to find these people, but the other half doesn't want to get my hopes up just to be disappointed."

"Let me help you. We will get through this together."

"I appreciate that more than you know."

"Well, you make things easy. I'm just comfortable being around you."

"Same here. Five hours feels like five minutes. I really have a great time with you. I was kinda hoping I was going to see you sooner than Wednesday. I mean, if they are still having church."

"Why, of course. I had planned to check on you today anyways. I mean, I had to deliver flowers." He smiled as we locked eyes, and for the first time, I saw the future looking at someone.

"You can come by anytime. Seriously, just walk in." We looked at each other with ease as we continued sipping our wine.

"By the way, dinner was excellent. Everything was exquisite."

"Thank you! I hope you are ready for some dessert."

After we finished dinner, we cleaned up the kitchen. We loaded the dishwasher, and I put the leftovers into Tupperware containers as he swept the floor and wiped the counters. Teamwork. We made the perfect pair, I thought to myself as I was standing next to him at the sink. Once everything was cleaned up from dinner, we immediately pulled out the ingredients for dessert. Even though it smelled like fresh lemons, the smell was going to fade, and it would turn into brown butter and chocolate.

"Everything is so organized. You even have a label with the expiration date," he said as he removed the flour and sugar from the pantry.

"I try. It makes it a lot easier to see what I have and what I need to buy at the store the next time I go."

From memory, I retrieved the eggs and butter from the refrigerator. I placed them on the counter next to the dry ingredients. There we stood, cooking dessert together for the third night in the past week. It was calming and just fun. We danced to music as we stirred the cookie dough and then scooped them out and placed them on the baking sheet. We always made two and a half recipes. This was to ensure Michael could take some with him after he ate one batch here. Half a batch was eaten during all of our "taste testings." Once the cookies were in the oven, he would grab the spatula and lick off the cookie dough. At one point, we were eating off the same one. I was so lost in the moment I didn't even realize what we were doing. It was just normal. Something I had longed for. But we were still just friends, remember?

One of the things I noticed whenever I hang out with Michael is that neither of us get on our phones or watch TV. We take in the moment and be fully present, talking and listening to each other, giving each other advice, like real friends should. Our days consisted of lots of beach walks, cooking, and dancing. We danced on the beach and in the kitchen. One of the things about my past was that material items came over each other. There was always something we had to watch or that required technology. Honestly, I wish social media would go away. I like the idea of being able to text, call, and take pictures; but that's it. I know, I'm old school. But it is the truth, and life would be more simple.

The evening turned into night, and the water was calm. It was still alive, but all of the movement came to a stop. The wind had died off but was going to pick back up during the early morning. We took advantage and managed to crack a window so we could smell the salt air. It was just another night of sitting and hearing each other's stories about our childhood and what we did to make the time pass. I told him how I would spend every day on the water during the summer. I would be at the beach, or we would travel down the Bahamas and do everything we could in a short week—from kayaking to zip-lining and even dolphin encounters. To no surprise at all, he also traveled a lot when he was younger. The similarities were scary. We traveled, attended church, and focused on our education to get us to where we are today. We kept saying, "So did I" or "Me too." It's like we had lived the same lives in another universe.

I thought to myself, I wish I had met him sooner, but I knew there was a reason God made me wait. It was to realize that when something good came into my life, I would know. I would protect and fight for it at all costs, and I wouldn't just let it run or push it away. I needed someone to stay—someone who wanted to make this work and fight to be together and not let anything tear us apart.

Around nine o'clock, it was time to call it a night. The kitchen was spotless, and I handed him a container with the batch of cookies I promised before he hugged me and went home. We are taking things slow. No sleepovers. Nothing that could interfere with what we already had and are continuing to build on. We haven't even shared a kiss. I knew that this was meant to last because of all the deep conversations and endless laughs we have shared. Having the same mindset and goals for the future was just extra confirmation. And one day I wanted to get married and raise a family, travel, and spend time together on the water. It was a dream I had prayed for my entire life; and now maybe, just maybe, it was my turn.

Chapter 11
LAND OF THE FREE

By the first week of July, everyone was in full swing to prepare for the upcoming holiday weekend. Fireworks were being sold under tents and grocery stores and even being advertised on TV. The market was jam-packed with people. Food Lion was nearly out of bread, chips, meats, and produce—everything you would need for a cookout. People were like colonies of seagulls. They would have ten packs of hot dog buns in their cart, not leaving anything for the next person.

None of it changed the flaming hot sun that nearly melted your skin off the second you stepped outside. The only downfall to living in Florida year-round is the extreme heat and lack of wind some days. It was so hot I considered going to the mountains for a weekend.

The summer had flown by. It was like one moment it was May, and then I blinked and it was the beginning of July. Things with Michael were as good as I could imagine. We had dinner almost every night together, switching between whose house we were going to. Some nights we went out while most of the time we opted to stay in and watch the sunset from the beach. It's like we were a *couple*—having dinner together, spending all day together on the weekend, going to church, running errands, and even working from home. He would bring his laptop to my house or vice versa.

One night he surprised me with tickets to a country concert. We took a road trip down to Miami to see the Zac Brown Band play. We danced and mingled with the crowd and afterward went to the condo he had rented. There were two bedrooms and two bathrooms, so we slept separately. Sure, I'm sure we both wanted something more but just weren't ready to explore intimacy with each other. We didn't want to have expectations or any regrets. But it didn't change anything; we were still best friends. And maybe something more.

We often rode our bikes on the beach and up hiking trails. I swear we rode up and down every side street in Orlando. Michael would look at me and say, "Where to?" and we would just ride and ride until we stopped to grab a bite to eat or went to a store. Along the way, we would stop for ice cream, drinks, and even smoothies. And if it started raining, we would wander into the closest gift shop. It became a tradition to buy matching magnets and Christmas ornaments. One evening, it was so chilly we bought matching sweatshirts.

We enjoyed each other's company but were still taking things slow. Just nice, long hugs, and we had even come up with a handshake. We kept things casual but also knew each other's expectations and boundaries.

Once we established them, they were never brought up again, and we had a mutual respect for each other that I couldn't describe.

Every Friday we would spend the afternoon together at LeeAnna's. She and Richard would leave while Michael and I read the girls books, played with their dolls, fixed them dinner, walked them to the park, and took them shopping. It's like everything was falling into place. For the first time, I felt that things were on my side. Spending time with them meant a lot. I loved being with them and seeing how good Michael was with children. It's like they had an instant connection. He treats them like kids but gives the same amount of respect as he would an adult. He read books in funny voices, completed a variety of crafts, and even played dress-up. I thought to myself, *He would be the ultimate girl dad.*

Things at the office were as normal as they could be. Summers were busy since there was no school, and it seemed like all at once work dropped on us like a bomb—driving an hour this way to meet with this family to another meeting and then a phone call. The days went by quickly, but the only thing I wanted to do was be with Michael and the girls. I wanted us to be the picture-perfect family. But I also thought, what if Michael doesn't even like me the way I like him? What if he just sees me as a friend or another fling? I thought I knew Michael, but in a lot of ways, there is still a lot more to discover.

The FBI was still going through the camera footage from the airport, and what they had already looked through was essentially useless. Just workers doing their jobs and no suspicious activities; people walking, sleeping, and eating; parents yelling at their children to stop running. Nothing yet. I felt so helpless. But I know nothing worth having comes easy.

Fourth of July was on a Saturday this year. Michael and I had plans like always to go visit the girls and do our evening routine. But LeeAnna asked if we wanted to meet the next day and go to the beach. Since they are too young to stay up late for fireworks after dinner, they would head home. By then, Michael and I would head to the boardwalk or watch from the beach. I thought to myself, *What a perfect day.*

Friday morning was beautiful. I woke up to birds chirping and the smell of the ocean hitting me as I walked into the bathroom to get ready. We had an easy day, just a few meetings before Michael met me to visit the girls. Robin was up to speed on Michael and me. She knew that we were talking and hanging out but at the same time knew we were taking things slow. She knew when to ask questions or to just ignore the situation altogether.

"So what time are you all heading to LeeAnna's today? I thought about coming by just to check in. I haven't been going the past couple of weeks."

"Probably around three o'clock, whenever Michael gets off. He is going to meet me at my house," I said confidently, knowing that I could say his name around Robin.

"That sounds like a plan. I'll let you know when I head that way. It probably won't be until around four or so."

"Great. Maybe you can eat dinner with us!"

"That sounds fun! How are the girls?"

"They are good. They seem really happy."

"I'm sure you and Michael have something to do with it. You seem happy too, and so does Michael. You guys are good together."

"They add another layer of life to mine. I mean, the girls are just sweet, and I love playing with them. And for Michael, he really does know how to hold conversation and just listen. He knows when to give me advice and when to listen." I noticed I was dozing off in a smile, trying to not blush.

During lunch, the receptionist came and got me. She said I had a delivery waiting for me. I thought it was the usual supplies we ordered every month and that I just needed to sign my initials. But when I walked in the lobby, there was a bouquet of flowers and a box with dessert along with a note that read,

Adaire,

These flowers made me think of you. And even though the box of desserts is not nearly as good as what you make, they made me think of you, too! I can't wait to see you after work today.

Love,

Michael

I just couldn't help but stare at the note. Once again, Michael made me feel so special. It's a new feeling that I never knew was missing. It's the little things he does for me daily. He always texts and calls me, opens every door, remembers the details about me, and just knows when I need him.

Robin walked through the lobby and gave me a wink. "What's in the box?"

"Michael sent over some desserts. I'm about to put them in the break room, so come and get one."

"They look heavenly. I might grab one of each."

"Please do. There's too many."

"This is the last thing I need to be eating, but after working with some of these people, it can't make my blood pressure go up any more."

Robin grabbed a plate and stacked a brownie, a few cookies, a doughnut, and a croissant on top of each other. She had grabbed a ziplock bag to put them in. She said she would take a bite of each and take the rest home. Anytime we would have leftover food from an event or if someone brought in something, she would also make a to-go bag so she wouldn't have to cook or go grocery shopping. Work smarter, not harder.

I headed out of the office at three o'clock to meet Michael at my house. He was picking me up to head to LeeAnna's. On the way, we stopped at the store to grab the girls some swimsuits along with some more summer clothes and toys for the beach. Michael enjoyed shopping for kids. We paced and wandered up and down the aisles looking at toys, clothing, shoes, and books. Everything was little, and my heart couldn't help but want to explode. The pops of pink and purple made me think about my own childhood and how I would browse the toy section for the perfect thing to bring home with me. There wasn't a ton of time; so we settled on a few outfits, sand toys, life jackets, and a pair of baby dolls with the accessories.

The last stop was the grocery store to pick up some things for dinner, groceries for the girls, and a few items we needed for the rest of the weekend. On our list were more formula for Isla and Lucy's favorite snacks. Lucy loves fruit, goldfish, and pasta. She sorts the goldfish by color and eats the red ones first. Michael noticed this, and since then, he has been sorting them by color for her. We were going to make homemade pizza for dinner and thought Lucy might enjoy it.

I took a step back. Michael and I were shopping for the girls and buying groceries for what seemed like a family dinner. For as long as I can remember, I prayed for the day when I would be married and have a family. This was the closest I had come to that dream. And maybe one day it will come true.

As we arrived to LeeAnna's, the sun was shining just as bright as ever, and the wind was subtle as if it was trying to whisper something to me. Richard came out and helped Michael with the bags as LeeAnna greeted me at the door with Isla in her arms. Lucy was watching cartoons but sprang up when she heard my voice.

"There's one of my girls," Michael said with a smile so big it melted my heart. He scooped Lucy up as if she were his. And in a way she is; she is *ours*. "We bought you some surprises. Do you want to see?"

She nodded her head yes, pointed to the bags, and said, "Pink. Dolls."

"Yes, that is a doll with a pink dress. You are so smart. Do you want me to open it?" She nodded yes, and he removed the doll from the box and handed it to her. He did the same for the other one and gave it to me for Isla. I had given LeeAnna a break and grabbed Isla. She was still sleepy but starting to wake up and become more alert, grabbing the doll from my hand. Michael helped Lucy dress her doll and give her a name; he even drew her on a piece of paper.

While he was watching them, which was the real test, LeeAnna and I started on dinner. She preheated the oven while I made homemade dough and pizza sauce, and we set out all of the toppings you could possibly think of. There were the obvious ones like cheese and pepperoni. But we also added an array of vegetables and meats.

Lucy wanted to dig in right away. It was like a giant craft you can eat. What gets better than that?

Michael helped her form the dough in the shape of a heart. I helped her with the sauce, and then we let her put whatever she wanted. She put a small mountain of cheese right in the middle; and around it she put pepperoni, black olives, and bacon. We left it just like she had it and hoped for the best. Everyone made their own pizza. Michael's and mine were nearly identical—cheese, pepperoni, bacon, sausage, ham, green peppers, and black olives. It's like we read each other's minds. The smell of firewood pizza filled the house, and Robin walked through the front door just in time.

"Dang, it smells like Domino's up in here."

"We saved you some dough, and all of the toppings are on the bar. Help yourself." LeeAnna took Robin's bag as she started creating her pizza. We fed Lucy first. Michael cut her pizza in bite-sized pieces while I gave Isla her bottle. Everyone was stuffed from dinner, so we just kept it simple and had ice cream sundaes for dessert. Lucy was covered from head to toe in ice cream toppings and pizza sauce by the end of it. After dinner, we gave the girls a bath, read them a book, and kissed them good night.

LeeAnna and Richard were filling us in on how well the girls have adapted to their new temporary home. They said how smart Lucy was for her age. She knew all her shapes and colors and could talk in full sentences. She knew how to pronounce the names of colors, shapes, her own name, and even a few phrases that she had heard around the house. Lucy was mild and timid, but around Michael and me, she became animated. I knew she loved Michael, and he loved her too. He was great with children and definitely chose the right career to pursue. He just understands them and what they need without even saying a whole lot. Isla, on the other hand, is a happy baby. She is always pleasant and smiling. She loves to cuddle and crawl everywhere and can even bring herself to stand. She sleeps well at night and takes long naps. LeeAnna said she's a dream. They both are.

"This is always one of the best parts of my week, spending time not just with them but with you too." He paused and opened the door to the truck as we waved good night to LeeAnna, Richard, and Robin. "I feel like time flies when we are with them. I just wish we could spend the rest of our weekend together."

"I hate saying goodbye even though we will see them tomorrow." I laid my head on his shoulder as we headed back to my house. "I also hate saying goodbye to you."

Michael dropped me off and helped me with the bags of snacks for tomorrow. He always kept a cooler in the bed of his truck for when he goes to the grocery store. He really does think of everything.

"Can I help you put those away?" he asked as he motioned to the bags of chips and boxes of crackers sitting on the counter.

"I think I'm going to leave them out for the morning. I know it is going to drive me crazy, but it will make it easier in the morning."

"Anything else I need to bring? I mean, besides the coolers and ice?"

"Nope! I've got everything already prepped. They just need to go in the cooler tomorrow."

"Perfect. You are always prepared. Well, anyways, I'll let you get some rest. I know we have an eventful weekend ahead."

He whispered good night in my ear as he hugged me from behind while I was washing my hands. I walked him to the door knowing it gets harder every time.

Chapter 12
FIREWORKS

The Fourth of July in Orlando was not taken lightly. The whole city was covered in red, white, and blue. Boats were being filled with fuel, gas stations were packed with people buying bags of ice, and everyone was up and running as soon as the sun rose. Especially the ocean and all of its creatures. Little did they know before too long, children would be running up and down the shoreline, fishermen would be casting their nets and fishing poles, tourists would be looking at treasure the ocean left behind the night before, and the noises of people would take over the sound of the waves crashing and wind blowing over the dunes.

I thought to myself, *I better enjoy the empty and quiet beach before it's ruined and taken over by all of Orlando.* I told Michael to meet me at my house around eight. I was making chocolate chip waffles along with parfaits and some bacon. I set up the table outside with a small arrangement of flowers along with plates and silverware. Just a nice and peaceful, relaxing breakfast to start the day. We may even be able to sneak in a walk before the girls get here at ten.

I went and slipped on a red one-piece bathing suit. It laced up on the back and had a flattering square neckline. It was pretty but not too scandalous. I tossed on a white beach cover-up along with brown flip-flops and had my hair half-clipped back with a claw clip. And I didn't wear a stitch of makeup, just sunscreen.

"It smells great in here! And you look stunning as always." Michael set the cooler down and approached me with a hug in the kitchen. "It tastes great too," he said as he reached for a piece of bacon off the plate and watched my eyes for a response.

"Good morning! It's great to see you. You look great too." I gave him a relaxed scowl but couldn't hold in the laughter. "Hey, that's for later. But I'm glad you like it."

"Anything I can help with?"

"Can you grab some glasses for our smoothies?"

We sat and stared at the waves. In a way, I studied the movement of waves and how when it is quiet, they are still, and when there is a lot of action, they go with the flow. And sometimes it all comes crashing down at once. The waves adjust to its surroundings just like humans do, and sometimes I think I am related to them and they are trying to speak to me, that they want to tell me the answers. Not just what I want to hear but the truth.

Michael and I had a conversation about what we were going to do the rest of the day. The plan was to spend the morning and afternoon with the girls on the beach, but after dinner, we were going back with LeeAnna and Richard. I knew they would be exhausted just from the heat alone. Since my house is right here, they could take naps whenever they wanted and could come and go as the day progressed.

I packed the coolers and beach bags with all of the necessities—beach towels, sunscreen, extra clothing and shoes, sand toys, water bottles and snacks, and a huge umbrella. Even though we were walking all of about two steps, I wanted to make sure we weren't running back inside and to feel like we were on vacation on our own island.

Michael and I went to claim our spot on the beach and laid out towels and set up the umbrella. The cooler was partly underneath in the shade. Michael and I were sitting on the picnic blanket. We applied sunscreen, and I helped Michael with his face. He hadn't rubbed it all the way and looked like he had a mask on. I couldn't hold in the laughter to the point he chased me into the ocean. I felt the cool sensation of the salt water refresh my soul. I felt the wet sand in between my toes. There was just something about the ocean—it makes you feel calm and paralyzed all in the same breath.

Richard, Lucy, Isla, and LeeAnna approached from the side of the house. LeeAnna grasped Lucy's hand in one hand and held a beach bag in the other. Richard held a small cooler in his other hand while he had Isla on his hip. They met us at the location where the umbrella was half buried in the sand. The girls were both awake and full of energy. At first, Isla had apprehension of the sand, and Lucy insisted on wearing the pink floats we had purchased for her.

We walked to the water's edge where the waves break at your feet and the tide gently washes it away. I wish I could go back and experience this for the first time. It's one of the best feelings in the world, and I'm glad I got to be there for Lucy's first encounter with the ocean. The ocean has always been my comfort and constant, and hopefully one day it will be hers too. Michael and I stood on opposite sides of her and held her hands. We lifted her so she could jump the waves. She would yell "up" when they were coming and would giggle when we pulled her up. She chased the waves for hours, following the shells that would magically appear until the waves hid them once again. I wish I could do the same, be invisible when I want to and reappear when all the bad things pass over.

Lucy and Michael built a sandcastle and dug a trench that led to the water. She put a few shells she had picked up on top of the castle, making it complete. Isla sat in my lap next to Michael while he was carving out the details in the sand. She grabbed some but knew not to eat it. The texture of the gritty sand didn't seem to faze her. Even though we had bought sand toys and a beach ball, they wanted to use their hands. I was the same way, hands-on. I used to tell myself I felt more connected to the ocean because I was able to swim and touch everything. I was able to explore the depths of what it had to offer.

Lunch was a blur. I was so content with being in the moment I had forgotten to eat. We fixed Lucy pasta, fruit, and goldfish while Isla gulped down an ice-cold bottle. In that moment, all was right in the world. It was the perfect weather, most of my favorite people, and the place that feels like home. We asked LeeAnna and Richard about what their plans are. They said they wanted to travel in a few years once the girls are old enough. LeeAnna works from home, and Richard works a nine-to-five as an accountant. They enjoyed the flexibility within their careers to be able to care and tend to the girls and give them all they need. Everyone was on the same page. The girls needed love, stability, and that constant home environment.

LeeAnna said that Lucy hadn't asked for her mom or dad. We think it is because she is too young to know anything else. Everyone wished their circumstances were different, but God makes everything happen for a reason. I never wondered where my birth parents were when I was little. I didn't know there was a difference. Or maybe I didn't want to come to terms with reality. But now more than ever, I wish I had advocated for myself.

The clouds took over as the afternoon rolled in. It looked like rain was going to seep through the clouds, but it held back and just sent a cool breeze. It kept us covered and out of the sun for a few extra minutes. The girls were having a blast, and Lucy was hallucinating from skipping her midday nap. She was laughing at everything. She would point and burst into laughter. It was so funny, but at the same time, we knew she had a full day. Isla, on the other hand, was lying on LeeAnna. She wasn't asleep but just content to be rocked.

We loaded up around four and ordered takeout. And just like our normal routine, we would come by on Friday, if not sooner. The girls were asleep. Richard and Michael carried them to the car as LeeAnna and I washed off the beach toys and chairs. My mind was gazing, and any recollection of my past was going down the drain along with the sand.

Michael had left some of his things in one of the guest rooms—a few changes of clothes, a toothbrush, toothpaste, and some toiletries. He never spends the night, but we are at the beach every chance we get, so it's easier than having to run back and forth to his house to change shirts or brush his teeth. Michael had bought me a toothbrush and a blanket for his house. He wanted me to feel comfortable and at *home* when we were together no matter where we were. We took showers and freshened up before starting on dinner. Michael had bought some fresh shrimp and mahi-mahi. I was allergic to raw seafood, so he did all of the prep work while I cooked it. I grilled each of them separately before adding them to a side of garlic fettuccine Alfredo with some vegetables.

I lit some candles outside and turned on the twinkle lights. I felt like we were in the Caribbean. Our eyes wandered as we soaked in the scenery before it transpired into the sunset. The sky was like a watercolor painting with multiple shades of red, orange, yellow, pink, and purple. Streaks of white shot from one side of the sky to the other, sending down a glow on the water.

"So, Michael, where do you see yourself in the next few years?"

"I plan to stay in Orlando for a while . . . unless something is calling me to move elsewhere. I mean, you can't beat the weather or atmosphere. What about yourself?"

Michael poured a glass of wine, handed it to me, and poured another, taking a sip. "Well?"

"I think I've settled down here for now, but I'm not saying this is my forever. You never know what life may hold."

"I mean, I love my career, but I also want a family and to travel the world. And normally having a fulfilling career and wanting to be dedicated to a family don't mix."

"I totally feel the same way. I love children and would love to have some one day. I just want to be married first and have a home. I want to raise a family in one place and not move around every few years."

"What's your dream house? Like if you had to build it from the ground up?"

"That's an easy question but hard at the same time."

"I get it. There's so many details. So go on, tell me."

"I want a white house with a two-car garage and a wooden door. I want there to be a bedroom for each of my children and then a guest bedroom. I want a wraparound porch with a swing. I want an office space to work, write, and paint. And in my office, I want there to be a wall with nothing but shelves to display all of my work. I want a large backyard for the kids to play in and a pool for the summertime. I want a big kitchen that overlooks the living room so I can see everyone and a window above the sink so I can watch the kids play outside while doing dishes."

"That's the dream, am I right? I love that you know what you want. You deserve it. And maybe it could be *us* one day. I know that may seem like a lot to say, but it's true."

"So does this mean you're taking notes?"

I continued with the details as we sipped on our wine until the bottle was a quarter of the way empty. I fantasized about what if. What if Michael was the one? But what if he wasn't?

"I've got it jotted in the back of my mind."

—————————●—◆—   —◆——●——————

As soon as the night took over, the fireworks were about to start. We popped a bottle of champagne and brought out the tray of cookies, brownies, and lemon tarts. To keep the red, white, and blue theme alive, I also made a fruit salad with watermelon, blueberries, blackberries, strawberries, and raspberries. The fireworks were incredible. It made me reminisce about the days I spent at Disney World. Their stagnant presence overtakes the noise they make. We stood on the sand and watched from my house. I noticed we put our glasses down on the table at the same time.

I walked over to him and melted into his arms. I stood in front of him as he kept me close, wrapping his arms around me. He slid his hands to my waist, spinning me around so I would face him. We locked eyes, and not only did I see fireworks, I also saw a man who kept me safe and made me feel *loved*. He moved his hand around my neck and tilted my head as we shared our first kiss. I felt the tenderness of his lips intertwined with mine. I could taste the sweetness from the wine. Magic. That's the only word I could describe this moment. Pure magic. I also knew it was worth the wait. I'm glad we didn't kiss on the first or second date. Then, we wouldn't have shared such a special moment. This will be one we will both remember forever.

"So that's what we've been missing all of this time?"

"Totally worth it, if you ask me," I said jokingly. We were giddy afterward, but it's true.

"I mean, you're not lying."

"I guess now we can kiss good night, even though I still want a hug."

"I mean, I do save them all for you!"

"You're the only person I want to hug. I mean . . . other than the girls."

"Woah, you scared me!"

"Gotta keep you on your toes."

We looked at each other once more, and I felt that we had relief knowing that our feelings were mutual. I guess that makes us more than friends. But we still didn't have an official label. For the first time in forever, I felt free—physically, mentally, emotionally, and everything in between. I felt I could be myself. Today, freedom has taken on a whole new meaning, and it's just begun.

Chapter 13
LOSS

Loss is a simple word. It has four letters and one syllable, easy to pronounce but can have an intricate meaning for some. You can even put a word before it and say something is a tragic or small loss. Some may say, "My team took a loss at the state championship" or "The company took a loss in profits last year." On the other hand, *loss* is a word that comes often to people; it's something that has defined their lives. That's all they hear; it's what they've succumbed to. They live in the waiting room of the hospital or lie at their loved one's bedside only for the doctor to say, "I'm sorry for your loss." They hear it so often it becomes a routine, embedded into their daily lives.

But I identify loss with myself. Some days I want to write the word *loss* on a white T-shirt with a red marker and walk around in public. I felt that loss was permanent, unfixable, and the only thing I had left in life. I had lost myself in more ways than one. I had lost the fight in my soul when I surrendered to Hudson's abuse. I had lost my way in the world when my parents disapproved of my decision to attend college out of state. But in order to gain something in life, you need to let some things go. So maybe loss isn't so bad after all. Maybe it's essential to survive and what makes us stronger.

The Monday after the Fourth of July was slow. A lot of people were out of the office and still on vacation. Robin opted to work from home, and I was going to do half a day. There were some files I needed to go through and organize. I added a picture that Michael and I took on our first beach walk. It was on my desk in a frame we had picked up when we were out doing errands one day. Every time I looked at it, I couldn't help but think about the night underneath the fireworks. Robin called and asked if I could bring her another mouse because the one she brought with her was dead. I packed up and was out the door. On the way there, I passed Michael heading to the hospital. He waved, and I held up half a heart with my left hand. He reciprocated, and it was our new thing. Robin was waiting by the mailbox, so I pulled in and talked about what happened at work that day. She was rung about one of the social workers and said he was slower than molasses getting back to her. I pulled out and headed home.

As soon as I parked in the driveway, I received a phone call from the Miami Police Department. The blood rushed through my body, and when I looked at myself in the mirror, I was as pale as a ghost. It was like I saw a ghost of my past. The last time this occurred was when the police told me Hudson was in prison for good. I was scared, anxious, and apprehensive. *Who is this, and what are they about to tell me?* I thought. Were they going to tell me that Hudson had been released, that someone in my family died? My mind was racing, yet I couldn't move. I finally came to and answered my phone.

"Hello." I was trembling, and my voice was slowly cracking.

"This is the Miami PD. Is this Ms. Carter?"

"Yes, sir, this is her. How can I help you?"

"Ma'am, I'm calling on behalf of Hudson Fisher. He died just this morning in his cell. It was due to suicide. *I'm sorry for your loss.* You were one of the last people he had any communication with. I just wanted to inform you."

"Oh gosh . . . I don't even have any words. I'm sorry he passed. Is the family aware?"

"Yes, his family has been notified. Do you have any further questions, ma'am?"

"If I may ask, what kind of suicide? I know that may be confidential, but at one time, Hudson was like family to me."

"He hanged himself, but when they found him, it appeared he also cut himself on the wrists and neck with a broken pencil."

"Oh dear, that's horrible. I don't have the words. Thank you."

"From his file, I knew he abused you, but at one point, he was someone you were close with. Again, *I'm sorry for your loss.* Have a great day."

Hudson is gone, just like that. I honestly don't know how to feel. Sad isn't the word, neither is karma or revenge. I guess you could say I was okay. I'm not relieved he's gone, but I'm also not heartbroken because he broke me long before that. I felt drained. I didn't know how to feel, act, or even what to say. I just knew now, he would never come for me or the people I love. I took a deep breath, knowing he would never find out about Michael or, if he did, what he would do. I replayed those atrocious memories as they danced in my head, and everything around me slowly faded away. The image of Hudson surged in my dreams as I tried to keep my eyes open. But when I was awake, they vanished. I was eventually able to control my thoughts and won the battle after all.

As soon as I put my phone down, it started ringing again. It was Michael. Everything in me was trying to hit the answer button, but I just stood there. After a few moments, I accepted it. I'm quiet when I'm in the state of trying to process my thoughts, especially difficult news.

"Hey? Is everything okay?"

"Michael . . ." I couldn't even form a sentence, and my voice cracked.

"Adaire, what's wrong? Please talk to me."

"Hudson committed suicide in his cell this morning. I just got off the phone with the Miami PD."

"Adaire . . . I'm . . . *I'm sorry for your loss.* I don't know what to say other than I'm sorry. I know he treated you horribly, but at one point, he was your person."

"I want to say thank you, but I also don't have any words. I'm in shock."

"I'm coming over. I will work from home the rest of the day."

"Michael, you don't have to do that. You love clinical days."

"But I care about you more. I'll be there shortly."

"Okay, I will see you soon. Thank you."

———————————————

I paced back and forth waiting for Michael. Even though it's been five minutes, it felt like a lifetime. It was just another thought trying to grab at reality. How did I get so lucky? Essentially, my ex committed suicide; and without hesitation, Michael dropped everything to come straight to me. I knew everything was going to be okay, but I didn't want to be alone. I wanted to have someone around me to talk and confide in but not just anyone, Michael.

He walked through the front door, and I just bolted into his arms, and we just stood there in silence as I cried. He rubbed my back and whispered, "I'm so sorry."

"I'm so glad you're here."

"I wouldn't want to be anywhere else." He brought me close to him. "I'm just so sorry."

"You are the most thoughtful person. You seriously didn't have to leave work, but I smiled when you were on your way."

"Adaire . . . ," he said as he tucked my hair behind my ear as he was staring into my eyes and then my mouth. "You never have to ask me to do anything. I want to. You deserve the best."

He then leaned in to kiss me, and it was like our lips knew what to do. I could smell the cologne around his neck, making this moment even more tempting than it already was. I grabbed his hand and led him to the couch. We sat beside each other on the couch and finished up work for the day. Afterward, we took a snack break and even watched a movie. I was cuddled up next to him on the couch about half asleep, and when I became fully alert, he was rubbing my back.

"If you keep doing this, I might not ever get up."

"That's what I'm here for. Take all of the time you need. Do you have any thoughts about dinner?"

"That hasn't crossed my mind. What are you up for?"

"Do you want to get McCullen's delivery? That way we can have time to make dessert and watch TV."

"Sounds perfect. I'll order it and have it delivered around five."

He then came and sat on my lap as a joke. "It's my turn for a back massage now."

"I have a better idea—lie on your stomach. It will be way more comfortable."

"So I have an idea for tonight. Do you want to eat dinner on the beach and then go for a long walk?"

"How did you know I was going to suggest that?"

"I just know you. Come here."

But in reality, he did. He knew me better than I knew myself. He paid attention to the details. He knew my order from every restaurant. He knew I liked my sweatshirts to be two sizes too big. He knew I was left-handed. He even came to know my home decor taste and would pick up something he thought suited me when he was out doing errands.

He motioned me to come lie beside him and be comforted in his arms. I lay in front of him, one of his hands resting on my waist and the other beneath me. We turned on the news just to hear some noise in the background until he pulled me on top of him. We just lay there. He was athletic and smelled like a cologne ad in a magazine. It was like he was a human-sized pillow. He looked at me with a starstruck gaze and started kissing my neck, then my lips, and went back and forth. Once again, it was like a numbing magic and a familiar feeling that only he had given me.

"I want to, but I made a promise to myself and to Jesus. And I just can't."

"I know. Me too . . . I wasn't trying to lead you on, and I respect your boundaries."

"Thank you. I know you do."

"I mean, if you don't want to kiss as much either, we don't have to. I like you for you. I enjoy our time together, and I never take it for granted."

"I mean, the kissing is great." We just stared at each other. "I'm glad we are on the same page about this."

"Me too! I'm glad we are able to have a civil conversation. This would not have gone over well with my ex. I hate to bring it up, but it is true."

"I mean, Hudson would slap me or one night tried to rape me when I was drunk, but I stopped him before he could do anything."

"I'm sorry . . . I feel like I've been saying that a lot to you. But same with my ex. I told her no, and then she wouldn't speak to me, and it would ruin the rest of the day."

"I'm sorry too. You should be with someone who respects and honors your boundaries and never leads you in the direction of crossing them."

"But I've found you, so that counts for something . . . right?"

At the end of dinner, Michael handed me a pink envelope. Inside was a note that read,

Adaire,

Who would have thought that I would have fallen for the girl that I ended up working with? Not me, but I am so grateful that I have gotten to know you. You have easily become my best friend and this is only the beginning. I love how caring you are, how you serve others, how much love you show everyone you encounter, how great you are with Lucy and Isla, and maybe one day they will have a mother just like you. The first thing that I noticed about you was your smile and how it lit up my entire world and I didn't even know that was possible. I didn't know my heart could open up fully until I met you. You made me realize what I was waiting for. YOU. You make me feel so seen and understood.

But to get to the point, I cannot go another day without asking you this question:

Do you want to make this official and be my girlfriend?

- Yes
- It's about time!

Love,

Michael

"Michael, I don't know what to say."

"Here is a pen. Take your time."

I grabbed the pen from his hand and checked off both boxes. I was crying happy tears as I knew this was reality and that I really deserved the good guy for once.

"I didn't check one . . . I marked both!"

"You about had me for a second, not gonna lie."

"I . . . I just want to hug you forever."

"Same here. I am *all* yours. But only if you are all mine."

"Sounds like a deal. Is it weird if I say I've always wanted to call you my boyfriend?"

"Not at all. I've always considered you *mine* anyways."

"But on a more serious note, Michael, you will never have to worry about loyalty with me. Once we are together, I only have eyes for you. Sure, I may have to work with other males, and some are part of the administrative team, but that is it."

"I know you are loyal. That is one of the first things I noticed. You are loyal and honest, and that's a few things I look for in my forever person."

"I do too. My last situation was the complete opposite, and I've just been afraid ever since. But when I met you, it all went away."

"Sweetheart, if there is one thing to know about me, it is to know I would never *lie* or cheat on you. I know that every guy says that up front, but you can trust me. Just know that I will never be able to find someone that even holds a candle to you."

"I wanted to ask you to come over the first day we met but thought and still think you are out of my league. Like what would a successful and handsome doctor want with me? I thought for sure you were married, but I didn't see a wedding band."

"Funny, because I thought the same about you. I couldn't keep my eyes off of you. I was like they are teasing me by putting me on a case with you. Like you seriously look like a model, like you are gorgeous, and I never want you to ever feel self-conscious about yourself around me. And if you want my opinion, I think you look stunning dressed up, but you are naturally gorgeous in my sweatshirt with no makeup and your hair up."

"I'm sure that is really attractive."

"Seriously, you never need to feel the pressure to put on makeup or curl your hair when I come over. We are a couple now, you know!"

"Now that we are laying all the cards out, I think you look *great* in a suit and tie, but you sold me with the studious glasses in the morning."

"I'm glad because I wear them around the house . . . I just didn't want you to think I was a complete nerd like yourself?"

"Hahaha, you are so funny, Michael. You are the real nerd. Mr. Doctor over there."

"Hey, I'm just trying to work, and now I'm being bullied by my girlfriend."

"You started it!"

"I'm messing with you. I love that we can joke around and take it lightly."

"I mean . . . life is just more fun with you."

"Life is great with you. I mean, I even have a whole bedroom and bathroom for myself over here."

"Man, I know! Your girlfriend must really like you . . ."

"Oh, I know she does."

———————————•— —•———————

We held hands walking down the beach. But this time we were officially boyfriend and girlfriend, and one of my dreams has come true. Out of everything in the world I could be, I wanted to be *his*, and I was. He vocalized his feelings and backed them up with his actions. It was the little things that just made sense. He never lets me touch a door handle or carry a bag. He never fails to tell me how beautiful I am, regardless of how I am wearing my hair or if I have any makeup on. He always buys me flowers and writes me handwritten notes. I find them on my mirror, in my car, and all over the kitchen and living room. He meets me for lunch during the week or if I am working from home. He will FaceTime me on his lunch break. He also remembers all of my favorite things. He knows my favorite artists, songs, what I buy at the grocery store, and even the shades and brands of makeup I use. He just knows.

We finally got to our spot and stood there staring out at the ocean that was just barely covered in the darkness with fog hovering over the waves. The moon was bright and glistened against the water, making it so I could see my reflection; and when I looked down, I saw Little Adaire saying, "You've made it."

Michael pulled out a small blue box from his pocket and handed it to me. There was a gold ring with a pearl in the middle.

"Michael, I don't know what to say . . . I mean, it is beautiful, but what is the occasion?'

"To me, this ring symbolizes the start of our relationship along with the promise that I will always take care of you. And one day I will replace this ring with an upgrade, if you know what I'm saying."

"I love it! Like it is breathtaking."

"You're breathtaking. This is just a ring."

I stood there with the pearl ring on my finger. I put it on that finger as a symbolism of promise. Not just a promise to Michael but also to God, that one day I may marry this man.

"Hey, Adaire?"

"Michael, is everything okay?"

"I love you."

"Michael . . ."

"Listen, I don't love you like I love the beach, my favorite food, color, or hobby. I'm in love with you. And I know we started dating today, but we've known each other for a few months, and I fell in love with you since I saw you in the airport parking lot."

"Michael, I love you too. I always have. And before you came into my life, I didn't believe in finding love. I just felt God thought it was best for me to be alone the rest of my life, and I was content with His plan." His eyes glistened like the stars as he stared into my soul and captured my heart.

"You never have to worry about being loved as long as I am here. You deserve a real love that lasts forever, and I promise I will give you that." I knew at that moment, this was a promise that was going to be kept.

Chapter 14
THE BITTER TRUTH

The truth can be brutal, but at least you have answers. The truth can be scary, unpredictable, and rewarding; but most of all, it sets you free. It frees your mind of the unknown, something you can't control. Most people I know would want total control of their lives. That everything happens perfectly and on their terms. But it doesn't work like that; only God knows your full story. He is the only one that has full control. He makes you take a wrong turn to make you realize that His ways are better and higher and will lead you to Him. Even though it might not be ideal, the truth makes you come to terms with reality. It wakes you up and keeps you more alert the next time the answers are standing right in front of you.

"Hey, Adaire! Are you coming? We have a meeting to get to." Robin shoved her briefcase to the brim with papers and jolted out of the door, just barely spilling coffee all over the new rugs in the lobby.

"I'm grabbing my laptop. I'll be out there soon." I was hardly awake, but the thought of him kept me awake enough to work throughout the day. We were heading to the airport because they found something in the footage and said we should look at it. Robin hated driving to the airport. She said it was just a tease and how if she could, she would buy a one-way plane ticket to Aruba and never look back.

"So what do you think those detectives found? I mean, it's about time they found something or at least finished going through footage. All they need to do is pop some popcorn and grab a soda and sit there. I mean, I would love to do that." She chugged her coffee and reapplied her lipstick once we pulled into the parking lot.

Robin hated detectives. She thought they were slow and took way too long to do anything. She thought they spent half the day watching TV and drinking Red Bull. And especially in this case, she thought they were useless. She said she could have walked around the world before they ever gave us any answers and not just another "I don't know" or "We're waiting for results." Just like me, Robin wanted answers.

An escort led us into a conference room; and there were police officers, detectives, and the FBI seated when we walked in. I felt like I was in a murder-mystery movie. I thought they were about to start questioning me, but I knew that if there were this many people here, it couldn't be good.

We introduced ourselves and went over the prior evidence everyone already knew but had to review anyway. I could tell Robin was getting impatient because she was doodling on a notepad. She was right—one of them was chugging a Red Bull. I thought he was going to shoot up from his chair. They pulled up the recording on these huge monitors that wrapped around the whole room. I felt like we were in the movie theater. On the screen, there was a man wearing all black and was walking toward the staff break room. He was in there for five minutes, then left with another person following behind him. They moved the footage back some more, and the only person who had gone in and hadn't come out in the same clothing was a younger lady with blonde hair, and she was carrying a tote bag, large enough to fit a change of clothes in. They walked out and went through the door where the pilots and airplane staff met before takeoff.

Another screen showed the two faceless figures walking to the plane with an aluminum can. There was no label to identify what it was. They were criminal masterminds; of course there was no identification. They also had on black leather gloves so they wouldn't leave any fingerprints, and like anyone wanting to commit a crime, they wore leather so fabric fibers wouldn't be left at the scene.

Sitting on the table in front of the monitor was the aluminum can, and the contents that were inside consisted of a poisonous gas mixture with fentanyl. It was concealed in a container so nobody else would inhale it. They traced every square inch of that room along with the break room. They looked for fingerprints, footprints, hair that may have fallen on the floor, DNA, and anything that would lead us to the suspects. In order to be this evil, you must also be smart—scary, intelligent, deadly.

One thing that they didn't think about was since they worked for the airline, they clocked in and out. They clocked in at the NYC airport and clocked out in Orlando. There were two planes that went from NYC to Orlando, and they were on the plane that arrived safely. The aluminum can was used to poison the pilot's cabin and then was brought back with them to Orlando in hopes of burning the evidence.

The poisonous mixture was sprayed in the cabin before it was loaded. There was video footage from the NYC airport of these same two people going into the workroom then loading the plane. They were loading their things on their plane, then went to the other and came out two minutes later. They had masks in their hands and threw them away. Even though the trash was long gone, their fingerprints were on the glove box in the supply closet closest to the airplane. Their names were also sent to us from the software engine that recorded their time. We had caught them, and they were in custody with the Orlando PD. They were in the next room handcuffed, waiting for us to go in and question them.

Their names were Steven White and Miranda Helm. They were in their early twenties like myself, had light-brown hair, and were stepsiblings. They looked like they were still high and were in orange jumpsuits with handcuffs around their wrists and ankles. They were hysterical and told us that they were trying to get revenge on the pilot for ruining their parents' marriage. Apparently the pilot and their mother had been having an affair for the past four years even though they had told their father. She said she broke things off, but it was a lie. They told their father, but he was too drunk half the time to do anything about it. They said that their mother abandoned them last year to be with the pilot. They hated him for stealing their mother away from them and that the only way to get rid of him was to kill him. They had been planning this for several months and had to create and mix up a poisonous concoction. They had to get jobs to work for the airline, coordinate the timing, everything. Every detail was set. The only thing left to do was wait until the pilot took his flight— his last flight. They were intelligent scientists. They made something so powerful yet odorless and left no trace of anything. They said it was poisonous, but it was a slow killing and had no side effects. One minute you are awake and the next you are asleep. The plane was headed toward a storm that night. Since all of the pilots were unconscious, they flew right into it and got struck by lightning, and the plane crashed immediately. There were no survivors. Well, there were two, and they were sitting in front of us.

They admitted to what they did and had no emotions. They sounded like recordings or like they were reading off a script. Their sentence was life in prison with no chance of parole or ever getting out even though they died long before that day.

We asked them how they felt since they took the lives of a hundred people. All they had to say for themselves was "At least he is dead. He did this to himself and took everyone else with him."

You could see the disgust in my eyes as they continued talking. They weren't boastful but just glad their mom's boyfriend was dead. Well, he was along with a hundred other people. Those people had families, jobs, and lives; and all of it was taken away because these two wanted revenge. I couldn't be in the room anymore, but sure enough, they gave us a break. I wanted to throw up or hit something.

"Robin, I've heard all I want. Can they send us notes on this, like I'm so upset right now. Nothing can be done. Those innocent people were killed. Nothing they can say or anything we do can bring them back. It can't bring Lucy and Isla their mother or father back like nothing ever happened."

"I know, but it's the bitter truth. Regardless of the outcome, we would never have been satisfied."

"You're right, if it could have been anything, but I wasn't wanting this."

"I think we should go. They can call me later this week if they need to. At least we know."

I was sick to my stomach walking back to the car. Thankfully, I could work from home the rest of the day and not have to sit in my office thinking about everything I just heard. Robin and I went through Chick-fil-A on the way back. We ate our feelings in the

Target parking lot where we stress-shopped for random things we didn't need. I bought some organizers for my kitchen, a few picture frames, snacks for Michael, and some soap. Robin bought her week's worth of Reese's and Diet Coke along with an eye mask, lotion, and an assortment of sunscreen.

I normally call Michael on the way home from work to see where he is or if he wants to meet me for dinner or go for a walk to watch the sunset, but I just couldn't today. I didn't want to worry him over the phone if I started crying, so I just told him to come over when he gets off.

He was waiting in the driveway. As soon as I turned in, he got out as I rolled down the window and came to the door.

"You're worrying me. Is everything all right?"

"Michael . . ."

"Adaire, talk to me. It's okay."

"They found out the truth about the plane crash!"

"Oh, gosh! Sweetheart, let's go inside, and you can tell me about it."

"Michael, I'm traumatized. I was numb in that room for hours. I felt like I was in a nightmare."

"I'm so sorry. I wish I could have been there with you. I can't imagine how you must have felt."

He followed me in the house and fixed me a glass of water before we proceeded to sit on the couch. I told him everything I could without breaking protocol. I told him their motives and their reasoning, but I kept asking myself why more than anything. Why did they do what they did? I know it was for revenge, but that is not a good-enough reason. Were they on drugs or so far gone that they had been drained for months? I knew the feeling. I felt the same way during the time I was with Hudson but never wanted to harm him. I traced the rim of the glass with my finger as my tears collected, making it look like I hadn't touched my water.

"The whole situation is heartbreaking, but just know that God has a plan. We just have to trust Him."

When Michael said that, I knew that eventually there would be light. It's just a matter of how hard we are going to have to fight for it.

Chapter 15
SOME ROADS LEAD NOWHERE

Andrea and Louis White were your stereotypical American parents. They had both been through a divorce and had one child from their previous marriage. Louis had a son named Steven who was twenty-two years old and attending community college. Andrea had a daughter who was the same age who had graduated from cosmetology school this past summer. Miranda and her mother had always been close because Miranda's father had never been in the picture, so it was always just the two of them. Steven wasn't close with his father, but they formed a bond when his mother left them to run away and be with her boyfriend. They were both drug users, and four years later, it was the same story. Andrea and Louis met on their children's senior field trip and hit it off immediately and found out that they had a lot more in common than they thought possible.

One conversation led to six months of dating before they decided to get married. Steven and Miranda were neutral about the decision, but regardless, they became joined at the hip and wanted their parents to find happiness. Steven got into some trouble and began using drugs, then influenced Miranda to do the same. They would get high together in the alleys at night and be too groggy the next morning to get out of bed. They chose drugs over their work and found themselves burying their feelings in a glass of vodka at the bar. They worked at the local McDonald's on the days they bothered to show up and for some extra cash sold drugs to their "friends" on the street who also wanted to feel high or nothing at all.

Drugs were their way to deal with their homelife. It was their coping mechanism. Since their parents got married, all they did was go on vacation and leave without notice, forcing them to fend for themselves. Drugs were the only thing that kept them going. Drugs became the only constant thing to bring them any sort of relief. It also suppressed their appetite and took the feeling of hunger away from them since there was hardly any food at the house. Most of the time there was a loaf of bread, bottled wine, and some crackers. They mainly ate out, but food didn't even faze them when they were high at 2:00 a.m. They had lost a significant amount of weight, their skin was splotchy, and their teeth looked like they were going to fall out. They were miserable.

When their parents returned, they would often be in a pleasant mood. They would stock the fridge and pantry with real food, and they would all sit around the dinner table like a *family*. Steven and Miranda saw a change for once and that there was hope. They thought their lives would turn out okay and not be another news article in the paper. This was all until they heard their parents argue about Ralph.

Ralph Lavoldo was a well-known pilot in Orlando. He was older yet charming, and Andrea met him one night at a bar. Louis was out of town that week for work, and instead of being home alone, she would go out and make friends. Andrea was an attractive woman in her early forties while Ralph was in his late fifties. There was an age gap, but all that dissolved after a few drinks. They met every night that week, and on Friday, she went home with Ralph and agreed to leave Louis when he returned from work. Ralph's wife had passed the year before from a heart attack, and this was the first woman who sparked his interest. They had fun and could talk about anything, but there was one thing: she was married.

A month went by, and she called Ralph every time she was alone and claimed to go on business trips but would Uber to Ralph's house for the weekend. The two were inseparable and wanted to get married. She promised she was going to leave Louis but was afraid of coming to terms with the consequences. After keeping it a secret for nearly a month, Steven and Miranda found out; and instead of dealing with the truth, they told Louis. Louis couldn't think straight from the alcohol building up in his system. But nonetheless, he was so upset and in denial. Andrea was the one, remember? She would never do anything like that.

Miranda liked Louis. She thought he was chill and was better than no father at all. Once she saw how ill he became, Stephen approached her with a plan: get rid of Ralph. They wanted to make sure that he knew to stay away from their mother. First, it was a threat, the second time they shot the window out of his truck, and the third was the plane crash.

They didn't want it to come to this but were so desperate and would settle for anything. At that moment, they only thought about themselves and their family. Nothing else seemed to cross their conscience. Every day they plotted and planned for months. They spent the following two weeks gathering the ingredients to mix together the "poison," booked a hotel in New York, and obtained jobs with the airline—everything. It all had to be calculated wisely so that nobody had an idea of what they were up to. Not only that, they had to think of what day they could sneak into the plane and plant the poisonous gas so that Ralph would inhale it. Even though they were high most of the time they were awake, it triggered something to make them criminal masterminds. Killing someone or in this case over a hundred people is one thing. But making sure all of your tracks are covered is another. It had to go *perfectly*.

When 99.9 percent of the details were finalized, the only thing left to do was execute the plan. They were smiling with revenge as they drove across state lines to New York. As the drugs and alcohol branched throughout their body system, all of their surroundings came to a blur. They were seeing double of everything and forgot what they were doing or where they were going. But the folder with a red skull drawn on it gave them enough memory to remember the purpose of this business trip.

They agreed to work the weekend to help out and told their manager they were going to visit their aunt and come in that weekend. They were assisting with stocking the flights with all of the necessary materials, from first aid supplies to food and drinks. This included the staff too and, lastly, the pilots.

To their big surprise, they were efficient workers, and the manager seemed pleased with their work, but it was only a matter of time before their plan would play out the way they wanted. They waited until they were alone, and Miranda made her way to the locker room where she stored her black attire and the poison. Steven followed her around ten minutes later. He was in a black hoodie but changed his pants. They exited and went into the area where only the pilots and flight attendants were allowed. This room also led to the plane where the staff boarded. This is where everything would take place. Ready. Set. Action. They stocked the plane with food and drinks with the mist underneath Steven's hoodie. Miranda bought masks in her pocket for them to wear as it was being released.

It was done, and nobody had any clue what they had done. For all they knew, they were loading the plane with supplies and going to the next one. Very casually, they walked out of the room before heading to the break room to clock out. To make them fit in, Miranda waved to some workers before they headed to the parking lot to go back to the hotel to finish out the following day.

They drove away from the airport both high and pleased with what they had accomplished. They thought to themselves, *It's over. We won. Nobody can mess with us.*

The next time they were talking about the situation, they were sitting across the table from us. They had been caught, and if I made sure of one thing, they were never going to do this again. The police had searched their house and car and found the papers of their "thought-out plan." It was labeled "The End of the Road." But little did they know, some roads lead nowhere.

Chapter 16
HER

The best things in life are unexpected, out of the ordinary, a breath of fresh air you didn't know you needed to survive. If you were to have told me six months or even a year ago that I would have met Adaire, I would call you crazy. I was just a guy trying to make it through residency with no intentions of ever falling in love. Not this way in particular.

I had been working in Orlando for about a year, and then one day Robin called me and asked if I could work on a case with her. That case turned into a few more and then the one where I met Adaire. I had no idea who she was. All Robin told me was that she was hired in January, a few years younger than me, and passionate about what she did. Robin also told me how she was adopted and didn't know any history about her birth parents. It only added to my curiosity.

I felt in a way we had met because I was also trying to find my way in this confusing world. But from the first moment I saw her, I knew she was meant to be in my life *forever*. I didn't know what role she would play, but I knew I would see her again. Our first conversation was professional but went smoothly; she could hold a conversation. She knew how to ask questions without giving too much information but also answering them. She talked with delicacy and ease, knowing she chose the correct words to say despite the situation. I saw how she advocated for children like they were her own. I noticed how much the girls clung to her, just like they once did for their mother. I had a feeling she was good with children since she worked around them daily like I did, but you have to have a calm and nurturing demeanor for children to trust you. It was one of the first things I learned on my peds rotation.

We had a small conversation about our careers, and I can hardly remember what we said because I was so drawn to her. Our eyes met, and in that moment, I knew I was in love. She was beautiful and mysterious like the ocean. She had a smile that lit up the room when she was in it, and I couldn't help but notice her figure. She was curvy but thin at the same time. I could tell she kept up with herself—her hair, skin, and appearance were clean and classy; and she did not use too much makeup. She had a polished look about her. Most women now like to get lip injections and facial piercings, dye their hair, have tattoos everywhere, and wear clothing that shows too much skin. But Adaire was perfect and had on a long-sleeved maxi dress that was fitted but also loose. She looked comfortable and walked with confidence and such poise. She had on closed-toed heels and her hair pulled halfway up just to keep it out of her face.

I wanted to ask her out on a date during our first conversation but didn't want to come off as desperate or startle her. How would an intelligent and beautiful woman like her not have a boyfriend or even be married? Robin did mention she was single, but it went over my head like everyone else trying to set me up with their friends or daughters. We kept the small talk going that day, and eventually I got the courage to ask her out, and I know over the phone sounds cheesy, but I didn't know when the next time I would see her. I had to shoot my shot, right?

Fast forward to our first date . . . I have never been that nervous in my entire life. Even though I knew she wouldn't notice, I deep cleaned the house all week and bought new dishware and wineglasses. I wanted everything to be perfect because she deserved it. I was more nervous than taking my MCAT or even interviewing for my first real job. It's not that I was scared; it was because I didn't want to screw this up. I wanted to make an everlasting impression. To be that guy for her. I wanted her to fall in love with me as quickly as I fell for her. I wanted to show her that not all guys are walking red flags, cheaters, and liars and only care about their bodies. I wanted her to know she was *the one*—the one person I have been praying and waiting for my entire life. I prayed for someone who loves, pursues, and accepts Christ as I do. I prayed for someone who is family-oriented, serves God's people, loves like Jesus, has a passion for traveling and learning, wants marriage to be the end goal with a family, is hardworking, and never gives up.

And from one date, I knew that was Adaire. She was unlike anyone I had ever come to know. She was sensational; she was like a rainbow that made my world fully light up. I knew that if I ever let her go, I would never find anyone who would even compare to her. I knew she was my once in a lifetime. And after that one night, it was like a dream.

The past few months we have spent a lot of time together but also make time for ourselves and our careers, since we love what we do and understand the dedication needed to excel in them. Even though we want to be together all the time, knowing time alone is also crucial. We share similar hobbies like going to the beach, traveling, and serving the community. We go on beach walks almost daily, cook dinner together, and on the weekends go for long drives and watch the sunset. Our weekends were spent relaxing and visiting the girls every Friday afternoon. And on some days, LeeAnna and Richard would meet us out to a restaurant or come over for dinner. It was that almost picture-perfect family I had always wanted.

One of the things I admire about Adaire is her willingness to serve others. She teaches Sunday school to the younger children, and they are all in love with her. Anyone who knows her can see how Jesus lives inside her. She radiates endless joy and beauty wherever she goes. She made me realize to stop existing and start living.

The night after our first date, I wrote a letter asking her to be my girlfriend. I also wrote another for the day

I ask her to be my wife. She doesn't know yet, but I am in the works of creating her ring. I want to take my time and perfect it. I want it to be special and significant. I want her to know how worthy and deserving she is of everything good that this world has to offer. This ring not only symbolizes marriage but also shows our commitment to God and each other. I want her to know that she is perfectly loved by Him, and I will always lead her to Him because He is our forever. I know it may seem so soon, but when you are content with Jesus and your partner is too, it is easy to talk and establish if you are compatible long-term or not.

The thing that made me say, "I want to marry her," was the moment I saw Lucy run to her the day we first met. Lucy knew that Adaire was warm and kind. I saw how great of a mother she would be, but I also saw how devoted she was to her work; she works 24/7. And despite all she has been through, she always overcomes it no matter how bad the storm is. She always pushes me to be a better person and loves me for who I am and what I have to offer. She listens and loves without judgment.

So to her, I cannot thank you enough for being such a light in my life. You showed me how to love and commit myself to you. You are my best friend, adventure partner, the one whom I want to wake up beside every morning and watch the sunrise. But at the same time, you are the one I want to ride around in our pajamas and watch the sunset. Now that I've experienced life with you, I cannot picture my life without you. You are part of my life, you are essential to my world, and you are what keeps my world spinning.

Until I met Adaire, I never knew what real love was. I thought it was with my ex, but it was far from it. Until you are loved right, you grasp at straws hoping that it lasts. Real love is formed with Jesus and is eternal just like Him. So know that if the situation you are in doesn't last, it is not a love from Jesus. She was living proof that there was hope. Now it's time to write our story. The one where the guy who was taken for granted met the girl who felt like she was impossible to love.

Chapter 17
HEAD IN THE CLOUDS

July slowly melted away into August, and the sun was as bright and hot and humid as ever. Every second I wasn't at work, I was on the water with Michael—from surfing, kayaking, tubing, snorkeling, and boat rides off the coast of Orlando to swimming with dolphins. We lived in a dream this past summer. Even though I felt like I had known Michael forever, it always feels the time we spend gets cut in half. There is always that itch of wanting more.

We spent many summer nights underneath the stars fantasizing about the type of house we were planning to build one day, and once that was established, we talked about children. I knew we wanted at least two. Once the kids were grown, we wanted to travel the world and eventually retire and grow old together. My gut was telling me that Michael was the one. I had never had any discussions about marriage let alone children with another man.

Michael had hinted about going back to China to help me find answers. I thought he had forgotten until one day he approached me with taking off some time to visit there and discover as much of the truth as I could. I never called the orphanage or even found out if my nanny was alive. I went to the attic and retrieved the boxes and sifted through the paperwork only to bring what was necessary. I made copies and organized them in a small black binder. I included both of my birth certificates, adoption paperwork, travel insurance, the hotels my parents stayed at, the names of the buses, restaurants, everything. But most importantly, the information about the orphanage and all the pictures I could find.

I felt I had all the pieces to a complex puzzle. I just needed help putting it together so I could see the whole picture. We had made arrangements in July to leave this week. I told Robin all of the details and that I should be back in two weeks. She told me that if I needed more time to just let her know and that everything would be taken care of. I would bring my laptop and get as much work as I could while we were on the plane or had some downtime. Two weeks is a long time in another country without your natural surroundings and what makes you feel at ease. It would also be the longest time without seeing the girls.

I spent my days after work packing and checking off my list, ensuring I had everything. I would need two weeks' worth of clothing, medicine and toiletries, money, my passport, the binder of documents I had accumulated, my technology case with convertible chargers, and an assortment of granola bars and trail mix. By Thursday night, I was ready to leave in the morning. Michael would pick me up, and we would head to the airport. I was excited, nervous, and anxious all in one as I lay in bed thinking about how this could change my life. I also thought a lot about the plane crash, and how I thought it could be us. What if we never come *home* again?

As Michael took my suitcase and loaded it into the back of the truck, he said, "That can't be all you're bringing. I know you."

"You know that one suitcase would last me two days. There is more inside."

"Oh, I know! So let me help you get the rest of this."

"I packed all of your favorite snacks."

"Really? You know me so well!"

"What are girlfriends for?"

"That was the whole reason I asked you in the first place."

"So I'm being used to buy snacks?" I cut my eyes at him, trying to hide my laughter.

"You know I'm messing and know how much I love you."

"I know. I love you too."

I had gotten creative and packed my belongings into a large suitcase, a carry-on, and a backpack. Michael had the same amount but decided to pack an extra suitcase with some extra food and bottled water just in case we couldn't find anything there that we were in the mood for. There were beef jerky, almonds and nuts, peanut butter, granola bars, and candy. There was even room to bring home souvenirs and other treasures we might collect along the way. I even hinted about after visiting China to go to Europe, but nothing was set in stone.

We pulled into the airport parking lot, and once again, that weary feeling set in. The last time we were here together was the day that we picked up the girls. But it was also the first time we ever met, so even though my stomach felt pains of grief, I couldn't help but be thankful because I have Michael. God placed us here at the right time to tackle this obstacle together.

One of the perks of traveling with Michael is that he knows everyone, which always makes it easier. He had a pass to keep his truck in the parking deck until we flew back. We unloaded the truck and luckily in one trip. I'm so glad we got to check three of the bags and hopefully will see them when we land in China. If not, we'll be in a scrape. I kept my toiletries, documents, money, and a few changes of clothing in my carry-on. Going through the airport is always a pain. I feel like I'm being rushed until my arms fall off. There are some people who are racing from point A to point B. Then you have those who have children screaming and crying and eating to run everywhere. Or you have those who are taking their sweet time not wanting to move out of the way, as if they're strolling through the park without a care in the world. Michael and I arrived in plenty of time so we could take our time, not feel the need to run, and grab something to eat before we boarded.

Great minds think alike, and we agree on Chick-fil-A. We bought bottled water and refilled our insulated ones. Once we boarded, there was no turning back. Michael surprised me with first-class seats, so we had more than enough legroom. Just like routine, the flight attendants made their announcements and went from aisle to aisle taking orders for drinks and passing out the premade bags filled with trail mix and crackers. They went over the safety features and showed us what to do if we were to evacuate. Michael saw me tense up and grabbed my hand; he just knew. And just like that, we were off. The next time I would step foot on American soil again would be when we returned. It would be after I was changed forever.

We didn't talk much. Instead, we watched movies and ate snacks just like we were teenagers on a summer night. Even though I was scared to be in a plane for the first time since we started this case, Michael gave me an unwavering sense of protection I had never felt before. I looked out the window and saw nothing but clouds across the horizon. It was sunny and not a sign of thunderstorms in sight. I knew then it was all going to be okay.

Changsha was located toward the eastern part of China and was part of Hunan Province, which is known for its rich and ancient history. Our first priority was to visit the orphanage that was recorded in my documents and see if any of the staff members would recognize my case. Hopefully they would be. Then again, I have no hopes or expectations to ever find out the truth. I mean, I've gone this long. I think I can go a lifetime. I knew that no matter the result of this, I had Michael through it all. But that was it. Did he have anything to do with it? It's a stretch, but it was his idea in the first place, and he even booked the flights.

"Michael, I have to ask you something." I couldn't even look him in the face and felt a stream of blood rush through my heart.

"Ask away. I'm all ears." He paused. "Adaire, is everything okay?"

"Did you know? Did you know who I was before we met? Was this a setup?"

"Adaire, of course not. Robin told me she hired you, said you were adopted from China, that you were single, and thought we might have a lot in common."

"Did she tell you to ask me out?"

"She didn't even know we went to dinner until she saw us leave church. I *promise*. I know you have doubts, but trust me, nobody had to convince me to fall in love with you. You're pretty impossible not to fall in love with, Miss Adaire."

"I'm sorry I even brought it up. I'm just nervous. There's just been a lot going on."

"I know, and it's okay. I'm here for you."

"I couldn't do it without you. You know this would be a different conversation if this were . . . never mind . . . I guess I'm not used to having civil conversations."

"It's okay. I know what you're saying. I know we said we weren't going to talk about our past, but it's part of what made us who we are today."

"You always know exactly what to say. And I've never thought about that. We are who we are today because of what we've been through. It's okay to talk about it. It means we're growing."

"See, the more you know, right? I want us to be able to talk about everything. There are no limits, and everything we say is between us."

"I feel like I can tell you everything and then some."

"I never want you to feel otherwise. You make me feel safe."

Michael started our third movie, and I felt the jet lag kick in. We had been sitting in these chairs not being able to get up and walk for almost ten hours. Thankfully, he found direct flights, so we didn't have to get off the plane and reboard. After they served dinner, I finally gave in and buried my head in Michael's chest and took a nap. I thought traveling isn't so bad when you're with your best friend who also doubles as a pillow. My head sank in his chest, and I realized my nightmares transitioned into daydreams. I could feel his heart beating as he wrapped his arms around me. It was a sound I recognized but was far from what I was used to. Michael's heart was beating like it was content and calm, just like him. I could sleep knowing that when I woke up, he wouldn't be angry or want to slap me for not setting an alarm.

I woke up to Michael massaging my back and kissing me on the forehead, telling me we were about to land.

"Did you get any rest?"

"I did, but I just couldn't take my eyes off you. You look like an angel when you sleep."

"Oh, I'm sure . . . I'm sure it's a scary angel."

"Seriously, you looked so peaceful. I didn't want to wake you."

"Well, it's because of you."

"Are you okay?"

"I'm good. I'm just afraid of the unknown, is all."

"I've got you—that's all you need to remember."

I looked out the window, and down below was a foreign country that had all the answers. And now we were just moments away from the truth.

Chapter 18
AT LEAST WE HAVE ANSWERS

The airport was more crowded than the entire city of Orlando. People were elbow to elbow just trying to get to where they were going. Some were yelling at each other in different languages that I couldn't understand. I was too exhausted to care. Michael surprised me and could speak some Mandarin. I followed closely behind him as he led the way. We had on our backpacks and rolled the carry-ons with us. And he was headed toward baggage claim and pointed to our luggage. He told me to wait by the bench, and he would retrieve them. And just like Superman, he grabbed three large suitcases like it was nothing. On the bright side, everything rolled easily just as it had legs.

Luckily, he arranged for a cab to pick us up and drop us off at our hotel. There was a gentleman with a sign that had a picture of a hotel and something written in Mandarin underneath. Michael approached the gentleman and showed him the documentation, and he motioned us to follow him. He led us to a black sedan outside. I felt like we were being abducted. He was super nice and spoke some English. Just like most cabdrivers, they asked us where we were from, if we were together, have we visited here before—the usual. I felt like we were being interrogated. I just wanted to go to sleep. Michael could tell I was tired and answered the questions. If it weren't for him, I would have wanted to scream and jump out of the car.

After about half an hour, we arrived at the hotel. It was nice and luxurious, and they even had workers come out and get your luggage. I went to the restroom and ordered room service while Michael checked us in.

"Michael . . . how many beds does this room have?"

"I reserved a suit that has two bedrooms."

"I didn't even think about it until now, like crap . . . but you think of everything. This place is gorgeous, Michael."

"I thought you might like it. I mean, it is classy just like you."

The lobby was clean and modern but had vintage charm at the same time. There were murals that lined the hallway of historical figures and well-known landmarks like the Great Wall of China. The carpets were red with a gold and black pattern and chandeliers that hung down from the ceiling. The elevators were smaller than what we are used to in the States but managed to squeeze in all our luggage along with the worker guiding us to our room. The suite Michael reserved looked like a penthouse. It had its own living room, kitchen, and a view of the city. There were two bedrooms that had their own bathroom on opposite sides. I could get used to living in a beautiful place like this.

After nothing but straight travel for almost thirty hours, we were exhausted and starving. I don't know if I wanted to eat or go straight to sleep. Our room service was delivered, and we devoured it like we had been living in the wilderness for two months. I had ordered an assortment of things to try from the menu, everything from rice to soup to dessert. Authentic Chinese food was so good but different from the Americanized version. We made a bet to use nothing but chopsticks for everything other than the soups. They included fortune cookies, but everything was written in Mandarin. Michael translated on an app and mine read, "Your destiny awaits." His read, "Now or never."

After a long nap that went into the next morning, we decided to dig through the files that I had bought. I found the address of the orphanage, and hopefully it was still there, or maybe someone in the lobby would know what happened. On a piece of paper, I jotted it down along with any names I saw on the documentation. There were two: Nina Li Wu who was my nanny and Shua Gi Lin who was the head of the orphanage. I had their names, but that doesn't mean they are still there or even alive.

The receptionist in the lobby said that the orphanage was still there and was one of the oldest in eastern China. She didn't recognize the names but called our chauffeur to let him know that we would be ready in an hour. I read through the papers over breakfast, seeing if any of the words written were trying to tell me something. Once again I stepped dead in my tracks, even though my thoughts were racing elsewhere.

The ride to the orphanage was only about ten minutes. It was sunny and a little windy but felt nice out to the point I removed my jacket. Michael held my hand the entire way as he felt me tense up. There were people walking along the sides of the streets just like they do in New York, and there were cabs coming and going on both sides of the road. There were lots of buildings. Some were modern, and others had lots of character from hundreds of years ago. In a way, it felt like I was in Epcot in Walt Disney World. We arrived at the orphanage, and the driver told us to take as much time as we needed.

There was a lady at the front desk, and Michael asked if she recognized the two names on the paper.

She replied back in English, "Nina Li Wu is actually here, and she is in the back. I will grab her, and Shua Gi Lin died of old age a few years ago."

"That would be great, thank you. I just have some questions for her."

"Sure thing."

The lobby area was painted with animals, and there were beautiful bamboo columns and furniture throughout. Even though they had remodeled, there were touches of vintage accents left on the walls that came to mind, sifting through my memories placing me here.

A shorter lady in her late seventies peered around the corner. She had white hair that was pulled back and had on a long silk dress. She surprised me by speaking English as she said, "So you must be Adaire?"

"Yes, ma'am. I was wondering if you recognized any of the information."

I handed her the folder that contained my birth certificate, pictures, and various notes and letters that my parents had collected about the orphanage. She skimmed through them, taking her time, and then paused.

"Oh yes, I remember . . . let's go down the hall." She motioned us to follow her, took us to an empty room, and went on, "Your aunt Sonia dropped you off at the front door. She handed me a baby carrier and a folder with your birth certificate and went on her way. I knew her from running into her at the market every week. We made small talk whenever we crossed paths, but nothing more was said about you until she gave me this." She handed me a letter written in Mandarin along with the papers she was given the day I was left at the orphanage. She had to translate it into English, but it read,

> My sister Sonia is leaving you with my first born daughter. Her name is Giu La Sha. I have no other choice but to leave her here. Her father has not been in the picture and she deserves better than what I am able to provide

her with. She deserves a house with a family and everything this world has to offer. I have inherited some money that was left behind but it won't change the circumstances. I don't even know if I am able to inherit the full amount or have to split it with other family members.

I am hopeful to start my life over again and have the same wishes for my daughter as she deserves a mother who is fully present, not one who is broken and running for dear life. I'm afraid if I stay, I will get harmed in the middle of it. Her father is a violent man and threatened to kill us both if I didn't abort the pregnancy. I wanted to go through with it because she deserved a chance so I left her with Sonia to later leave with you at the orphanage. I wish things could be different and maybe we will cross paths one day. I just hope she finds peace and lives a life full of experiences and chances, something I was never given.

—Lynn Wi Sha

I was teary-eyed as I read it. This was the true meaning of sacrifice. She gave me up because she loved me. It takes a lot of strength to give up something you love and put your whole heart into. She did this for me, so I could truly live.

"Do you happen to know if she is alive?"

"Adaire, I'm sorry. She passed away a few years ago from cancer. I heard her sister left the country to live in America to give her two daughters a better life."

"Were they involved in a plane crash?"

"Yes, I'm afraid they were."

"I know her children, and I know this might break all kinds of laws, but Michael and I visit them. I'm one of the foster parent recruiters on their case."

"Oh my, well, what a small world."

"They are beautiful, intelligent, and so sweet."

"I know they love you. You look like their mother. She had dark silky black hair like you. And your eyes sparked the same way hers did."

"Oh really? I always wondered where I got certain features from. But anyways, I just wish I could have met my mother. Do you know who my father is?"

"Your mother said once she got pregnant, she disappeared when he threatened to hurt her, so she ran away after she left you here. I don't know where she lived until she died, but I do know they did eventually inherit the money from your ancestors. She received her portion around ten years ago. Sonia most likely has hers left, and if that is the case, you and the girls will inherit it."

"I'm angry at my birth father, and I don't even know him."

"From what your aunt Sonia told me, it was just a matter of time before he killed her, so she fled to another town about ten miles away. She wanted to visit you but was afraid of getting hurt, and by the time she had received the money, you were already in the States. She didn't want to cause any confusion. After she accessed the money, she asked if I had heard anything from you, and that was the last time I heard anything from her until Sonia said she died from cancer and that she inherited all of the money because her daughter was adopted. I could make a phone call and see what is going to happen to it."

"This breaks my heart, but I am also grateful for the life I have today. Eventually I feel like we would have been okay, but I would have done the same thing. I mean, if my ex was threatening to kill me and my unborn child, I would want them to have a better life even if it meant I wasn't the one raising them."

She looked at me and squeezed my hand. "I think any mother who loves their child would give them up, meaning they get to be safe." As she handed me the paperwork, she added, "Let me make a phone call, and I will be right back."

Michael couldn't even say anything; he just sat there in silence and disbelief because neither of us were prepared for what we just heard. I thought this was going to be another situation where there were no answers to be found. Another dead end. But if I took anything away from this, it was that all my mother wanted was for me to be happy, loved, cared for, and free. She wanted me to have the best life even if it meant sacrificing her relationship with me.

The only thing that was more intriguing than my mother's story was how she inherited a small fortune. I mean, if she left that much money after her death and it was signed over to me, I could do so much. I would start a nonprofit, donate to schools and the community, retire my parents, travel the world, build my forever home—the dreams are endless.

I walked back to the lobby to gather my thoughts and had been sitting with numbness the entire time. I felt like I was in a state of confusion that I couldn't escape. Michael was by my side the entire time. He wasn't judging or asking questions. He was just there. He was my new constant that felt abnormal because I was used to facing everything alone. But for the first time, I felt at ease and comforted regardless of the outcome.

After half an hour, Nina walked back to the lobby and waved for us to come back. I walked hesitantly, and Michael followed.

"I was able to speak to your mother's and Sonia's attorney, and as far as they know, the money, property, and all of their belongings belong to the next of kin, which is you and the girls. Sonia and her husband sold their home in China and bought a house in Texas. All of the details are on this document, and the property belongs to the girls along with their parents' money. Since some items were destroyed in the crash, we cannot replace those, but they did inherit 100 million dollars. Your mother's belongings were left with Sonia, and they had their things shipped to the US and delivered to their home in Texas. Half of Sonia's inheritance came from your mother, and the lawyer signed off, stating that you are entitled to half.

"So, Adaire, despite all you've been through and everything you've learned, you are about to become very wealthy. Sonia's bank account was set up in the US a few weeks before the move, so it should be fairly simple to transfer your portion. After a meeting with the bank and some signatures, you will have 50 million dollars. No taxes or anything being taken out. The lawyer agreed to stop by to get your signatures on some things so it can be easier when you return home. And since Lucy and Isla are so young, all of that money is yours, and when they are old enough, you can give it back to them if you would like."

"I'm speechless. I've never even dreamed of having that amount of money or what I would even do with it all. I want to do something good with my share, but I want the girls to have their portion when they are old enough to understand. And I would be happy to wait for them to come by so we can get this transition started."

"Great. I will give him a call. It should be just a few minutes. He is located a few miles away."

Once again, I was in shock. But not in a bad or disgusted way; it was different. I was content, and as harsh as this may sound, something good was bound to evolve out of all this. I thought, *I never have to work another day in my life if I don't want to.* In just a few weeks, I'll have 50 million dollars. The lawyer showed up just moments later; he was accompanied by a financial advisor. I told them my story and why I wanted to return to China to learn the truth. But they said my mother didn't die from cancer. Sonia just wanted to give them a cleaner story. But the truth is she was shot and killed by my birth father's brother in hopes of inheriting her money and fortune. My birth father had committed suicide a month before she was shot. My uncle thought he would take her money and run away since he was the only family member left. But my mother was smart and planned ahead; she had already signed her belongings to Sonia and me. Once I was born, she never changed them back; and since we were still alive, he would not receive any part of it.

Another can of worms opened, and my mind became even more confused than before, more questions than I could ever think of. We went over the paperwork to sign all of my mother's and Sonia's money and belongings over to me. When I return to the States, I will set up accounts for each of the girls. I want them to inherit what was meant for them to start with. The only thing left to do is transfer the funds to me, and then it will be mine. I contacted my accountant back in Orlando, and she was already on it. She was making sure all of the paperwork was being set up for me to sign electronically and making the necessary phone calls. She told me that in a few weeks, my checking account will have 50 million dollars in it. I told her I wanted 45 million to go directly into savings and investments. This was all new, and I had no idea what I was doing, but it was going to work out.

We left the orphanage with more answers than I could have hoped. Even though both of my birth parents were dead, I felt content knowing that I will get to know them better through the remnants of their belongings. I was starving, so we walked about ten minutes to the downtown area and explored the shops and booths lined up on both sides of the street and even grabbed some lunch at a local restaurant. I felt like I was in Chinatown in New York. China was beautiful, but I felt like a ghost was following me the longer I stayed. I felt a shadow watching over me.

Chapter 19
THE GREAT WALL

It was officially our first night in Changsha, and we got to experience the city alive at night. It was quiet, but once we drove farther, you could see it beam with the activity of people. There were tall modern buildings like you would expect to see in America. We visited museums and shops and even stopped in a nice sit-down restaurant. A cab took us to the city, but we opted to walk as we explored the streets. Ever since we were dropped off, I felt a sense of urgency to check my surroundings. I felt like someone was watching me, but I didn't know who.

———————

Steven was pacing back and forth in his cell trying to accumulate ways to plot his revenge. He wanted to make them pay for exposing who they really are. *How dare they! How did they know, and much more do they know?* he thought to himself. Anger. Disgust. Hatred. Those were the feelings running through his mind as he stared at a cement wall. His friends Aaron and Dimetre Rodgers were brothers and visited him often. They had gone to the same high school and would get high on the weekends. They were acquaintances as you might call it; they were also evil-minded, and the word *death* didn't even faze them. They had code names and phrases so the guards or other inmates wouldn't know what they were scheming up.

The plan was for them to fly to China and hunt down Michael and Adaire. Their friend worked at the airport and was able to tell them exactly where they had landed, so it would be easier than looking for a needle in a haystack. They couldn't fly with any weapons or drugs because they would have to go through airport security, but instead, they would find their location and then pick their poison—drugs, knives, guns. The options were endless.

They can't fool us. We are too smart for them. Who do they think they are? They laughed with slight evilness under their breath, and at last, the final details were set. In less than a day, they would be grinning from ear to ear with ease knowing that they had found them. The next part was easy—destruction.

———————— •— —• ————————

Michael and I were going to explore all that China had to offer, so we booked a short flight to Beijing to visit the Great Wall. It was just as long and narrow as you could imagine and mirrored what they would show in movies. Nothing could have prepared me for being on it, walking casually and taking pictures. I felt like the real-life Mulan for a second. It was sunny with just a slight overcast and was a beautiful day. We wanted to embrace Chinese culture by going to as many museums, gift shops, and restaurants as possible. Michael was smart enough to bring Chinese currency so we could pay them in cash. We took pictures in a photo booth in the museum for around $0.25 and then bought postcards, magnets, Christmas ornaments, other knickknacks, and silk dresses for Lucy and Isla. I felt like we've been everywhere together, but this time we could add a stamp to our passport.

———————

The day flew, by but the baggage claim in Beijing was taking forever. Demetre was aggravated, and Aaron was thinking, *The more time we waste here is more time they could be getting away. We have to finish what we started.* To calm their nerves, Demetre went and got sandwiches from one of the convenient shops in the middle of the airport while Aaron stalked the conveyor belt. Finally two silver suitcases peered around the corner. Aaron grabbed them and waited for Demetre to get back. The two of them called a cab, and they were on their way to the hotel, which was just a few minutes from the Great Wall. Just steps away from them. And just like that, it would be over, and they could claim victory.

———————

All of the museums and attractions made China more intriguing and mysterious than ever. I learned a lot about the history of China, read about the rulers, saw some ancient artifacts, and bought an authentic silk robe. It was a part of who I was even though it is like meeting someone you are related to for the first time. They are a part of you, but you've never seen their face or interacted with them.

Michael supported me through everything. He never complained about being anywhere for too long. He was just there encouraging me every step of the way, telling me that everything was going to be okay and we would face anything that came our way together. This was a different change of pace because I was so used to doing everything alone. Or even if I had friends or family surrounding me, I still felt invisible. I felt judgment and scared for what the future had to hold.

———◆—————◆———

And just like that, Demetre and Aaron arrived at the hotel. They checked in with nothing more than a black duffel bag in each of their hands. They were dressed in all-black suits to make them *fit in* so nobody would even think about questioning their presence. They looked like businessmen. Who would stop them? Walking through the lobby, they admired the war paintings hanging on the wall. *The war has just begun.* They had unpacked their belongings that consisted of more black clothing, a map of China, their laptops, rope, and duct tape. They couldn't bring weapons or drugs, but before they left for China, they contacted a dealer and made arrangements to buy drugs, guns, and knives—all of the things they were ticked about not being able to bring with them from their home. They changed into their black sweat suits, grabbed one bag, and took a cab to the city. *We're here. You can run, but you can't hide.*

———————•— —•———————

The sun was glistening, not a cloud in the sky, and there was a slight breeze. What could get better about this day? Michael and I were taking in every moment, sight, and just being in each other's presence while being together. We were walking, talking, and pointing to everything that was new to us but nothing special to those who see it every day. I always feel cautious especially when I am visiting any area for the first time, but I felt like someone was watching us. I blinked and saw two dark figures and then blinked again and they were gone, but something in my gut was telling me that I was right. *Trust yourself, Adaire. Trust yourself.*

"Michael, can we talk?"

"Is everything okay?"

"I feel like something is wrong, like there is someone or something following us. I just have that feeling. That unsettling feeling that you are right when you want to be wrong."

"Everything is going to be okay. I've got you." He pulled me in and kissed the top of my head. "Do you want to head back to the hotel and order room service? We have another big day tomorrow."

"That honestly sounds great."

———————•— —•———————

"Look, there they are," Demetre said with enthusiasm as he pointed toward Adaire and Michael.

"Perfect timing. I'll follow them, and you go and find the items we talked about."

"Sounds like a plan. I will call you when it is done."

Aaron walked briskly but at the same time tried to blend in to not draw any attention. He followed them but not too closely. He stayed a healthy distance away from them so they did not feel watched. He interacted with the people at the stands on the side of the street and even bought a drink to make himself look like a local. He thought to himself, *They are so boring. They came all the way to China to just walk around?*

He kept his distance and continued following them until they got in an Uber. He followed the car until he couldn't and could only walk so fast on foot. And just like that, they were gone.

I will have to come up with something else. There are only so many hotels here unless they flew from another part of China or spent a lot of time in an Uber. He thought like them and knew they were too smart to spend all day in a car. He called all of the local hotels and nothing; they must have flown. He called an acquaintance to see if it was true, and they did. They flew from Changsha to Beijing, so they must be flying back. He got off the phone and did more research to find hotels in Changsha. That's it, there was the hotel. He figured they were staying in a hotel close to the city but was also nicer, somewhere people with money would stay. He called the hotel impersonating a travel agent, retrieved the address, and gave Demetre a call. *Sooner or later*, he thought to himself.

———————————— -•- -•- ————————————

We Ubered to the airport so we could head back to the hotel for the rest of our time in China. There wasn't much else to explore or that I wanted to anyways. Sure, China is where I was born, but I've found my answers, and now I'm ready to move forward. China will always be a part of who I am, but it is time to leave the past behind. Michael and I were in agreement to spend the rest of our time in Greece. Tomorrow I will leave China and never look back. To me, it will just be another place on the map.

———————————— -•- -•- ————————————

"Aaron, how did you let them get away like that? Now we have to start over from square one."

"Not exactly, I know the hotel they are staying at. Since you already have the goods, we are going to have to take a cab. We can't go through security with guns and drugs."

"I'll rent a car, and we can leave in a few hours once we collect our things at the hotel. Let's pick up some more beer and cigars for the drive. I miss the loose feeling it gives me."

"They can't fool us. We are smarter than they are! What idiots! Am I right?"

"Tricking us into coming all the way out here. Little do they know, we know where they are staying."

After a long, exhausting day, I finally got to take a shower while Michael ordered room service and was working on flights and accommodations to Greece. I had contacted Robin about what our plans were and what had happened since we got here. I left the part out about the money. She told me to bring her back a shot glass and to have a good time. I should be back to work around the same time I had originally planned because we cut our visit to China short. I just wanted to go to another country that I had no ties to. I wanted it to feel like a vacation.

After what felt like an eternity, they arrived in Changsha. They thought it was like stalking prey, or in this case, they knew where they were going; it's just a matter of time before it was over. They stared at the scenery as they were driving through. It was all just a haze, and all of the colors were running together the drunker they became. They were smoking and popping pills like they were candy. Their diets consisted of fast food, alcohol, and drugs—all of the most unhealthy things to put in your body. Their surroundings came to a freeze as they pulled up to the hotel parking deck. They said boastfully, "Ready or not, here we come."

I was packing up the rest of our things so we could head to the airport after dinner. Michael and I were clean and organized, so it was just a matter of putting everything in our suitcases and sitting them by the door. Michael was in the shower, and I couldn't get used to the fact that it was normal to be around someone like this. Dating a person that you can do day-to-day things with, like eating meals, doing laundry, and cleaning the house or, in this case, our hotel room. Normal began to take over my life. It was a lifestyle that I had craved but thought I was already living. But instead, I was living scared. I was tiptoeing around trying to be perfect so I didn't get slapped while I was eating dinner or had to speak in a soft tone so I wouldn't provoke him. I didn't have to be afraid that he would pick me up and slam me up against the wall. I felt like I could breathe.

Room service showed up with the last authentic meal we would eat in China. We savored every bite before heading down to the lobby. I was soaking in the final minutes until we got in the cab and never looked back. It was quiet this time of night. Everyone was settled in their rooms. We even opened a window and noticed that the rest of the world was asleep too. There was hardly any traffic, and I thought that this was the best time to leave for our next destination. But ever since I landed in China, I had an overwhelming sensation that someone or something was here, watching me, watching us. I didn't know their motive, but I just knew. I kept it to myself because I didn't want to worry Michael, but we made a promise to never keep secrets.

"Michael, I have an unsettling feeling that someone is here watching us. My gut is telling me something while my mind is trying to convince me otherwise."

"Do you know who it could be? I know we are in another country, but today has felt off. Not with us but our surroundings."

"I've felt the same. I just don't know. Should we call a cab so we can get out of here?" I was shaky and tense. Michael came over and held me to see if anything would make it go away.

"I made arrangements earlier. Our driver should be here any minute. Let's head down."

"I'll sleep better tonight, knowing I can leave everything behind." I grabbed the room key and headed out the door. "It is finally over."

"I think we will have some time to relax in Europe. You are not allowed to work next week. Deal?"

"Sounds like a plan!"

———————— •◦ ◦•————————

Demetre and Aaron were getting frustrated the longer they had to wait. They didn't want to cause a scene or arouse any suspicion and wanted to fit in, like they belonged. So they decided to wait in the car. A cab drove up to the front of the hotel. Michael walked out with the luggage while Adaire followed closely behind. They headed toward the trunk of the car to put in their luggage, and in just a matter of seconds, there was a gunshot. And then another. *Boom. Boom. Pow.* Everyone was in shock. People were screaming, taking cover behind cars, and running inside. It's like the world flipped upside down in just minutes.

I couldn't even wrap my head around what just happened. One second we were loading the cab to head to the airport, and then the next moment I was staring at Michael lying on the ground. He was still conscious but not able to move. He was shot. Luckily it was in his shoulder and not his head or chest. The adrenaline inside of me was just making me more delusional than normal. I couldn't think straight. I couldn't even form a sentence. I fell to my knees and put Michael's head on my lap as we waited for the ambulance. He kept telling me everything was going to be okay. I just lay there with a glassy look in my eyes, stuttering that I loved him. I came back to reality as the blood was consuming us in a puddle. And after a few minutes but in what felt like an eternity, the ambulance arrived. They loaded us up in the back and headed off to the hospital. Michael was going in and out trying to hold on for me, but I knew it was impossible with the amount of blood he had lost. He was still breathing, and the paramedics were doing everything they could until we reached the hospital. They rushed him inside while I was greeted with the police and detectives.

Aaron and Demetre took a deep breath as they drove off in the distance, leaving Michael and Adaire there to suffer. They were grinning with spite from ear to ear, smiling in victory. They had gotten away with it, for now. They drove until they were high enough that they lost their train of thought and pulled over to get some rest. Who was going to suspect anything from them anyways?

———————•————•———————

As I sat at the hospital going through everything, my brain would allow me to comprehend. What happened? We were walking toward the cab, and then Michael was shot. I had no recollection who shot him, how many there were, or whether they were on foot or in a vehicle. I didn't know their motives or reasoning, if it was planned or a freak accident. I felt helpless when I woke up that morning. I had everything I had ever wanted, but now, it was all stripped away from me, and there was nothing that could be done.

Chaeli Smith

Chapter 20
THE WAITING ROOM

The term *waiting room* is what it sounds like. It is a room in which you have to wait for answers, good or bad. It is a room that you have to sit in and go mad until someone comes to tell you if your loved one is alive or not. It is the room that could change your life forever. It is the room where you sit and think about what went wrong and if there was anything you could have done to prevent it. And that is exactly what I was doing. I was alone, in a foreign country, sitting in a waiting room praying that Michael was alive and that someone would come and give me an update. I was praying to God, knowing that everything happens for a reason. But I was questioning everything in my existence, begging for Him to tell me why this was happening. I was suffocating in my own memories, trying to keep them lucid.

I paced back and forth. I even went to the cafeteria to see if I could focus away from the pain by eating. The sight of anything made me nauseous. After two hours, the cab arrived with our luggage. The driver was super nice and offered to grab me anything I needed. I thanked him and asked if it was possible for him to bring our luggage to me. Moments later, he sat them in the waiting room. I eventually asked one of the receptionists if there was a room where I could store our belongings until further notice and if there was an update on Michael. She told me that he was alive and still in surgery and that she would help bring the luggage up to the room he will be staying in until they release him. Great, so I was moving from one waiting room to another. The only difference is that I was one step closer to seeing him.

The receptionist walked me to the bathroom that had a shower so I could wash the blood off my body and change into some new clothes. I felt everything in me being washed down the drain along with any memory I had about the shooting. I tried to remember, but there was a part of me that wanted to remember the details while the other side of me wished it would all go away and Michael and I were on a plane to Europe. Two police officers pulled me to a conference room to question me. I told them everything I could, wishing they would be able to catch whoever did this. I told them what we were doing and gave them the details about the hotel we were staying at so they could review the security cameras. This was my last hope.

Another hour passed by, and the same two police officers came back and said that they had everyone out searching for a small black car that matched what they saw on the monitors. As soon as the gun was shot, a black car scurried out of the parking lot and headed west. They were going to drive everywhere and get everyone on the same page. They were going to check at gas stations, hotels, restaurants, and even the sketchy parts of town to make sure they covered their tracks. I told them to do everything. I don't care what it takes. It is one thing to mess with me but another to hurt someone I love, or in this case, the only person I have ever truly loved. Now that I had Michael in my life, I couldn't picture it without him. I mean, I could, but my world would be black and white. He is the perfect addition to my life, and I am so grateful for everything he has done. He has shown me how to live life and to always look at the beauty in every situation.

Sitting here made me think back to all of the times he would be next to me, whispering that everything would be okay. But he was not; he was in surgery trying to hold on and live another day. I would die right here in the waiting room if I were to receive any bad news. I finally gathered myself enough to call Robin. I didn't spare any details and told her that I needed to be with Michael until they released him. Again, I didn't know what the future held but told myself I would take it by the hour. No update was better than a bad one. Robin told me how sorry she was and that if she weren't across the world, she would fly here. She told me to take all the time I needed, to not worry about work, and she would handle everything.

I also called the airline and hotels and canceled our reservations in Europe. Everyone was understanding and said to give them a call once we wanted to rebook. The last thing to do was to call LeeAnna. She was so heartbroken for me and wished she could fly to be with me in a matter of minutes. I told her the only thing that was keeping me together was knowing that she, Richard, and the girls were safe. I also informed her about the money I inherited and if she could go by the bank to see if they could call me to complete the paperwork. I wanted the money to be transferred as quickly as possible so if anything were to happen to me, they would inherit it all.

"Ms. Carter, Michael is in the postoperative care room down the hall if you would like to see him. He did great. He should make a full recovery with the help of some physical therapy."

"Thank you! I would love to see him. Do you have an estimated time of when he will be released?" I took a deep breath as I was so relieved. I could feel the shock leave my body as I stood up.

"If everything goes as planned, a day or two. But he cannot lift or strain his muscles for four to six weeks. He will need physical therapy daily. He can lift up to five pounds but needs to keep the movement minimal unless otherwise stated by the doctor in the US."

I walked cautiously behind the doctor and passed by nurses, patients in wheelchairs, and loved ones visiting their own. As I peered around the corner, I saw Michael lying in the bed with a nurse standing beside him checking his heart rate. He was sitting up and was able to talk to the nurse. When our eyes locked, it was like the first time we met. My memories came back, and my mind reminisced about that day. I slowly approached the bed and sat at the edge, grabbing Michael's hand.

"Hey, sweetheart! I hope you are okay. I don't really remember what happened."

"I was worried sick about you. I would have died right here if I was never going to be able to see you again."

"I told you nothing is going to prevent us from being together, I promise."

"How do you feel? How bad is the pain?"

"I feel good, sore though. But it all went away the second I saw you."

I lay beside him crying, and I couldn't help but think how lucky I was that he was okay. I would never recover if he had died, especially not in this way. I never got a proper goodbye or an "I love you." I know he does, but something about him saying it pulled at my heartstrings unlike anything else.

As I nestled my head in his chest, I let out a soft sigh. "I don't know what I would have done if I never saw you again. To tell you I love you, to hug you, to walk on the beach with you, to cook dinner together, to play with the girls, and to drive around at sunset."

We lay there in a calming silence as my tears began to dry on my cheeks. "Do you need me to get you anything?" I asked but remained at his side.

"Just you." He grabbed my hand. "Do you remember anything that happened?"

"I remember we were packing up the car. I heard a gun go off, and then I was sitting with you on the ground. But other than that, my mind went blank." It was like my thoughts were underground and I was walking on top of them. "The police and detectives are searching for the person or people who did this. They said they are searching for the black car that left the parking lot immediately after the gunshot was fired. They didn't tell me much. Otherwise, they would be in contact with me if they find anything."

"I wish I was there to be there for you. This is all my fault anyway. It was my idea to come here in the first place."

"Michael, never blame yourself for this. This is not your fault, and you are the one who got shot, not me. I guess we can look at this as another obstacle God put in our path, and the only thing left to do is to conquer it together."

"How are you so strong? I'm so lucky that I have you by my side."

"I learned from you. The doctor said if everything goes well today, they will release you in a day or so."

"I'm feeling good. I just wish we were in Europe roaming the streets of Greece and dancing underneath the stars as live music plays."

"Me too. I called the hotel and everyone we made reservations with, and they said we could give them a call when we're ready. So I guess we do get to explore

Europe together. I just want you to be better so you can enjoy it and not hold back."

"How about this, when the doctors and physical therapist clear me, we will plan to go for a month."

"Sounds perfect! Are you thirsty or hungry?"

"Too bad we are not home so you could bake or cook anything."

"How about if I surprise you?"

"Can't wait!"

I kissed him on the cheek and walked down the hallway to the elevator and down another hallway and eventually ended up in the cafeteria. It was like a maze trying to get there. I was lost and in a foreign place where I didn't know anyone let alone speak the same language. I bought a bag full of Chinese snacks, ice cream, bottled water, and two bowls with their dish of the day. It looked like a version of sesame chicken with rice. It looked decent for hospital food.

———————•— —•———————

"Did you buy the whole cafeteria? But whatever you have smells good. I'm starving, and the doctor said I can eat whatever I want."

"I didn't know what to get, so I got a variety of snacks with some real food . . . so what do you want first?"

"I guess whatever I smelled when you walked in here!"

I sat next to Michael and helped him eat. It really wasn't as bad as we thought it would be. Then we moved on and tried all of the snacks and washed everything down with some ice cream. We made the most out of it and tried a ton of different snacks. I even went to the gift shop and bought some games and was able to pull up Netflix and put on a movie. By that time, it was late afternoon, and the doctor and nurses came in to evaluate his shoulder. He was able to stand and walk across the room on his own, but he was still sore from surgery. They said that everything went as seamlessly as they had hoped and that we would be discharged in the morning. I was terrified of going to another hotel and especially without Michael, so they wheeled in another bed beside him so I could stay with him. We ordered more food from the cafeteria and had round 2 of different Chinese snacks and candy, played card games, and even spoke to Robin and LeeAnna. They were working on our flights the following day, so we could head home. I told Robin that I wanted to work from home when we got back so I could take care of Michael and help him get used to not carrying or lifting anything. I knew this was going to be challenging because he was used to doing everything, and now it was my turn to serve him.

"Demetre, do you think we escaped? I mean, I think we did our job and fled the scene in the midst of complete chaos that nobody will suspect anything, especially from us."

"I mean, that was record timing. We shot one of them and flew out of the parking lot. We haven't been caught yet."

"Let's reward ourselves with some drinks, and then we can get high and hit the road again. Back to America, land of the *free*."

Aaron and Demetre rode to a local convenience store, picked up some junk food and liquor, and headed back to the airport to fly home. Home sweet home. They had drunk themselves until they couldn't even form a full sentence and stuttered until they came to their senses that they needed to sober up so they could blend in at the airport. They didn't want anyone to suspect them of anything and were just a plane ride away from being back to America where they can go on and pretend like they never left. And that life was normal and neither of them felt anything.

The cops searched west, east, north, and south to find the black car that had left the hotel. Nothing. They might as well have not even started. It's like they didn't know what they were searching for. The blind leading the blind. I knew that God would eventually bring this to light because He never lets anyone go without His final judgment. They searched for hours on end that night and until the early morning. They set up cops on every block and in all of the main places people would go—the grocery store, the mall, hotels, restaurants, and, last but not least, the airport. They had security check every car that came through the entrance and exit. They started checking passengers for suspicious behavior, people wearing black clothing. They were examining everything like their lives depended on it. The time went by slowly, but one of the security guards' suspicions grew when a small black car entered the parking deck and two guys dressed in black hoodies carrying duffel bags got out and went up the stairs.

Just like most cops trying to catch a criminal, they notified everyone but kept the scene calm until they were able to approach them without causing too much of a confrontation. At the top of the stairs, two police officers stood waiting. They were armed and had on bulletproof vests just in case. When they rounded the corner, they knew they had been caught. They tried to walk past the guards but were stopped and handcuffed. They were taken to the police station and questioned about their purpose for being in China, why they were at the airport, and if they knew Michael and Adaire. Being the intelligent criminals that they were, they claimed they were there for work. They were being searched along with their belongings and their car. A knife, a gun, a duct tape, a rope, drugs, and black clothing were found in their trunk. They were both still high and somewhat admitted to what they did. They were being charged with several things including the shooting and the possession of weapons and drugs.

I received a phone call from an officer telling me that they had Aaron and Demetre in custody, who they were, and what their motives were. I was sick to my stomach that they were after me, us. I couldn't wrap my head around why they would do such things for their friends. How does this benefit anyone other than them getting the satisfaction of watching other people suffer? But on the other hand, I honestly felt sorry for them and that their life had come to this point. All they lived for was getting high and committing crimes for friends and receiving nothing in return. I mean, what type of money do these people really have? Did they think they were going to inherit the money? What good was coming from this? At the end of the conversation, the officer said they were going to send them to the Orlando prison, and they would never bother us again. He also said a cab would pick us up and drop us off at the airport, and there would be workers waiting for us so they could escort us to the correct location.

Michael handled everything like a champ. Once we were discharged from the hospital, it was time to fly back home. Everything with the bank went through even though I have to go in person when I get back. LeeAnna and Robin were going to meet us at the airport to help with Michael and get his truck. This plane ride felt different than the one coming over here. My life was never going to be the same, from learning about my past to the shooting. As a movie played on the screen, I couldn't help but trace my thoughts to something else. I thought about what if? What if we never came? What if I never met Michael? What if I never met the girls? What if I chose a different career? There were all of these other paths that I could have chosen, but I decided with this one. I wonder if Michael ever regretted that he met me, and then none of this would have happened. I noticed he was in a daze focused on the movie but saw him glance up at me. The warmth in his eyes melted my heart. I could tell he was tired, but as he always told me, at least we were together.

Neither of us got much sleep. In fact, I think I would have been more comfortable if I were standing up. The turbulence was loud. People were having sidebar conversations, dogs barking, and kids screaming. I knew it was the next morning and that this would all be over. The sky was beaming as a rainbow was peeking through the sky like it was a welcome-home banner. I looked out the window and saw a blur of green and blue, but I knew that it was home, and we were finally here.

Chapter 21
CHINA DOLL

July 12, 1999

Lynn and Phau Wi Sha were just an ordinary couple living in Changsha, China. They went on about their day-to-day lives. Between working and attending school, there wasn't much else to have time for. In the late summer of 1999, Lynn discovered she was pregnant and, a few weeks after, found out it was a girl. Deep down, she was excited but had to keep all the joy she was feeling inside because she knew that her husband wouldn't be thrilled since he had always envisioned raising a son. Boys were worth more than girls because they could serve in the army, and by law, you could only have one child.

Lynn was due in January and knew she couldn't keep this a secret much longer because she was going to gain weight and was sick most mornings. Her husband didn't really pay her any mind because he would get up and go to work. When he wasn't working, he would be reading books or outside exploring. Phau found out about the pregnancy soon after and beat Lynn because she didn't tell him. He asked about the gender, and she claimed she hadn't found out yet. When she finally told him it was a girl, he was furious and was blaming her for everything, claiming she wanted a daughter more than a son, and would abuse her. He would drink and hit her. He threatened that if she would keep the baby, he would kill them both.

So one day, she planned her escape, her only way out alive. She was playing the game of survival, for her and her unborn child. She referred to her daughter as a *china doll*. She knew the only way they would stay alive is if she would leave, have the baby, and then have her sister drop the baby off at an orphanage. She thought that her husband would have no idea that she even had the baby, let alone know where she was. Lynn cashed out some of her inheritance, made a plan, and never looked back. She wanted to raise a daughter of her own. She loved children and always dreamed of being a mother but thought that her daughter deserved the very best and to have two parents who loved her. She wanted her daughter to be raised with a family, not growing up to the noise of her father abusing her mother or worrying about if she could go to sleep at night. She loved her daughter, so she gave her up. She wanted her daughter to live the best life possible, so she left the inheritance money to her so that maybe, just maybe, they would find their way back to each other in another lifetime. She had written her sister several letters with instructions, a birth certificate, and a copy of her will.

Once she gave birth, she swaddled her baby in warm clothing, put her in a basket along with the documents, and left her with her sister. She was clothed in a purple handmade blanket from her aunt Sonia. They were made out of the same material of Lucy's and Isla's blankets. Sonia then read the letters and followed the instructions to keep her promise, and that was that. Lynn's daughter was safe at last; she was free. She was free of all violent outbreaks of her father. Her innocence remained unwavering as new hope was unraveled through adoption. If anything stayed true, it was that her daughter found the love and freedom her mother had always wished for. And deep, deep down, her heart would always be a part of her mother's; and she would always remain a china doll.

Chapter 22
POLAROIDS IN A BOX

The next few weeks flew by, but the days seemed to run together. Robin and LeeAnna picked us up from the airport and brought us to my house. They helped unpack, wash clothes, and put away everything. Michael was doing physical therapy Monday through Friday and was exceeding the doctors' expectations. He couldn't lift anything over five pounds for two weeks, but that didn't stop him from playing with the girls. Isla would play doctor and listen to his heart with a plastic stethoscope. She would run from one side of the room to the other, bringing Michael toys to play with. Michael will always claim that being with them is better than any medicine that a doctor would prescribe. It was the twinkle in his eyes reminding me what it would be like if we had our own children and how great of a father he would make.

We worked from home the following few weeks and were adjusting to our new daily routines. In a way, we were living together. He would stay in my guest room for a few nights, or I would go to his house. Michael was limited to the activity he could do but could go on walks. We still cooked and danced in the kitchen just like on our first date. I thought to myself, *Through thick and thin.* And there was nobody else I would want to do life with. I knew that if we were able to make it out of this better and stronger, we were meant to be. And as weird as it may sound, Michael has yet to meet my parents. He met Ellie briefly over FaceTime, but that was it. But it was just normal to my parents because I have never brought home a guy before let alone a boyfriend, so I guess I was just holding back.

But things were different, and I wasn't the same person I once was. In just a few short months, I had become fiercely independent and stood up for myself. I also met the person I was searching for. There was a reason for having a void in my heart. But I found the person who adds value to my life. It was Michael. Everything made sense. I finally stopped searching when I met Michael, and I didn't even know it.

After about a month of being home and fully being able to process everything, it was time to go through all of the things that Lucy and Isla's birth parents had arranged before they came to the United States. Michael, LeeAnna, Robin, and I flew to Dallas. We looked at the property they bought along with the furniture that was already delivered. It was a gorgeous house but still needed to be put together in order to live in it. There was a lot of stuff in boxes, and most of their belongings were shipped to a storage unit about ten minutes up the street. It felt as though their whole lives were thrown into the shed. There were boxes of clothing, books, toys, furniture, antiques, and other knickknacks that were carefully placed and wrapped. Everything looked like it was packed by a woman—the cursive handwriting, everything perfectly placed and organized. I thought to myself, *Is this where I get all of my organization skills?* There were little quirks and mannerisms about myself, and I wondered where they came from. Did I just pick up on them from my adoptive family, or were they genetic? One of the things about being adopted is that you will wonder where your personality comes from or why you pick up certain habits.

After spending all day rummaging through the storage unit, we made a few different piles: keep, trash, and donations. We kept all of the vintage and antique pieces and clothing. We kept the girls' toys and clothes, all of the documentation, pictures, and some furniture. There was so much, we didn't know what to think. We donated the items that weren't going to be used. It took all hands on deck and a few days to sort through everything.

One of the most important things we found was a box of old pictures that were taken over twenty years ago from when their parents were in their teens. We even found pictures of my birth mother and father and some other relatives that I'd discovered were dead. I had my mother's hair and eyes, yet I hardly resembled my father. I guess that is a good thing after all. I also looked like my aunt Sonia from the side. She too had long black hair, and we even shared the same smile. I couldn't believe everything I was discovering just by sifting through old pictures. A picture was worth a thousand words—or, in my case, a lifetime's worth of searching. Sonia was just like me and wrote the dates on the back of each card. She also wrote recipes, passwords, and even notes about the girls. She had made them each a scrapbook, and it was unfinished. I knew that she had intentions of finishing them due to the blank pages, so that is what we agreed to do. We dug through boxes of baby clothes, books, CDs, jewelry—you name it.

In the end, we decided to sell the property and save the money for the girls. All of the money was now in my bank account, and it didn't feel real looking at the numbers. I had 50 million in my account and 25 million each in the girls' accounts. I had put most of mine into savings and even invested some of it, but I did tell myself I could do what I wanted with 5 million. I could buy a house, a new car, or a boat; travel the world; start my nonprofit; start a company; or all of the above. I could even cash it all out and retire if I wanted to. But I knew that I was destined for more than just lying underneath palm trees on some private island.

Michael and I had a conversation on the plane back to Orlando about what we wanted to do. I came up with all types of ideas like buying a bigger home, going back to Europe, and even leaving Florida altogether. He said that he would support me no matter what I decide and would come with me. I hinted that we would start the process of building our dream home, starting my nonprofit, and planning a mission trip overseas for next year. I had also always dreamed of starting my own business. I couldn't make up my mind if I wanted to go into fashion or home decor. I told Michael that the one thing I wanted more than anything was to be a mother and raise my children until they were old enough to go to school. I always said to myself, *A girl can dream, right?* But now all of those dreams are finally coming true.

Michael saw how overwhelmed I was just thinking about it all and told me that we could do one thing at a time. First, we could start on the design of our house and buy a piece of land. Once that was started, we would look into funding a mission trip and keep adding things until they were all checked off. I mean, I have a lifetime to accomplish all of this. He balanced me out more than I realized; he was the calm to my storm and would always tell me that everything would work its way out.

LeeAnna and I talked about the accounts for the girls, and on paper, all of the money belongs to me since I am the eldest and the only one legal to sign for the money, so I made them accounts under my name. The money will remain untouched until it is needed for a car, education, or medical expenses. I want them to do whatever they dream in life and to have the resources to achieve them. If they want to cash it all out and travel the world, go to college, or even start a business, the choice will be theirs to make. I let LeeAnna know that if she needed me to write her a check, I would. She smiled softly as she told me to keep it safe and sound.

Chapter 23
BECAUSE OF YOU

Thanksgiving was only a few days away. It would be the first major holiday I would be away from my parents. They called and told me they were going on a cruise and that I could go with them, but I told them I wanted to stay in Orlando with all of my close friends and Michael. At this point, they knew about him, but they had never met face-to-face, only over the phone. I even offered them to come here, but they already had plans set in stone. For the rest of my family, we don't really see each other. We talk here and there but not enough for me to fly home for Thanksgiving when I've already committed to hosting this year. LeeAnna, Richard, the girls, Michael, Robin and her family, and some of the ladies I go to church with were all planning to eat at my house around two. There were about twenty people coming over. Michael agreed to help me set up the tables inside and out, grocery shop, and clean the house. Everyone had signed up to bring a dish or two so not all of the weight was on me.

I was extra thankful this year. Michael and I bought a huge piece of land a few minutes down the road. It was a few acres and was right on the water. It was the perfect place to build our forever home. I knew the style of house I wanted and the features. I wanted at least five to six bedrooms, a large kitchen that opened up into the living room, a wraparound porch, a swimming pool and gym, a garage, and a huge backyard that overlooks the water. I had hired a contractor and builder, and they said that the best bet would be to build a three-story home. Our basement would have a gym and a man cave. On the second story, there would be the kitchen and living space, and the top story would be all of the bedrooms. I loved fantasizing about these things but find it intimidating when it comes to committing to the actual design.

Michael and I spent a lot of time preparing for all our guests. We moved the furniture around to accommodate twenty people. I even bought more silverware and dishes. The grocery stores were packed like sardines in a can. There was just enough room to breathe. As we were going from aisle to aisle, Michael and I observed all types of people—from those who had children with them to those who were shopping alone or had their spouse. Most people's carts had the Thanksgiving essentials like turkey, ham, mashed potatoes, and assorted vegetables and produce. Then you saw some that had the most random things. It was like they were blindfolded. One older lady had soda, bread, and ten different types of cookies. I wondered if these people were just buying snacks or if they even had anyone to celebrate the holiday with. Michael and I opted for self-checkout and headed to the truck. In the parking lot, Michael stopped to help an older couple load their groceries into their car and even put the cart away. What a gentleman. Who knew this simple gesture would make my heart do a somersault in my chest?

"Two days until turkey day!" Michael said as he opened the bed of the truck.

"I can hardly believe it. It looks like we are feeding fifty people."

"You technically are. This is a lot of work. I'm impressed!"

"Don't say that. The real work hasn't even begun."

"I know you will handle it with such grace, just like you do everything else. You make everything look easy."

"Well, that is because I have you. Don't worry, there is plenty that needs to be done. The tables and chairs need to be set up, the decor needs to be spread out, the food needs to be prepped and cooked, and so much more. I love it though."

"It will be a learning experience for us together to see if we want to do this again next year or if we want to escape and go out of the country."

We finished loading up the back of the truck. Michael drove slowly on the way home so we could take in the view. It was slightly overcast and not too hot. So we opted to grab sandwiches on the way home and go for a walk on the beach. I realized that I needed a bigger refrigerator once all of the groceries were laid out.

"I hope we have everything because nothing else will fit in here."

"Dang, are you going into hibernation or something?"

"When we get back, can we prepare some of the food to make more space?"

"Absolutely. You're the chef."

———————————— • —————— • ————————————

As we walked down the beach, Michael's hand was locked into mind like they just fit. It's like our hands were magnets, bound together every time they touched. Whenever we held hands, I felt safe. *Safe*—a word I could now say with ease rather than suspension. We talked about Thanksgiving, seeing the girls and how big they were getting, and our excitement about building our first home. The only thing was we are not married. I thought, *Are we going to live in the same house but have separate living spaces like we are college roommates?* But I guess we will cross that bridge when we get there. I mean, the house isn't going to be move-in-ready for another year or so. So there is still time. If you know what I mean.

"Michael, if you were to have told me that we would be walking on the beach together let alone be building a house six months ago, I wouldn't have believed you."

"Well, why is that you may add? But I do agree with you." He just stared at me. "I could have never dreamed this. It is more than a dream. It is part of God's plan for us. And that to me is better than any dream I could ever imagine."

"Same here. And before I met you, I never thought I deserved to find anyone let alone be happy. I just thought I was destined to be alone."

"Trust me, someone like you is never meant to be alone."

"Because of you, I was able to add the perfect addition that I never knew I needed to my life."

"You mean more to me than you will ever know."

We looked at each other and communicated through our eyes just how we were feeling as the sun was trying to emerge from the clouds just like our hearts were doing for each other. The one thing about Michael and me is that most of the time, we just know what the other is thinking by our facial expressions or actions. We don't even have to tell each other; we just know. We know when the other is happy, sad, excited, or overwhelmed or just needs a quick beach walk to ease our mind. I feel that within the next few days, I was going to feel a lot of things, especially overwhelmed. But at the same time, he knew what to do and say to cool my nerves. Just looking at him, I knew that everything was going to be all right, and we needed to just keep moving forward.

The waves were making a delicate slushing noise as the wind died down. This was my favorite time of day—just before sunset and dusk and when the ocean went to sleep. I loved watching nature transform into the still environment it does at night. All of the creatures on land and in the water know it is time for bed. But I got an unwavering sense of energy when the world was asleep and I was awake. It makes me feel like I am watching and protecting the world before it wakes up.

Michael and I got back to the house and began chopping up all of the vegetables and premeasuring all of the dry ingredients and putting everything in separate containers. Then we grouped together the ingredients for each recipe. We put all of the ingredients for the pies in a container, then the cookies, etc. You get the point. We walked from one side of the kitchen to the other, moving to the sound of the music in the background. We were humming, singing with spoons as microphones, and dancing. It was just easy. It was fun.

Chapter 24
LOVE LETTERS

The next morning, Michael and I came up with the idea to make a scrapbook. We wanted to make a time capsule so that in the future, we could dig it up with our children. I think it would be cool to reflect back on how things have changed and how we have grown. There would be pictures, knickknacks we had picked up from places we had traveled to, notes we had written, concert tickets, shells we had picked up along the shoreline, and lastly love letters. We spent an hour or so apart writing a letter that we would open and read when we were older. I'm normally a pretty decent writer. I compose emails and letters for work and leave Michael notes all over the house. So why was this one letter so difficult to write? Because I wanted it to be perfect. I wanted to capture our entire story together, from when we met to all of our date nights, trips, the shooting, everything. I wanted it to summarize everything we had conquered together but wanted to tell him how much I love and appreciate him. I wanted to sound romantic but not cheesy. I wanted to write our inside jokes and funny moments without losing focus on the real reason why I'm writing this. This letter isn't for me to just say "I love you." It's a thank-you letter. Thank you for loving me, thank you for choosing me, thank you for all of the endless beach walks, thank you for taking the girls in as your own, thank you for putting up with my crazy ideas, thank you for being my travel partner, and, last but not least, thank you for being you.

I had written a sentence, then would think of something better and trash it. I had about fifteen pieces of crumpled-up paper lying beside me with the words *what if*. But finally, when I looked out at the ocean and touched pen to paper, the words just started to flow.

Nov 27, 2024

My Dearest Michael,

50 years from now, I think about where we will be and how we ended up. If we stayed in Orlando or if we moved to another state or country. I wonder where we will be when we read these letters. Will we have children or grandchildren? Will we be on vacation or just at home in each other's company? But one thing that will remain unwavering is my love and endless gratitude for you.

Who would have thought that six months ago my life would change forever? From the very first day I saw you, I knew that there was something indescribable about you. I saw your gentleness and patience with Lucy and Isla, I noticed your bright smile and sparkling eyes as we had our first conversation. I saw how easily we fit together, I saw your professionalism in your work but also how you empathize with others, and I saw my potential to possibly be yours.

When we first met I wasn't looking for love; it was searching for me. At the time I was lonely, scared, and depressed. So I ran. I ran from everything I ever knew. I ran away from home, relationships, and the idea of finding my person. And then I met you. You turned my life around. You were accepting, understanding, caring, and loved without judgment. You loved me for me. Then, I felt my heart slowly opening up to you, and before I knew it, I felt something I never felt before. Real love. To be in love with someone. Since then I have fallen more in love with you with every second that passes.

During our first conversation I wanted to ask you out. But I hesitated just like I always have. I figured a tall, handsome, and kind doctor like you must be married or engaged. I didn't want to cross any professional boundaries and figured if we were meant to be then we would. I honestly thought that we would never see each other again after that day. And that day was one of the first that I toyed with my ring finger. It was the first sign of hoping. Of wishing and thinking "what if."

Fast forward to our first date. It was magical. I mean, it may have seemed simple to you but it was the picture-perfect date. No having to deal with the public, no waiters or waitresses, no strangers, just me and you. We talked, we laughed, we were present with each other underneath the stars. We had deep conversations like we had been best friends for years. It's like we knew each other in another lifetime. We ate dinner and cooked dessert, we danced around the kitchen, and then you drove me home, and before I went to sleep that night, I knew that this was going to be the start of forever. A thousand thoughts raced through my mind and the only thing that I could feel was my love for you. Forever.

Since that day we have spent endless hours together. I would stop at every green light to talk to you and I would run every red light just to get to you.

We have explored the beach and ocean, cooked and tried new foods, traveled to quirky towns, gone across the world together, experienced heartbreak and tragedy, and lastly we have bonded with two beautiful little girls that I wished were ours. And in a selfish way, I pretend that they are. Despite what we face, we do it together. You have helped me though more than you could ever imagine. If it wasn't for you, I would still be searching. I would be lost because I would not know what to look for. I believe that you must suffer loss in order to gain your greatest blessing and you are just that. You were able to open my eyes and help me see that there was so much more to life. I knew that God was waiting until I was ready before He intertwined our worlds together. And because of you, I knew that God was listening to all of my prayers.

Life with you is so much fun. It is a dream come true to fall in love with your best friend. But it is even more special when you look into their eyes and see a future. When we locked eyes for the first time, I saw my future. I saw someone who I had dreams about when I was little. I saw a man who was gentle and kind and someone who I thought I didn't deserve. But you made me feel so seen and loved and you still do. Every day. Every day when I wake up I feel like the luckiest girl on earth because when we are together you make me feel like we are the only two people left on earth.

Michael, thank you for asking me on our first date, thank you for making me believe in forever aside from Jesus, thank you for asking me to become your girlfriend. Thank you for always choosing me and loving me. Even on the toughest days, you choose me. I cannot wait for our future together. Our story has just begun. And I will love until the end of time. And this may sound cheesy but I hope I die before you so I never have to live without you. So cheers to a lifetime of beach walks, traveling, and serving Jesus together. You & Me, Always & Forever!

I'll love you until the day I die,

Adaire

———————

Adaire was sitting and writing on the beach towel just a few feet away from me. I could just tell that she was pouring her heart out on that piece of paper. But honestly, if I were to write a letter to her about how much she means to me and our journey together, I would never stop writing. But the only thing I could do now was start. I didn't know what to include or leave out. I did want it to sound authentic, and when she reads this fifty years from now, I want her to smile as the memories play live as she reads it. I want her to relive these moments of us in our twenties and remember how young and in love we were. The older we grow, the stronger our love will become. I also thought to myself that if I had made a different decision in my life, I might not be where I am today. So thank You, Jesus, for leading, teaching, and loving me in the way that You do. Your timing is perfect.

The saying "Good things come to those who wait" couldn't be more true, because Adaire is the best thing that has ever happened to me. She was my answered prayer that I have waited a lifetime for. I fell in love with her before our first conversation. I saw her smile, mannerisms, and interactions with others. I saw a light that surrounded her wherever she went. I saw Jesus. I know that He is alive because He lives in her, and it is so easy to see.

Adaire always tells me that whenever I have doubts or am unsure of something, I should look to the ocean for answers. Even though you don't say a word, it will make you feel an unwavering sense of calmness that delivers in the right direction. So I took her advice often and especially today when trying to compose a letter. I know, I'm distraught about a letter, but I know that hers is going to be perfect, and I want her to feel special when she reads this. Adaire cautiously chooses the words she writes to make you feel like she is in the room with you. So I glanced at the ocean and began writing. I thought to myself, *One sentence at a time.*

Nov 27, 2024
Adaire,

My sweetheart, as I'm sitting here writing I can't help but look up and see you doing the same. You are much better than this than I am. But you are easily the most influential person in my life. You have taught me the beauty and joy in all aspects of life. You have shown me faithfulness and forgiveness. You have given my life a whole new meaning.

Who knew that God could change your entire world with one person? I believed in Him but you are living proof that He exists. My whole life, I knew what I was praying for but didn't know who until I met you. Our paths came together and became one. You have taught me sacrifice, service, and love through God's eyes. You swept me off my feet from day one. When I first saw you, I was afraid of getting shut down again. I was afraid of starting something new and getting hurt. I was scared. But from our first conversation and date, it all went away. And my heart opened itself again. I wanted to flat-out say, "I want to marry you one day," but held back because I didn't want you to run.

But since you will be reading this in 50 years, I think I can say this. I haven't told anyone yet that I have a ring that is being made. Because, Adaire, I love you and I cannot picture my life without you. I want us to be together. The ring doesn't captivate all of my feelings and love for you. It's a symbol that I want to love you forever. It is a symbol that we will continue to serve God the rest of our days.

I don't have all of the details planned but it needs to be almost as extraordinary as you my love. I want it to be a day you remember for the rest of your life. I want you to know how much I love you as much as you love me and everyone else. I tell you often all of the things I love about you but here are just a few.

1. Your love and passion for God and His people, this is my all-time favorite thing about you. You love and serve everyone so well. Just being around you makes me feel special, seen, and loved.

2. Your willingness to serve others, whether it's volunteering on your only day off or taking a

month to take care of someone. You serve God's people and make Him proud.

3. How authentic you are, you are always true to yourself and never let anything change you!

4. How hardworking you are. Your dedication and attention to detail never goes unnoticed. You work so hard and despite where you are, you will always drop anything and everything to help others.

5. Your kindness and generosity. To know you is to love you. You are kind to all of those you encounter. You would go out of your way to help strangers and would do anything for anyone.

6. Your infectious joy and beauty. Anyone who sees you says, "Wow, she is stunning." Because it is the dang truth. You are easily the most beautiful and exquisite woman I've ever laid my eyes on.

7. Your sense of adventure. You love exploring new places, restaurants, and challenges. You make learning something new so much fun!

8. The way you celebrate others. Even on your special days, you make everyone else feel so seen and loved!

9. Your love for Lucy and Isla. Watching you with them is magical. They love you so much. You have raised the bar on what a parent or guardian should be and so much more. You teach and care for them like they are your own!

10. And lastly, your willingness to give me a shot. We always argue about this but you are way out of my league. Thank you for saying yes.

Adaire, I would be here forever if I wrote everything I love about you. You are beauty, you are grace, and you are mine. And I cannot wait to continue building our life together.

My love is yours forever,

Michael

I folded the paper into thirds and placed it in an envelope. I wrote "Michael" with a heart on it and sealed it with a sticker. Michael had bought a waterproof lockbox, and we placed the envelope along with other treasures inside. Lastly, Michael put a scrapbook on top and told me not to open it until I read the letter . . . in fifty years. He said it would make sense then. We drove to the land where we were building our forever home, and in the left corner of our soon-to-be backyard, we dug a hole about a few feet deep and placed the safe there. As we piled the dirt back on top, all I can think about is all of the words that would be enclosed for another half a century before we are able to read them. I tried to forget yet knew it would be in the back of my mind until that day.

Chapter 25
SWEETER THAN PUMPKIN PIE

Growing up, I would always go out of town for Thanksgiving. My family would travel to Mexico and Hawaii, and last year we went on a cruise. My parents used this as an excuse to go on a vacation so my mother didn't have to cook an entire feast or get sucked into hosting. My mom said if we didn't opt to go somewhere, she would be stuck in the kitchen making a bunch of different dishes she didn't like just for them to be half eaten and then be thrown away a few days later. And the truth is, I didn't blame her. Plus, I always enjoyed getting out of town and visiting new places. Everywhere was packed, and Charleston would be invaded by tourists and college students coming home. Even the locals couldn't go to the grocery store, get gas, or go to their favorite restaurants and shops. It was like vultures preying on Charleston. So my memories included going somewhere tropical with family and friends. After a few years, we adopted it as our tradition.

This was the first Thanksgiving since elementary school that I woke up in my own bed. The morning started out peaceful. Around 5:00 a.m., I did my daily workout, a quick Bible study, and continued preparing and cooking the few dishes I had left. I was in charge of the ham, mac and cheese, mashed potatoes, bread, and a few desserts. Michael set up everything before I added the decor and floral arrangements. Everyone else had signed up to bring the turkey and additional sides that would complete the picture-perfect Thanksgiving meal. I had made mashed potatoes and gravy the night before. Everything was prepped for the bread and mac and cheese, and the ham was in the oven. It was just a waiting game now.

Michael showed up around 7:00 a.m. to join me for our morning beach walk before we got tied to doing this and that. There was seating inside and out on the patio, but regardless of where you sat, you could see the ocean—my personal favorite. I had arranged the tables with the flowers in the middle and had a place setting for every person. I wanted it to feel welcoming and that I had put in some effort into being a good host. I had cleared the bar so people could place their dishes there, and along the wall that entered into the kitchen was a long rectangle-shaped table where we would set up the buffet once everyone arrived. I had the napkins folded to match the decor and arranged the silverware and the plates accordingly. I could finally take a deep breath, knowing that the hard part was over. I finished the rest of the morning by getting ready and doing miscellaneous household chores. Michael made sure there were ice and drinks. Then we found a room for where we were going to put Isla's high chair.

Around one o'clock, LeeAnna, Richard, and the girls arrived. Lucy was excited to see all of the decorations since she had never celebrated Thanksgiving before. I wanted it to be extra special, so Michael and I made sure that there were decorations everywhere and lots of activities to do, everything from arts and crafts to playing games. Despite the holiday, I tried to make everything a big deal. I mean, it only happens once a year. The girls were playing in the living room with Michael. I stood back and smiled knowing that my dream was right at my fingertips yet so far away at the same time. I was trying to grasp reality, wishing I could understand what it felt like.

LeeAnna and I were finishing up heating the remainder of our dishes before Robin and her family arrived. Robin had a casserole dish in one hand and a Diet Coke in the other. Her family poured in behind her along with some of our friends from church. Everyone was introducing themselves. There were lots of noise and distinct chatter and sidebar conversations. The mingling continued as everyone was coming into the kitchen trying to help set up for dinner.

"Thank you, everyone, for joining us today on such a special holiday. Before we dig in, it is a tradition to go around and say what you are thankful for. I'll start by saying that I am thankful for all of you and your friendships."

Michael went next, then Robin, and so on. Everyone said they were thankful for friends and family, the ability to eat together, being able to be by the beach, and just your normal cheesy Thanksgiving stuff. Richard said the blessing, and we all started to form a line. The kids went first so they wouldn't get restless while waiting. I walked through the line with Lucy, and she pointed at everything she wanted. She pointed at the turkey and ham, mashed potatoes and gravy, macaroni and cheese, cranberries (mostly because she liked the color), and bread. Just like your normal child, the vegetables didn't look or sound appealing. She insisted on sitting beside Michael. I found that adorable, so we moved her chair next to his. Michael sat next to her after he went through the buffet. She even waited for him to sit next to her before she started to eat. She would point at something, and he would cut it into smaller pieces. He taught her how to use a fork and spoon. I sat on the other side of her, and she was a surprisingly clean and good eater. She ate everything on her plate. On the other hand, Isla was still being warmed up to eating solid foods. She had milk and a few bites of mashed potatoes.

Michael and a few of the guys went outside with the kids so we could finish and start to clean up. I was able to eat and talk with some friends for the first time in a while. We caught up about life, work, and everything in between. I even talked to Robin about Michael and the girls a little bit. We were talking about the house plans, what we were doing for Christmas.

Robin pulled me aside and asked, "So when do you think the house is going to be finished?"

"I'm not in any rush but within a year or two."

"Where do you see you and Michael going?"

"I think he may be the one, but we don't have a timeline. We haven't talked about getting engaged and haven't even been going out for a year."

"But when you know, you know. Everyone who knows you says you are the best couple. Y'all are perfect together."

"I think he's pretty great. But I'm also scared. I've never been *in love* before. I just don't want to screw things up."

"Trust me on this, I don't think you will. He is head over heels for you. He tells me all the time how happy you make him."

"Well, he makes me happy too. It's like everything disappears when we are together. He makes time stop."

"I know both of you, and I couldn't pick two better people for each other."

Evening came upon us like no time had passed. All of the food was just about gone, and the kids had eaten nearly all of the dessert. Luckily most of the casserole and side dishes were in throwaway containers, so there weren't a lot of dishes. A few of the ladies from the church washed the plates and silverware, as I boxed up the remaining food and took the trash out. Everything was cleaned and put away in an hour. Richard folded up the table and chairs and loaded them in the back of Michael's truck for him to take back to the church. We all sat outside watching the kids play while we sipped on some wine. The breeze was just right, not too cool but just enough so we wouldn't get hot, and it kept the flies away. I tucked my hair behind my ear, and out of the corner of my eye, I saw Michael smiling and playing with all of the kids while Lucy stayed at his side. Isla was asleep in Robin's arms. Robin's demeanor changed around kids. Don't let her fool you, but deep down I think she is fond of them. I saw this whenever we would work on cases and especially with Lucy and Isla. She softened her tone and even played with them.

Everyone eventually trickled out until it was just Michael and me. We put away the last of the dishes before crashing on the couch with some dessert and watching TV. Around 11:00 p.m., Michael headed home. It was late, and the next morning we had plans to get up and go Black Friday shopping. I wanted to look for some furniture and miscellaneous items for our future home.

What a day, I thought to myself. It was a long day but also felt like I blinked and it was over. I would trade a cruise or any other luxury trip for this every year. I get why my parents wanted to get away, but I also understood the people who host every year. Yes, it is a lot of work, and half of the day you are running around forgetting to eat yourself, but it is all worth it when you see your loved ones relaxed and enjoying every moment soaking it all in.

I was lying in bed as I was barely able to keep my eyes open. I reminisced about the past few days—cooking, cleaning, having a full house, being surrounded with family and friends, and walking on the beach. And I thought to myself, *I could do this every year.*

Chapter 26
MAGIC

The holidays were officially upon us. All of the Christmas decorations were displayed around Orlando. There were lights strung on the light poles, wreaths hanging from every door, and Christmas music playing as you walked down the street; and even though it was still warm, it felt like Christmas. I considered the sand as our snow. Michael and I spent the first two weeks of December Christmas shopping and decorating each of our houses. We had put up our Christmas trees, lights, and miscellaneous figures around the house. There was a manger scene on one of my side tables and garland draped across the mantel with stockings hanging in front of the fireplace. This was the first time I saw other people's names beside mine. I thought back to when I was little. I dreamed about what Santa would bring but also rejoiced because it was Jesus's birthday—two of the best things in my opinion. I loved Christmas. It made me think of my grandparents. It made me believe in magic, that anything could come true.

Michael and I went overboard with the shopping. We had bought the girls a bunch of toys and necessities and even shopped for LeeAnna and Richard, coworkers, friends, and family. As I wandered down each of the aisles browsing for the perfect gift for each person on my list, I thought to myself this is the first Christmas I am picking out a gift for a boyfriend. Normally I help my friends or cousins buy for their significant others. But this year was different. It was all brand new and something I never would have thought would happen, especially this year. I had bought mostly everything except I had to order Michael's gift. I had ordered him a watch. He mentioned it was something he was going to buy himself eventually but couldn't ever decide. So I went online and ordered him one I think he would like and could wear to work and on the water. It also had a dressier look to it so he could also wear it to church. It was silver and waterproof and had great reviews. Along with that, I had bought him some shorts and T-shirts to wear on our upcoming trips. One of our Christmas presents for the girls, Richard, and LeeAnna was a trip to Disney World. We leave next week to get back in time for Christmas Day. The following week, Michael and I were planning to spend a few weeks in Europe to make up for what happened the last time we decided to leave the country. We were planning to visit Greece, Italy, France, and Croatia.

I looked up and saw Michael looking at ornaments. He was studying the different opinions, thinking about which would be the best with the rest of the decor.

"What do you think about these?" He smiled as he held up a box of red ornaments.

"I like those a lot. I think they would go great on the tree! We should get a box or two."

"Do you think it will look complete after we get done putting these on?"

"It looks great now, but it will brighten the tree up with some red."

"I know we are by the beach, but I can't imagine Christmas without it."

"I'm glad we are on the same page. Look at that over there." I headed to the shelf of miniature figurines. There was everything, from snowmen to Santa Claus, reindeers, and manger scenes. For some reason, I am drawn to anything that is miniature and you can add to it every year.

"I think that would look great on top of your nightstand or even dresser. You should get it." He eventually added the box with the village scene to the cart along with everything else.

"I swear we always come in here with a plan and then get sidetracked into buying more stuff we don't need."

"I guess that is the beauty of shopping."

We strolled down each aisle to make sure there wasn't anything else we forgot. Even though we had most of the items saved from our previous trip being canceled, I felt it would be wise to purchase anything we would need for the forthcoming travels, such as toothpaste, shampoo, conditioner, toothbrushes, and chargers. We even got a few things for the girls since we wanted to give Richard and LeeAnna one less thing to worry about. One of our favorite traditions is to buy snacks once we're done shopping and eat them on the way home. So I grabbed some holiday-themed chips and cookies to enjoy as we drove back.

———————————————

The next week LeeAnna, Richard, and the girls came over for dinner. We played games and rode around and looked at Christmas lights while drinking hot chocolate. The twinkling lights, blow-up characters, and decorated trees really made us feel like we were up north in the cold when in reality it was in the 80s in Orlando. When they were about to leave, we gave them each a box with Mickey ears and a T-shirt. Lucy was superexcited; she was jumping up and down, and Isla was just messing with the box, not having a reaction to what was inside.

"I can't believe it is next week. How did you guys pull this off?" LeeAnna asked as she shared her excitement.

"It was all Adaire. She is a professional planner."

"I enjoy planning trips, and I love Disney, so it was fun and easy to do."

"Well, I know the girls are going to love it, especially Lucy. She wears her princess dresses around the house," Richard added as he was examining the pair of sparkly ears.

Michael asked Lucy, "Are you excited to go to Disney World and to see all of the characters?"

"Belle . . . ?" she said softly.

"Yes, that is right! We will see her there. Did you know we are going to the castle and you might get to meet her?"

She blushed as she was pulling the T-shirt over her head. Michael and I looked at each other with a sigh of relief, knowing that we did good.

"It is Disney day," Michael said as he called me at four in the morning.

"Well, it's a good morning to you too! Did you even get any sleep, or are you too excited?"

"Both. I'm tired, but I am ready to get the day started. It's not a far drive at all. Have you thought about getting annual passes?"

"I actually have. I think that Disney would be a great date night!"

"That sounds really fun. We should definitely go for a weekend. Do you want to go on a walk before we head that way?"

"Sure. What time should we tell them to meet us there?"

"Seven? I mean, the gate doesn't open until eight, but we'll need time to find parking. I want to get a full day in."

"Sounds like a plan. I will see you soon."

———————— •— —• ————————

Luckily for us, we live in Orlando, so it takes us about thirty minutes to get there. LeeAnna and Richard were driving separately so if we end up buying a few things, we want to make sure we have enough room to bring it back. And after we get done at the park, Michael and I might go out and listen to live music.

The traffic wasn't terrible for Orlando, but once we got to the gate at Disney, everyone came to a dead stop. Everyone had the same idea. Who doesn't want to see Disney all decorated at Christmastime? When we walked through the entrance, there was so much to look at from the castle to the big tree and all of the buildings covered in garland and colored lights. Lucy and Isla looked around without saying a word. It was like their brains were overstimulating just like ours were. There was so much to do and look at that we didn't know where to start. So we headed in the direction of the rides. I thought ahead and bought a pass to skip the long lines, which was nice, so we were able to ride what we could with both girls. Some rides we would just have to take Lucy while someone stayed behind with Isla.

We rode everything from the carousel to It's a Small World and watched a few shows and met all of the characters. Lucy was fond of all the princesses. She got her picture with all of them along with their autographs. By the end of the day, she had too much sugar—from ice cream to candy. I was convinced that is all she was going to want. But she ate a few bites of pasta and fruit for lunch.

The afternoon flew by as we rode on more rides, walked in all the shops, and ate at the castle for dinner before the fireworks started. The girls seemed to enjoy it. Lucy was pointing at them as they burst into the sky. She was also lured into watching the video on the castle, and her favorite part was when Tinker Bell flew in the sky. I looked down at her and saw a younger version of myself. I remember my first trip to Disney. I was five years old and felt like I was in another universe. I felt safe and free and that all was right in the world.

Even though we live close to Disney, I wanted the girls to have the full experience, so we booked rooms on the property. After the fireworks were over, the park was about to close, so LeeAnna and Richard headed to the room with the girls while Michael and I went to Disney Springs. We listened to a live band at one of the adult-only bars and walked around in some shops.

The next two days were filled with going to Epcot, Animal Kingdom, and Hollywood Studios. We rode every ride that the girls could go on. Michael and I even went on a few roller coasters. And my personal favorite—walking around the entire World Showcase in Epcot. It was perfect weather and not too hot. Lucy kept pointing at everything and wanted to go into every little shop along the way. She picked out another princess dress, a few stuffed animals, dolls, and books. Michael and I tried a new food and drink in every country. The taste buds on my tongue were exploding.

Growing up and even today, Epcot has been my favorite park. Unlike the others, I felt like I was traveling around the world. I mean, you basically are. For the most part, the workers in each of the countries are actually from there and speak in their native language. They are knowledgeable about the food and other customs. In Italy, the waitress was an exchange student, and she had come to America for the first time a few months ago. It was refreshing seeing Michael talk to everyone and getting to know them. He made friends everywhere. Seeing the way he chose his words for each person he encountered and the way he looked them in the eye showed his ability to hold a conversation. It was one of the things that sparked my interest. He was warm and inviting and could talk about anything to anyone.

We spent our last full day back at Disney Springs picking up some last-minute Christmas gifts, trying new restaurants, and soaking in the last of Disney. It had been a fun few days, but we were all exhausted. I even told Michael I wanted a massage for Christmas.

"Well, was it worth it?" Michael said with tired eyes.

"Oh, 100 percent. I think you had just as much fun as the girls." I paused, not knowing what to say as I was trying to catch my thoughts. "I mean, we all did. I'll never stop loving Disney. It makes me feel like a kid all over again. It makes me believe in magic. Just like Christmas."

"Well, this was the perfect gift. They will remember this forever!" LeeAnna added. "This was the best trip, and the girls were so well-behaved the entire time."

I leaned in to hug her. "They were so good, no crying unless they were tired, and they seemed to have fun with whatever we put in front of them."

We headed back to the car to head home, thirty minutes that will feel like an eternity. Michael drove as I sat in the passenger seat, reminiscing over the past few days. I felt safe and cautious at the same time. Ever since the shooting, I've been on my toes. I pay even more attention to my surroundings, people's body language and what they say, and where Michael is, because I worry about him too.

Christmas Eve is one of the most magical nights of the year. Children all around the world prepare cookies and milk to leave out for Santa Claus in exchange for the gifts they put on their wish list. Aromas of roasts and gingerbread fill the houses on every street. Christmas movies and music are being played on repeat. People are roasting marshmallows for s'mores. But since it's too hot in Florida for that, we opt for the microwave. And my favorite part—reading the story of Jesus and how He was the most perfect gift given to us. He is the reason we celebrate Christmas. He is the reason for the season.

This year looked a little different. I had visited my parents and family a few days ago in Charleston. We did all of our annual traditions. This included our gift exchange, going to see our church play, our gingerbread house competition, and last-minute shopping. Everything felt right, as if I had never left. But one thing weighed on my mind, Michael. I couldn't help but think about him. He should be here, but I know he's with his family too. We decided to spend a few days with our families so we could spend our first Christmas together in Florida with the girls.

I sat on the couch with my cousins, making small talk. I had grown up with them since I was little. We saw each other on birthdays and holidays and kept up with each other over FaceTime. Lana is probably the one I'm closest to. We're the same age and have similar interests. In elementary school, we were in dance class together. We text here and there, and I've mentioned Michael to her without giving too many details. She and I had some girl time while we sipped on our hot chocolate.

She had moved to California for a business internship and was also in a long-distance relationship with her longtime boyfriend, Jackson. Lana and Jackson had been together for three years. They met in undergrad and continue to see each other on the weekends. He lives in Arizona, and the flights aren't too long. She never mentions him because she didn't want to make me feel like I was a third wheel. Lana was good about making me feel included, and when we were all together, I would tag along. He was good to her and treated her with respect, something that I was numb to. She would always tell me, "When the time is right" or "You're still so young." But every time I heard her or anyone say those words, I wanted to punch the air.

"So tell me more about Michael." She sipped on her mug and gave me a look.

"I met him on a case, and we have been seeing each other ever since." I wanted to tell her I loved him and he was the one. But I didn't want to get either of our hopes up. I took a short breath and another sip of hot cocoa. "He's different, you know? He's humble, incredibly kind and caring, and we just have fun together. After spending time together, we discovered we had a lot more in common than we thought."

"That's awesome, Adaire. So when are you going to bring him to meet the family?"

I paused and took another sip to think about what to say next. "Umm, honestly, I don't know. Things are going great, so if they continue that way, the next time I come home, he will be with me."

"Well, I think you will make the right decision, whatever it may be. I trust your instincts. But I know we will all have fun. We can go to a game, see a movie, go bowling, or even just to dinner."

"Honestly, that sounds great. I know everyone will love him. He's just one of those people." I felt different, but in a good way. I wanted everyone to meet Michael. The only thing I may regret is not introducing him to my family sooner.

We caught up on work, relationships, and just life. It's like no time had passed and we were in middle school having sleepovers. Lana and I stayed up all night. We made holiday cookies, watched movies, and ate s'mores. I fell asleep dreaming about the past few days and how in just a day I would be back *home* with Michael.

———————————————•——— ——•———————————————

I enjoyed Christmas Eve just as much as Christmas Day. It was the anticipation, excitement, and all of the preparation. I enjoyed the weeks leading up to Christmas. Some people would say they were overwhelmed; but I looked forward to the last-minute Christmas shopping, baking, and cooking. I loved wrapping gifts and giving them even more. Just like my mother, I had a wrapping theme. This year I went with neutrals with pops of red and green. I would gather everything together and wrap while I watched Christmas movies. The nostalgia.

This year was the year of many firsts. My first Christmas away from my family and Charleston. My first Christmas having a boyfriend. My first Christmas getting to play Santa Claus. My first Christmas getting to play that mother role. Something I always prayed about. I prayed about my future husband and children daily. I prayed for their protection, and I thank God for giving me these thoughts. But in a way, I saw my future every time I looked at Michael, Lucy, and Isla.

Michael was coming over around noon to help me finish setting the table and cook the last few dishes. LeeAnna, Michael, and the girls were coming over around the same time to decorate gingerbread houses before the rest of our friends arrived. A few of the ladies from church were coming over along with their children, and Robin and her family were going to stop by. As much as I love a quiet, clean house, I also couldn't picture my Christmas Eve looking like anything else—friends who have become family, making small talk, eating lots of delicious food, and the children playing.

"Where would you like me to set these?" Michael asked, holding up the silverware.

"We can start setting up the placemats for everyone, if you want." I tossed him the pack of napkins. "Here you go. I'm going to grab a few more things. I'll be right back."

There was a red-and-green table runner on the dining room table. I wanted something festive, but it wasn't overwhelming. There were flowers in white vases on the bar where the food would be served buffet style. I grabbed the salt and pepper shakers, plates, and serving spoons and placed them accordingly. Then I placed all of the name cards on the tables along with stands for the desserts and other dishes.

"Perfect! We make a great team." He smiled and continued to set the table as I brought him more stuff to sit out.

"I mean, I can't argue with you. Everything is looking amazing. The table setting and decor are coming along. Thank you for helping by the way!" I tried to hold back my excitement.

"What are boyfriends for?" We locked eyes, and he gave me the same look as we continued.

"It's fun having someone to do this stuff with, like everyday things." My thoughts went five years in the future, hoping this would be us each year.

To make it feel even more like Christmas, I turned the AC down low, and we were all going to wear Christmas sweaters for photos. Mine had reindeer while Michael's had Santa and elves. His even lit up when you pressed a button. Lucy and Isla are going to love it.

"I like your sweater. The lights are the perfect touch." I stood there and admired him. I loved how he was going all out.

"I wear this during the holidays at work. The kids love to touch the button that turns the lights on. It also helps distract them if I end up having to draw blood or give them a shot."

"That's sweet. I love that! I'm just really glad you're here."

"Me too. Like I mean, we're having fun setting up for dinner and listening to Christmas music. What's better than that?"

"I can't think of a thing."

———————— •— —• ————————

LeeAnna, Richard, and the girls arrived. Michael sat down with Lucy and helped her decorate her gingerbread house. He glued it together with icing while she put sprinkles and other candies on and around it. He made sure she didn't eat too much sugar. Isla sat in her high chair and played with graham crackers and icing.

But he made her one too. He was patient and let Lucy design it the way she wanted. He was there, looking at her like a father would, in awe and drawn to her every move.

"You are doing a beautiful job, Lucy!" He handed her the bowl with sprinkles as she continued.

"I'm covering the snow with sprinkles!" she exclaimed.

"Do you want to make a snowman out of marshmallows?" She nodded her head as she stuffed a cracker in her mouth.

"You do it." She pointed to the bag of marshmallows.

"I'll give it a try."

I was mesmerized by how concentrated he was trying to make everything perfect for her. He cautiously piped the icing onto the marshmallows and used black sprinkles for the eyes and buttons and an orange one for the nose. He used pretzel sticks for the arms and a piece of sour candy for the scarf.

"Wow, Michael, I'm impressed," LeeAnna complimented him as she walked by to give Isla her milk.

"I guess I should have gone to culinary school," he joked but remained concentrated on the snowman.

The gingerbread houses were finished and displayed for everyone to see. They were filled with sprinkles, peppermints, gumdrops, and several other types of candy and icing. It was the little details that Lucy added. She covered the roof with cookies and sprinkles and gave the snowman a hat. She used every color sprinkle and scattered it all over the snow. I saw a younger version of myself in Lucy. She believes.

And just like that, our guests arrived. Each of them brought a covered dish and a gift for a game we were playing later. It was great seeing everyone come together, but I was really smiling because of how well everyone was getting along. The girls were also in a good mood and playing with the other children. We finished setting out the food and making the drinks. The thing that brought me the most joy was hearing Michael say grace. I started to tear up because it was a new sound to my ears. Hearing him pray in front of a room full of people he barely knew only made me more sure that he is the one. You can hear it in his voice and the words he chose. You can tell he is sincere and authentic. You can tell that Jesus lives inside him.

The company, the food, and the stories that were being told were wonderful. I never wanted this evening to end. There was everything—from ham to several different vegetable dishes, bread, and too many sides to name. We ate until we ended up lying on the floor, eating dessert with our Christmas sweaters on. The kids played with the toys and watched movies. It's like they had been friends forever. We adults did the same; we kept an eye on the kids while playing card games and drinking hot chocolate. We did our white-elephant gift exchange but with a twist. Everyone opened a gift, but instead of stealing each other's, we gave it to the person it reminded us of. This would teach the kids the importance of giving and sharing with others—teach them selflessness and thoughtfulness. The moon shone through the windows and faded away into the pitch-black sky. I guess that was our sign to end the evening and for all of the parents to go play Santa Claus.

"Adaire, thank you for hosting. Everything was perfect!" Virginia exclaimed. She was a lady from church and took care of everything while her husband was in the army. She hugged me tight, "We definitely need to get together sooner than later."

"Thank you for coming, Virginia! It was great seeing you guys again. Come over anytime!" I leaned down to hug the kids. "Seriously, just give me a call."

Michael and I stood at the door as everyone was heading home. We made sure they all took leftovers along with their gifts and dishes. And just like that, the only ones left were LeeAnna, Richard, and the girls. It was around eight o'clock or so, and Lucy and Isla were lying on the couch with Michael while LeeAnna and I were packing up their things.

"Wow, it looks like you had a full day!" LeeAnna said to Michael as she was walking toward them.

"It was, but also so much fun," he replied softly to not wake them as they were falling asleep. "Adaire made everything perfect."

"She is just the best. I'm glad you two are finally together." She looked over at the clock and then back to the girls. "We better head out and put these two to bed so Richard and I can play Santa."

Michael carried Lucy to the car while Richard followed behind him with Isla. They were dead asleep. LeeAnna and I loaded the trunk with everything else.

"Thank you both again for everything," she said. She paused and waved. "We'll call you in the morning!"

"We should be up early anyways. Text me anytime!" We waved as they all drove off. What a day, I thought, but at the same time, it was perfect.

———————•— —•———————

"Adaire, thank you for this. It was everything I needed. It was . . . it was all perfect, just like you." Michael grabbed my hand and pulled me in close to him. "I knew we were going to wait to exchange gifts tomorrow, but I have to give you one tonight."

"One of them?" I paused. "We agreed we weren't going overboard."

"Well, I know you. And I know you got me more than one thing too." He reached into his pocket and pulled out a black David Yurman box.

I had a shocked look on my face, not knowing what was inside. Is it an engagement ring? A necklace or bracelet? "You didn't have to do this, seriously." I reached for his hand. "What did you do?"

"It's honestly not enough. I wish I could repay you for all you have given me. But what you have given me you can't buy or see. It's intangible."

He handed me the box. "Here, open it." He smiled as he waited for me to unwrap it. "Well, go on. I hope you love it almost as much as I love you."

"Michael . . ." I froze as I looked at a gold necklace with a round pendant with an *M* and another with an *A*. "I . . . love it, but you didn't have to do this."

He grabbed the box and proceeded to remove the necklace from the box. "Here, let me put this on, only if you want."

"Of course you can. I love it! It's gorgeous." I couldn't help but blush knowing that his first initial was around my neck as I was waiting for his last.

"You're absolutely breathtaking." He kissed my forehead. "This is just a nice accessory."

"Here, I have something for you too." I walked to the Christmas tree and picked up a box wrapped in green paper with a Polaroid picture of Michael and me. "I'm not going to be able to wait until tomorrow."

"You definitely beat me on the wrapping. I don't want to ruin it." He hesitated and carefully removed the picture, then the ribbon. "Adaire, is this what I think it is? I love it!"

I had ordered him a watch a few weeks back. I picked what I thought he would like and guessed on the size. Thankfully, I could return or exchange it.

"Well, put it on! Does it fit?" I helped him clasp it around his wrist.

"It's perfect! This is a really nice watch!" He looked up and kissed me, bringing me in closer. "You really know me, don't you?"

"Well, I have my ways! I figured you wanted something you could wear to work, the beach, and fancier occasions."

"Let's not forget about impressing my girlfriend too." He winked and led me to the couch. "Let's watch a movie before we head off to bed."

We sat on the couch and watched the Hallmark Channel, one of my favorite traditions. I popped some popcorn and brought a tub of ice cream and then went back to make hot chocolate. Michael and I agreed we have never eaten so much food in our entire lives, but calories consumed on a holiday don't count. The movie finished, and I went to my room while he slept in the guest room. That was our normal and was going to be for now. We both understood and didn't talk about it much, nor did we tell other people. We were both waiting until marriage. It symbolized commitment to God and each other and represented more than anyone could ever comprehend.

———————— ·•· ·•· ————————

"It's Christmas morning!" I yelled with excitement as I woke up but still half asleep in bed. I stayed up later to fix Michael's, Lucy's, and Isla's stockings. Michael hinted he would do mine. Normally, my mom and I would make a huge breakfast, but this year it was more quiet. We had a peaceful morning and took a tray outside and ate as the waves were just starting to stir and birds took over the sky. There were flowers on the table in the living room, all the stockings were filled, and a few gifts Michael must have added after I went to bed.

We did our gift exchange before we went to see the girls. It was special and intimate; and we got the chance to talk, laugh, and spend time together. He made me go first. He bought me running shoes, a few dresses, workout clothes, and some dinnerware for the kitchen. He had really good taste, I might add, and knew what my style was. The last thing I opened was a picture frame. There was a collage of us along with the girls. It was so thoughtful, and I displayed it in the living room first thing. Michael loved all of the clothes and shoes I bought him. I had saved the book I made him for last. I titled it "Volume 1" because it was the first of many. He loved it, and we shared a long hug afterward. I had put a variety of toiletries, snacks and candy, earbuds, cologne, and other small gifts in his stocking. I loved how excited he got over the small things. I would also say he pays attention. He had put all of my favorite makeup and skincare products, some small kitchen tools, a pair of small gold hoop earrings, socks, and perfume. I sat there and realized we knew each other more than I thought. We memorized each other's favorite things and took notes. It didn't matter if we were in the store or said it out loud, not thinking the other person would remember.

Driving up to their house, I couldn't help but notice the wreaths hung on the windows and multicolored lights draped on the fence. There was a Christmas throw pillow in each of the rocking chairs along with the swing. Richard greeted us, and when we came through the door, Lucy was playing with her new dollhouse, and Isla was in the kitchen with LeeAnna. I had placed the groceries we had bought on the counter while Michael went to go and give the girls their last few surprises along with their stockings.

"Hey, Adaire, LeeAnna, come in here! I have a surprise for you guys." Michael gave us each a jewelry box. "Open them at the same time," he motioned.

LeeAnna, Lucy, and I unwrapped the boxes as Michael helped Isla. Lying in the box were matching gold chain bracelets with a dainty cross pendant.

"Michael, they are gorgeous! Thank you!" LeeAnna said with excitement as she clasped it around her wrist.

"Oh, Michael! I love it. These are so special. Thank you."

He helped Lucy put hers on. Now, all of us were matching, it was just a sentimental moment. We will now have a tangible item that will tie us together. This was the most special piece of jewelry I've ever received. Regardless of where life takes us, we will all be connected in some way.

When I went to bed that night, I felt nothing but ease. I felt the muscles in my heart loosen, and the walls I had formed started to gently dissolve. And it was then at that point that I knew I had the family I always dreamed of.

Chapter 27
POSTCARDS

The following week flew by. I wish I could freeze time. The more time I lived in Orlando, the easier it was to call home. But it wasn't the scenery, attractions, or even my job. It was the people, specifically Michael. Not to mention I had the girls, LeeAnna and Richard, a few coworkers, and my church family. I had a blank thought that if I had made a different decision along the way, I wouldn't be here. What if I listened to my parents and never left Charleston? What if I would have stayed in Miami? What would have happened if I stayed with *him?* I wouldn't have ended up where I am today. I blinked and refocused on what was in front of me, the strong winds of the ocean blowing and stirring around the furniture on my back porch.

It was Wednesday, my last day of work for a few weeks. Michael and I fly out on Friday to head to Europe. I cleared my inbox and voicemails, finished my filing, and sat through the last of my meetings. Everyone in the office knew I was going to be gone, but I opted to bring my computer anyway. There were a few things that had to be done before I left. I had to finish packing, run a few errands, and make sure we had everything so our flights were as smooth as possible.

———————◆— —◆———————

On Thursday, the only thing left to do was zip up my suitcase. I had all of my clothing sorted and organized into packing cubes, and put all of my medication and technology accessories into my backpack along with my valuable items. But most importantly, I made sure I had my passport, wallet, and driver's license. I had gone through my entire suitcase twice just to ensure I had everything.

LeeAnna offered to drive us. We were able to spend a few minutes with the girls before we were off. On the way to the airport, we stopped to grab a bite to eat and a few snacks. If you know, you know that snacks at the airport are ten times more expensive—$10 for a small package of candy? I think not. Our flights were at an off time, so traffic wasn't terrible. Normally the cars are bumper to bumper, people running red lights with no hesitation, and honking like there is no tomorrow.

"So where are you two going?" LeeAnna asked as we were pulling up. "I do know for sure—we are all going to miss you."

"Croatia, Greece, Italy, and France! We will be back in three weeks. But it will feel more like three years leaving y'all." I had to refrain from letting a tear roll down my face. "But we will send lots of pictures and FaceTime."

"Adaire and I are going to miss you guys. Don't let the girls grow up too much while we are gone!"

We unloaded the car, kissed the girls, and waved goodbye. There wasn't a huge line, but we were on the way to check our luggage and go through security. I wasn't a fan of airports. It brought back memories of the crash. It also reminded me of the last flight I took out of Miami to start over. And even though I was too young to have any recollection of it, I thought about when I was a baby coming to America.

The day I moved, I remember running on two hours of sleep the night before. How exhausted I was from being scared to sleep, class, my parents, all of it. But it also symbolized a new beginning, a fresh start, and how you never know who you are going to meet along the way. Whenever I'm at the airport, I sit and wait, and then I think of the most random topics. How about if we didn't have airports? There would be limited traveling or we would have to travel everywhere by car or boat. I sat there and weighed the pros and cons. Michael and I brought up where different languages originated from.

"If we all originated from the same place, did some random person invent the language, alphabet, and symbols?" He paused. "Who invented the names for things?"

"Good question. How did we all learn to talk in the first place?" I couldn't keep up with my own thoughts. "I wonder what the first word was."

This conversation went on, and I felt more confused than I did before. After security, we lined up to board the plane, and there were a lot of people heading to the same place we were. Michael had upgraded our seats so we would have more legroom. It was worth it, and I didn't find it too bad. This was the largest airplane I've been on, and there was an eight-hour plane ride ahead. We ate snacks, watched a few movies, worked on our computers, and took a nap. When I opened my eyes, we were in Croatia.

It was hot and humid like Orlando, but the stunning views made up for it. I felt like I was in another universe that didn't exist, kind of like Narnia. We grabbed our bags and met our Uber driver. As we were driving to the hotel, I was taking in the scenery. Most of the buildings had a charming feel to it. They kept their original architecture and details. I could just see the history and how each of the buildings had their own story. I was jet-lagged, but my mind came alive when I saw the water. The water was a dreamy blue; it was an outdoorsman's paradise. There were boats of all different shapes and colors sprinkled in the water. I felt like I was in a movie.

Time is a thief, and the week went by so fast. Korcula was heaven on earth. Our hotel was modern but still had remnants of the European style. The people were friendly, and we even had the same waiter every day who knew our order. It was only a ten-minute walk to downtown. The streets were made out of beautiful cobblestone with shops and restaurants intertwined throughout. We picked out a few souvenirs of course—everything from T-shirts to jewelry, as well as a few things for the girls. We held hands as we walked through the streets of Korcula. I felt like I was in a dream I never wanted to wake up from. The food was out of this world. I could tell they used authentic ingredients because I didn't feel sick from eating pizza for once. I could also live off gelato if we ever moved here.

"This is one of the best things I've ever tasted," I commented as I finished my last bite. "I'm kind of glad I can't eat this every day. I would gain a hundred pounds."

"Who would have thought gelato was our entire diet? We buy it at least twice a day."

"I would move here just to eat this every day. Other than gelato, what has been your favorite?"

"I love food, so everything! But pizza and pasta are two of my favorites."

"Mine too!"

———◦— —◦———

We went to a nearby beach and winery, did a hiking tour to the waterfalls, rode on a private boat cruise, and even did a walk-through of the city with a guide. It was unbelievable. There were fun restaurants on the waterfront and bars that stayed open later so we could explore the nightlife. Fun fact, they eat dinner late in Europe, so everything is open until midnight. I might have convinced Michael that we need a piece of property here because I could spend the rest of summer exploring, trying new foods, and visiting every city on the map.

But that was just it; our trip had just begun. We were off to Greece to stay in Athens and Skiathos for a week. Athens was hot, and there was no water in sight. I felt like I was in New York City 2.0. It was crammed, and there was not a lot of character in the heart of the city where most people were. There were some old churches we walked through; but for the most part, we ate at nice restaurants, did some shopping, and lay out by the pool to recover from Croatia.

"Wow, what a week." Michael nodded as he sipped his smoothie by the pool. "What's been your favorite part?"

"Honestly, all of it. I heard this quote once that goes 'It's not the journey or the destination. It's the company.' So anywhere with you!"

"I love you, and I wish we could travel together forever." He paused and grabbed my hand. "You just don't feel real."

"I love you too! And I'm already looking into more trips for later this year."

"Oh, really? Where to next?"

"Possibly a cruise. I've also thought about Switzerland."

"I've heard it's really gorgeous." He pulled out his phone. "And according to Google, it's also really safe."

"Another one of my lifelong dreams is to travel abroad on a mission. I want to build homes and churches and teach the Word of God."

"That is beautiful. I would love to go with you."

"You could even provide health care, Mr. Doctor, over there."

"Seriously, that sounds perfect. Let's do it."

"I guess we are." I looked out into the open and saw the city of Athens. "When we get back, I'll call a few of the ladies at church to see if they would be interested."

Michael and I finished getting ready to explore since it was our last night. We walked the streets where there were shops up every alleyway and a gelato shop at the end of every street. We decided to try different foods and snacks rather than a sit-down dinner. There was a lady playing the piano in the middle of a shopping center. She was extremely talented and drew a crowd of people around her. I couldn't help but notice that she had her baby lying beside her. It's like the music was mesmerizing and stopped everyone in their tracks. After that night, I thought about the woman playing the piano and how she played. Was that her full-time job, or was that something she did for fun? I wondered about her story.

The airport in Athens was busy. There were cabdrivers holding up signs, people running in both directions trying to find their way, and people even sleeping out in the open. There were places to grab food but not like in America where they have McDonald's and Cinnabon. The airport wasn't tiny but nothing compared to Miami. When we boarded the plane, I couldn't help but feel a little unsettled. I don't have a fear of flying, but I do have a fear that someone is out to get me. Ever since the plane crash and the shooting, I've been reserved. But at the same time, I am not going to let those things define me. I don't want to let my fears overcome my dreams and consume my life. It was something I had experienced once and never planned to go back.

Skiathos was a dream. I could feel the breeze from the ocean pierce my skin as I stepped off the plane. I had missed the sensation of knowing that the ocean was just a few miles away. I realized that being in Athens made me feel claustrophobic and made me miss the water. It made me think of *home*. We had to rush to baggage claim to pick up our luggage or we were going to miss our Uber. Unlike Athens, I didn't feel like I was being caved in. I could see water for miles, the people walking up and down the sidewalk, the kids wandering around. It made me think of the girls and the beach back in Florida. I was homesick and feeling adventurous all in the same breath.

There was no time once we arrived at the rental house. It had three bedrooms and two bathrooms, a full kitchen, and a pool and was just a few minutes from the waterfront. There was a sailboat waiting for us in an hour. Nothing tests your speed like being jet-lagged and having to rush. But we wanted to see as much as possible. Once we changed, I packed some towels, sunscreen, and snacks and ran out the door. It's just like we were home and are always on the move. The water was a gorgeous turquoise color and was clear, so you could see all the way to the bottom. I couldn't tell if it was five or fifty feet deep. There was not a fish in sight. The water glistened against the sunlight like it was trying to smile.

The boat went to several of the smaller islands, and we were able to jump off and swim into caves and walk along the pebble beaches. I felt like I was on another planet. It was unreal. I thought they were going to press a button and a green screen would come up and there would be nothing. It reminded me of Soarin' in Epcot. We enjoyed each other's company and talked to the people who were also on the tour. There were a few people who were local while some from the UK, South America, and even Australia. It was a unique experience getting to meet people from other countries, yet we all shared a love of travel.

It was around five o'clock when we arrived back at the dock. Michael and I didn't have any plans for the night because we weren't sure of what time we would return.

"Do you feel up for eating dinner on the waterfront?" He paused, looked at me, and nodded. "They have gelato."

"That sounds perfect. There was this really beautiful shop that had postcards. I was thinking about buying a few to frame."

"We can grab gelato, shop, and then dinner."

"You know the way to my heart."

If you've never been to Europe, they don't rush you whenever you eat at a restaurant. Every night since we've been here, we've politely asked for the check. And there was one incident where our waiter disappeared, so we had to go up front and pay.

The place we were staying at was very nice. It had a waterfront view, and I could see the entire city. It was very clean and updated but not modern. I stayed upstairs while Michael stayed downstairs. But we mostly stayed in the living room. While I was getting ready, I couldn't help but think about the girls. Even though we FaceTime once a day, it is still hard knowing I'm halfway around the world. I slipped on a yellow maxi dress and sandals. I left my hair wavy and applied light makeup so you could see the glow from the sun.

"You're breathtaking," Michael said as he cuffed the sleeves of his shirt. "I love the yellow. Are you ready to head out?"

"You look handsome. I love the white with the navy shorts." The sun on my cheeks helped the blushing not look so obvious. "Let me grab my bag."

"So do you have an idea of what type of food you're in the mood for?"

"I could eat anything honestly. When we want to grab something later, we could look at the menus and decide if it's worth a try."

"Sounds like a plan." He opened the door for me and then grabbed my hand. "So are you ready for gelato?"

"I could eat it 24/7. I can't describe it, but it's way better than ice cream."

I soaked in the walk to the waterfront. And the nightlife was just getting started. The restaurants, bars, and shops were open with people forming lines down the street. There were cars roaming around everywhere and people on scooters flying down the middle of the road. In America, pedestrians have the right to cross the street first. But here, the laws aren't as strict. People run out in the middle of the road, and there aren't as many street signs. The cops roam around rather than sit at every block waiting to pull you over. I also noticed that the people here are happy. Everyone was friendly and inviting. It felt like a slice of home.

Strolling down every street was different. Some had nothing but shops while others had restaurants. I held on to Michael's and was making the most of every moment. When are we going to be this young again walking around in Greece? Probably never, but you never know. There were lots of unique gift shops. One had nothing but magnets while there was another that was head to toe in hand-stitched bags. There were wind chimes, T-shirts, and hats all in the windows. Another thing I observed was that there was luggage in several stores. I guess they know we can't resist shopping.

As we kept looking around, there was a restaurant that had a nice ambiance with string lights and delicate music playing in the background. The food looked amazing, so we opted to stop for dinner. We had a perfect view of the water that overlooked the entire island. I wish everyone could see it. As we sipped our cocktails, the flames of the candles in the middle of the table danced to the beat of the music. Our conversation continued over dinner and into dessert as we savored every last bite. As we finished dinner, all I could think about was sleeping in the cool AC, but the night had only just begun.

On the way back, we listened to live music and walked among the crowd and just people-watched. I didn't realize how much more simple life is here. There weren't as many people on their phones or riding in fancy cars. They didn't believe in AC as much as we do. They are just present and not focused on materialistic things, and that is one of the reasons I love Europe.

The next few days consisted of the beach, walking downtown every night, and relaxing by the pool. One morning we woke up and jumped straight in and ordered room service. We lay out all day and went to a restaurant for lunch and bought every snack you could think of to try. LeeAnna also called and checked in, and I showed her the view and even talked to Lucy. She asked when we were coming home because she wanted to play and draw. This made me want to catch the next flight home. But sooner rather than later, I would be heading back to Orlando. On our last full day, we decided to do the sailboat tour again. It was just as fascinating as the first day. I wanted to bottle it all up and take it with me.

Italy and France were the perfect additions to the trip. For the most part, everything has gone perfectly.

The weather has been warm but with a breeze, except in Athens. The people were welcoming and made us feel like we belonged. All of the food was fresh and made out of authentic ingredients. No wonder people vacation and live here. I might make a phone call to have my things packed. Just kidding. It is fun to think about. Our last week was split between Venice and Paris. I felt like I walked around the world as much as we were able to see. I captured every moment and stored it in my brain.

From churches and museums to famous landmarks, we tried to hop from one place to the next. We walked most places but sometimes opted for a cab. There were lots of boat tours, so you could really see the different cities. Venice could be the cover of a magazine. The one thing about Venice is that there are no roads; you have to get everywhere by boat. Michael booked a private gondola ride down the Grand Canal. I was amazed at all of the boats we passed. It's like they were copies of each other yet unique at the same time.

St. Mark's Basilica was one of the most popular tourist attractions. Inside the cathedral was fascinating, from the walls and ceiling to all of the details scattered throughout. We were told that it's connected to the city through religion and makes up a lot of Venice's heritage. As I was observing the details, I asked myself how long it took them to build this. How much has it changed, and what have they updated or left the same?

The flight from Italy to France was smooth. I could see every cloud in the sky. I almost felt like we were floating on them and they were guiding us to our destination. I could see the Eiffel Tower from our hotel. It was taller than I expected. When we arrived in France, it was early morning, so it wasn't crowded. But as the sun started to rise, the crowds increased, and people circled around it and lined up to get their picture taken. I always wondered if people understood the meaning behind the landmark or if they were just snapping their camera because they saw it being surrounded.

"Hey, Adaire, I have a surprise for you," Michael said as he handed me the key to my room.

"Oh my gosh, this is amazing. This was the best surprise ever. How did you pull this off?"

I leaped into his arms as we left our luggage in the hall. My room had a connecting balcony to his; and on the table were a bouquet of flowers, snacks, and a note Michael had arranged beforehand.

"I have my ways." He walked behind me to the table. "Open it and see what it says. It's your first clue."

I could not help but admire the bouquet of purple flowers. The note read,

Adaire,

When I think of Paris, I think of romance and how in under a year my life has changed. It wouldn't be what it is today without you. You made me realize that tomorrow only gets better as the days pass and fade into memories that will last a lifetime. Thank you for always showing me God's love. I couldn't imagine being anywhere else, especially without you. You have done so much for me and now it is my turn. So, cheers to us! And I promise I'll tell you where we are going.

I love you,

Michael

"Michael, I love you too."

"I'm so glad you love it, but I'm taking you to the city to explore, and we are going to have a picnic in front of the Eiffel Tower."

"Let me change, and we can head out."

I grabbed my denim dress and red slingback heels and headed to the restroom. Michael headed to his room to change. I felt like a whole new person after changing out of my travel attire. I ran a brush through my hair and applied some blush, mascara, and lip gloss. Nothing makes me feel more gross than sweating with a pound of makeup on my face.

On the way to the park, we stopped at a bakery to grab a few things for our picnic. Michael had even bought a blanket for us to sit on. In every store we passed, we had to stop by and look around. I ended up purchasing some postcards, a magnet, and a jewelry dish for LeeAnna. It was a small circular shape but not a complete circle. It had different shades of blue with gold accents and white flowers. In another store, I picked

Robin up another mug for her office. She collects them on a shelf in her office, and when the time comes, she will wash out all of the dust and pour coffee in it. I can hear her say, "It saves space in my kitchen."

There was a perfect spot left in front like it was made for us. Even though there were people around us and we could hear their conversations, I only heard and saw Michael. It's like time froze and it was just the two of us. Nothing else mattered. We laid out the blanket and began eating all of the different food we picked up along the way. There was a variety of pastries, sandwiches, and candies. I felt like we were two high schoolers who were nervous and giddy like it was their first date. I know I haven't been dating Michael that long, so I hope the honeymoon phase never wears off. We took lots of pictures of our surroundings and selfies of us acting silly. I blinked, and two hours went by. That's what happens whenever I'm with Michael. I think everyone should be with someone who makes time freeze yet you feel like you need to press the pause button. Lying on and facing Michael reminded me of how we fell in love under the sun and moon and spent every possible second getting to know each other. Michael told me that he wanted to know me. Not what my favorite colors or hobbies are but why I like them. He wanted to know my heart and soul and what I desired in life. And I wanted to know the same. I wanted to know what his biggest dreams were, how he was chasing them, and what I could do to support him.

For the remainder of the trip, we took the tourist role seriously—taking pictures and Polaroids, eating at all of the recommended restaurants and shops, and spending most of the evening sitting on the blanket in front of the Eiffel Tower. We fell in love even more with every word we spoke to each other. A few feet away was a couple who just got engaged. I saw the light in Michael's eyes as it reflected my own. I thought to myself, *Could that be me one day? Could that be us?*

Chapter 28
FOREVER AND ALMOST ALWAYS

The following couple of months flew by, and I could almost see the hints of early spring. We spent the winter embracing the cooler breezes and at night would run on the beach just to feel the velvet-like sand in between our toes. The girls were growing up way too fast; it felt like we just picked them up from the airport. I never knew the definition of life before I started living and stopped existing. I didn't allow work to consume me and focused on what was important.

I still couldn't process the amount of money I had inherited. I felt like it wasn't there because I couldn't physically see it; it was just a bunch of numbers on a screen. I told myself a while back I could do whatever I wanted with 5 million dollars. So I decided I was going to fund a mission trip to the Philippines and Africa. This was going to be next year, but some of the friends I went to church with were helping organize it. The first thing was to order supplies and gather volunteers.

I made donations to local schools and food banks to feed families in need and wrote my parents a check so they could take the trip of their dreams. Lastly, I bought a piece of land right on the water. It was a few steps away from the ocean but still had a large backyard and would be finished by the summer. I had picked out roofing, paint, floors, hardware, and furniture—everything. It was just a matter of time. On my days off, I would spend time running errands and meeting with the contractors, builders, and painters. Every last detail was thought of and written down.

———◆— —◆———

It was the middle of March, and one day Michael told me he had a special date planned. All he said was that he was picking me up around six on Friday and that we were going to a nice dinner and meeting up with friends later. I really didn't think much of it because we make plans all the time, and there weren't any holidays coming up. But I felt it in my gut. Something was off. I spent the whole week at work wondering what the surprise was or if Robin knew anything. I didn't ask, but I would have been able to tell because Robin can't hide anything by the looks she gives.

Every three weeks, usually on Thursday, I get a mani-pedi. I normally get red on my toes and a neutral color on my fingernails. I was focused on so much that I just opted for my normal. Rose is my nail tech, and she does the same shape and cut every time. And she can even predict the color I want and that I like them short and oval.

I took Friday off work to meet with the builders. I was going to do a walk-through before they added paint and floors. It was hard to picture it without either, but I was excited to see the progress. When I got home, I showered and got ready for this mystery date. He said "fancy"; so I threw on a white sundress and heels, curled my hair, sprayed perfume on my wrists, then rubbed it on my neck. I put on the necklace and bracelet Michael had gifted to me, and lastly, I threw my lip gloss in my purse before he pulled up in the driveway.

A few months back, I had told LeeAnna and Richard that I was planning to propose to Adaire, and I wanted it to be a surprise. I also preferred to do it when there wasn't a holiday or birthday. She also wouldn't want to be melting in the hot sun, so I opted for the time of year when it was perfect. I had the ring designed and waiting at the jewelry store. I was scared she would find it or I would lose it. It was an oval-cut diamond with a solid gold band. It was classy and timeless, just like Adaire. LeeAnna helped me reserve a spot on the waterfront where everyone would be waiting. The Bay was an upscale restaurant at the end of the waterfront and right where the sailboat was going to stop. She didn't know, but I invited all of our friends and family to be here this weekend—our parents, close cousins and friends, and her best friend, Ellie. They would all be watching from afar and waiting. Ellie asked me how I managed to pull it off without her finding out. If you know Adaire, she figures out everything and doesn't like being surprised.

Adaire thinks we are going to dinner and meeting up with some friends. But little did she know what was coming. I made sure everything was in check. I called Robin and asked if Adaire was getting her nails done and if not, to convince her. One of the things Adaire wanted was to have her family there. I made sure everyone was at the right place at the right time. All of her family knew to unshare their location with her and, if they communicated, act like they were back home. I had written my speech; picked up the flowers, champagne, and blanket; and had a leather Bible engraved with her full name. It read "Adaire Wren Carter Bennett" in the bottom right corner. I made sure the photographers were there. One of them was disguised as a sailboat worker. The photographer on the boat laid out the blanket but hid the rest of the items to the side so I could pull them out when it was time. I wanted it to be a surprise and didn't want there to be a giveaway that it was happening. And when I looked up, I was sitting in Adaire's driveway knowing when we returned, she would be my fiancée, and nothing would be the same.

———————————

I ran out of the house with overwhelming excitement and curiosity. Michael got out of the truck and opened the door. "So are you ready to know where we are going?" He shut the door cautiously as he was placing my dress inside.

"Most definitely, I think we're going to dinner somewhere. But I know you always have a trick up your sleeve." I was all smiles. "You're all dressed up.

You look very handsome." Something was definitely up. He was wearing leather shoes, and he only wears them to church or a formal event, but I decided to keep quiet and not ask too many questions.

"Why, thank you, sweetheart. I know you always dress perfectly, and you look exquisite as always!" He ran his hands through my hair and touched my shoulder as he kissed me on the forehead.

"Well, let's get going! I'm excited."

We drove into town and farther than normal. Usually, we parked away from traffic so we could take in the scenery and enjoy each other's company.

"So here is the first surprise." He pointed to a gorgeous sailboat waiting at the dock. "We are going to take a sailboat cruise before dinner."

"Michael, this is the perfect way to end the week. How did you even book this? Normally there is a waitlist."

"I called a few months ago because I know how busy they are. And I scheduled a private tour so there won't be anyone else."

I grabbed Michael's hand and walked with ease toward the sailboat. There was a blanket spread out toward the bow of the boat. It was the perfect place to sit and take in the view. There was just enough wind to move the sailboat but not too much to knock us over. It was golden hour, and the water was glistening as you could see fish just below the service. There were even a few dolphins as we were riding up the waterfront. I could tell something was happening by the way Michael was acting. He wasn't saying much, and then he prompted us to stand up so we could take a selfie with the water in the background.

When I turned around, he grabbed both of my hands and took out a piece of paper and started reading, "Adaire, my sweetheart. When I time-travel and look back through our journey, I can't do anything but rejoice in the Lord and thank Him for letting us cross paths. This past May, my life changed forever. That was because it was the first time I ever laid my eyes on you. It was the day we had our first interaction and conversation. I saw how soft-spoken and delicate you were with your words. I saw how beautiful and classy you were. After that, I thought to myself, 'I understood why God made me wait.'

"I used to think that 'love at first sight' was overrated until I saw you. I was lovestruck. You have had my heart since that day, and it's been beating fast ever since. It's been beating for you. You had me at our first hello, the first time you smiled at me, the first time you looked into my eyes, the first time you ever said my name and 'I love you.'

"When we first met, I wasn't looking for love. In fact, I didn't know what I was looking for, but I knew something was missing. But since that day, I knew you were the perfect addition to my life. The one God knew I needed. And after our first conversation, I knew that I wanted you in my life forever. There has always been such a draw to you that I couldn't explain. We went

Chaeli Smith

from friends to best friends, and finally, you became my girlfriend. Thank you for saying yes.

"I will always cherish our relationship, and the urge to love you even more only grows with each day that passes. Now with certainty, I know that it was God who placed you in my heart—to love your joyous and ageless soul and timeless beauty. To appreciate your easy, calming, and nurturing demeanor. He knew that we would become best friends but also become each other's deepest loves other than Him. He knew we formed an unbreakable bond with Him at the center of our relationship. He knew that we would push each other, overcome trials and tribulations, stand tall and firm in our faith, and serve Him daily. He knew that we could love each other as He loves us. I thank God for the way my life has panned out because if I had made a different choice, I wouldn't be here with you. I thank God every day for you, especially your love and passion for Him and His people, your tender and servant heart, your humor and wisdom, your adventurous soul, your discernment, your willingness to overcome anything that comes your way, and your acceptance of others.

"The mystery held within your eyes still remains the same. Every time I look at you, I am reminded of all of the prayers I have prayed to find my forever person. I am reminded that true love still exists—God's love. And most importantly, that I deserved to find it. Thank you for loving me. And thank you for choosing me every day. We have gone through the heartbreak and tragedy of losing loved ones. But we have also celebrated and witnessed too many answered prayers that God has blessed us with. Despite our ups and downs, I am so thankful that we have stayed true to God and each other on His timing and direction because it has made us better and stronger. It has made our relationships what it is today.

"I believe that it is time to pour out all of the love and intimacy in my heart that I have been longing for, for so long. There is no one else that I would rather spend the rest of life with. To continue our journey. To laugh, to cry, to rejoice and worship, to serve, to mourn, and to love. Adaire, you are my very dearest friend and one true love. You are my comfort, my home, my travel partner, and the best thing that has ever happened to me, and I can't go another day without asking you this question . . .

"So, Adaire, will you marry me? Will you spend the rest of your life with me serving Jesus together so that we can walk and grow in love? Will you be my wife?"

As he finished the last few sentences, he got on one knee and pulled out a box with the most beautiful ring I've ever seen. I bent down toward him with tears flowing from my eyes. "Yes, of course, 100 percent yes." He scooped me up and twirled me around as he kissed me. Then all at once the barriers around my heart dissolved, and I was finally free.

He then pointed to the restaurant where all of our friends and family were waving and cheering. As we were pulling up to the dock, the sun was setting; and he pulled out the champagne, some of my favorite flowers, and lastly . . . a Bible with my soon-to-be new name. I couldn't even process what had happened the past ten minutes. I was so excited and filled with so much love. Part of me was still in shock.

"So do you like your ring?"

"Are you kidding? It's perfect." He held my hand as we both admired it. "You did so good."

"The minute I saw it finished, I couldn't wait to see it on you."

"And our families? How . . . how did you get them all here?"

"Let's just say it's been a few months in the making, so were you surprised?"

"You got me, but oh my goodness. The ring, the sailboat, my family, how did you know?"

"Because I know you, Adaire."

The boat pulled up to the dock, and our families were racing down. I ran to my parents first; then I saw Ellie, my cousins, the ladies from church and work, Robin, LeeAnna, Richard, and the girls. I even saw a few of the workers from different restaurants we ate at often. Everyone could hardly fit on the dock. I thought it was going to sink. But we all eventually made it to the rooftop where they had decorated it. The waiters were bringing out drinks and appetizers. I was still in complete awe.

"Ellie, I thought you were heading out of town but not here." I hugged her so tight as we were both crying.

"This was the hardest secret I've ever had to keep and from the one person I tell everything to."

"How? What? When? When did you all get here?"

"Michael messaged me a few months ago over Instagram and then talked on the phone about dates and getting everyone here."

"I can't believe you're here. How long are you down for?"

"For a week. Michael said I could stay with you, but we couldn't tell you."

"We're going to have the best time. I can't wait to show you around and take you to all of my favorite spots."

"Adaire, I love you, and I'm so happy for you! Michael is everything and more."

"I love you too. I'm so glad we get to hang out next week. I'm taking you to all my favorite shops, restaurants, and our spot on the beach."

I walked around to speak to everyone and thanked them for coming and how much it meant that they could all be here. We took photos, ate dinner, had drinks, and listened to everyone's speeches. It was fun to go down memory lane as Robin told everyone how we first met. It felt like a lifetime ago, but at the same time, it felt like I blinked and it was yesterday. The night came to an end as everyone went to their hotels or back home, and we were all going to meet at the beach in the morning.

The next morning, I received a call from LeeAnna asking if we could all get together for breakfast. So they ended up coming here, and we enjoyed staying in. This was easier as the girls got ready for the beach. I also felt like staying in my pajamas. Ellie and I started making the waffles and pancakes while LeeAnna started on the bacon. The guys were in charge of putting sunscreen on Lucy and Isla.

Once it was ready, we gathered outside and took advantage of the sunshine before it became blistering hot. We talked about wedding plans and where we wanted to go for our honeymoon. But Michael and I decided that we wanted to go ahead and get legally married, go on our honeymoon in a few months, and have everyone come to celebrate with us after our house was built and host it there.

"Well, it sounds like you two have everything figured out." LeeAnna took a long pause. "With that being said, we have something to tell you."

My thoughts were racing, my pulse elevated, and I felt like she was going to say they were giving the girls up.

"LeeAnna, is everything okay?"

"Oh yes . . . the last couple of weeks we've been talking with Robin and decided that it would be the best thing for the girls if you both adopted them. The judge agreed. You just have to come in and complete a bunch of paperwork."

Michael grabbed my hand as tears poured out of our eyes. My voice was cracking, "Are you serious?" I paused. I couldn't even form a sentence.

"From the first night we saw you two with them, we just knew it was meant to be." She grabbed my arm. "There are no better parents for them other than the two of you. We were just letting them stay at our house until you brought them home."

"Wait, really? LeeAnna, but how did you know we were going to end up together?"

"I just knew. We all did. So, Michael and Adaire, what do you think?"

"A million times yes!"

Michael nodded as he grasped my hand tightly. "Of course! This is the best surprise I've ever received."

"Well, okay then." Robin paused. "Let's get to work."

Within the next few weeks, a lot had changed. Michael and I had gone to the courthouse. This would make the adoption process more smooth. And instead of a honeymoon, we opted for a weekend trip to Amelia Island. But don't worry, there will be a reception at a later date.

Lucy and Isla moved into my house, and so did Michael. This was just until our dream home was ready. It had three bedrooms, so it was perfect for the time being. Michael sold his house and moved the rest of his things over. The furniture that there wasn't space for went into our storage unit as it waits for our new house to be built. Our new home is going to be double the size with six bedrooms, six and a half bathrooms, a master kitchen, a huge backyard with an in-ground pool, a gym, two offices, a movie room in the basement, and a playroom for the girls.

We had established a good routine with the girls, and I was able to work part-time when needed, but otherwise, I was on maternity leave, and so was Michael. I also wasn't concerned about money since I had saved so much and still had part of my spending money left over. Our routine consisted of eating breakfast, lots of playing and learning, lunch, beach time, dinner, bath, and bedtime. Some afternoons LeeAnna and Richard would stop by, and they did often. We considered them family.

Since we were home, I was able to go and work on the house. We were able to soak up sunrays any chance we wanted. Our days were filled with beach walks, swimming in the ocean and lying by the pool, another Disney trip, and spending time with friends and family. There were lots of sleepovers in the living room and watching the same three movies on repeat, but I wouldn't have it any other way. It's like my world had turned to color all at once, and I was able to see clearly.

Chapter 29
I AND LOVE AND YOU

Spring of 2027

One of the questions I ask myself the most often is "Why can't we just go back in time?" There are some moments that I just need to live through twice, while there are others I wish had never happened. But in some way, they were meant to occur. If they hadn't, I wouldn't have Michael, Lucy, Isla, and our newest addition, Elle. The past few years have flown by. But they have been exceedingly and abundantly full of nothing but straight joy.

Lucy is in kindergarten, Isla started pre-K, and Elle just turned one. Since they are all so young, I want them to remember these days and reminisce about their childhood. I work from home three days a week and have a sitter come the other two days. Michael is finished with residency, so his hours are more structured, and he is home most weekends. We see LeeAnna and Richard every couple of days, and they always know they are welcome to come over. One evening after dinner, we asked them to be the godparents; and when we did, their eyes swelled.

Lucy had started her first official year of school. She is well beyond her years and could even skip a grade. She can read fluently; recognize all her shapes, numbers, and colors; and solve some word problems. She knows her multiplication table up to 12. And we have even taught her fractions. We started teaching her the fundamentals, and she ran with it and enjoys learning. She has even taught Isla some things like shapes and colors. The girls have an extensive knowledge of vocabulary and repeat a lot of what they hear around the house. They learned the names of household items like a vacuum and mop and have picked up on how they are used. One day I went to the kitchen and pulled out the blender, and Lucy knew I was making a smoothie.

The house was finally complete. We added a shed in the backyard, a huge fort for the kids to play on, and an outdoor shower. I enjoyed the house being full and watching them play outside as I washed dishes and looked up through the window. We hosted our friends and family whenever they came to town. It was always nice being in each other's company. We talked, played with the kids, unplugged from our phones, and were present in the moment. I never take these moments when they are young for granted because the next time I blink, they will be off to high school, then college.

Michael and I sit on our front porch every evening at sunset as the girls are sleeping and enjoy talking about how our day was, what the plans are for the next day, and about our future. But it felt like yesterday when we got engaged. I remember that day. It was perfect, and we were a few years younger, still trying to piece together our future. But I also felt in many ways my life was complete. I had found the love I had been yearning for my entire life. And at the same time, we were adjusting to parenthood.

This year I had plans in place to establish our nonprofit that assists children and parents in foster care or going through adoption. This includes clothing, food, housing, transportation, and medicine. I was constantly in and out of our new office ordering supplies, meeting with families, and working with businesses to support the "why" in our organization. Aside from our nonprofit and assisting Robin, I meet with our church community to plan and help fund mission trips once a year. Every year we decide on a country and get a collective idea on our plans, resources, and budget. This lets me know that there is still hope, that there are people out there who want to know, serve, and teach God's Word. So far we have been to South Africa and the Philippines.

During the few weeks we visited each place, we reconstructed homes, churches, and schools. And if needed, we rebuilt the entire building. With the money donated from fundraising, we were able to furnish and stock what was necessary. There was a set amount for food, medicine, and clothing. Every day we would prepare a meal, play games with the kids, and teach them how to read and write. Even though they couldn't control their situation, I wanted them to know they were loved and cared for and that they were placed on this earth for a reason. God wouldn't give you a situation you can't handle. He is your backbone. He is your Shepherd. He is your light.

───────────────•─   ─•───────────────

One of the activities our days were filled with was riding in the boat and soaking up the sun with endless beach days, just like I did as a child, and whenever I look at them, I remember my childhood, and these were the days. They chased the waves as they met the shorelines and saw the magic of shells appearing then vanishing as the tide came in. We would build sandcastles and decorate them with shells. The day would fly by, and we would eat dinner on the beach and make s'mores. It was the moments like these that would remain imprinted in our hearts forever.

───────────────•─   ─•───────────────

Every year Michael and I write letters to each other, and on our anniversary, we open them. We included what we were proud of, highlights of everything that happened, what we learned, our goals, and, most importantly, how we grew with God and each other. This year specifically I highlighted all of the places we've traveled, including Japan, Switzerland, Germany, and Fiji. I was able to see just how diverse the earth is. I learned so much about the different cultures and how we take a lot of things for granted, from living conditions to the ability to have freedom. I fell in love with the world all over again. I fell in love with Michael again. I fell in love with us.

Chapter 30
ECHOES

Summer of 2037

God is like an echo. You may not be able to see Him, but He is always there. He is in your conscience, guiding you through every obstacle you encounter. So believing without seeing is a gift. It's something only a handful of people get to experience in their lifetime.

And just like that, our lives had changed. The girls grew up, and so did we. Lucy is fifteen years old and a sophomore in high school. She skipped a grade when she was younger, yet she handles everything with such grace and doesn't let it overwhelm her. Her focus is on school with hopes of going to college to become a pediatrician. She excels in academics and joined several clubs. She also plays tennis and has a part-time job babysitting. Just like Michael and me, she had a love for the ocean and traveling. We showed her the pictures from when we were younger and told her stories about the different museums and sites we visited. And of course, just like every teenage girl, she asked a million questions. She asked about the weather, the people, and lastly how we met. We told her the abbreviated version.

She knew she was adopted and that her parents had passed away but nothing more. I was also hesitant because I didn't want to lie to her either. So we told her about the plane crash and that some malicious people caused it. I could hear her heartbeat as I was sitting next to her. Whenever she asked us anything, we were transparent and didn't sugarcoat anything. But we didn't shove information down her throat or have expectations of what we wanted. Michael and I didn't want our children to feel like they had to fit a certain mold or felt like they had to make a decision that jeopardized their happiness.

Isla was thirteen and in middle school. It felt like it was yesterday and she was eleven months old, wrapped up in a blanket. But she was strong and into basketball, tennis, and painting. She didn't know what she wanted to do when she grew up. She hinted at something in business or even becoming a physical therapist. But Michael and I told her she had plenty of time and that whatever she chose, we would support her. She loved marine life just like I did. On the weekends, she would volunteer at the local aquarium. She would also help babysit Elle even though they were a few years apart, but they would never be alone. Isla loved the water, and she spent more time wet than she did dry in the summer. I would always tell her she was going to turn into a mermaid.

Elle was still in elementary school and enjoyed anything that had to do with science. She loved writing and would even write short stories for us to read at night. I couldn't get over her imagination. She wrote a story about sea animals adapting so they could live on land. It was realistic and had every last detail. Just like me, she would take her journal or iPad and write as she sat on the beach hearing the ocean in the background.

My kids are grown, and Michael and I grew up in a lot of ways together. Our marriage remained a strong unit, and we never stopped dating each other. We always made time to talk and sit outside underneath the stars like the first summer we met. We laughed and smiled more than anything. And you should when you're with your best friend. Every time we are together, it's like I time-travel back to the day we met. There is never a day where we stop learning about each other. Michael is the best husband and father I could have ever dreamed of. He doesn't let work control him. He makes time for family and vacation. He knows when the girls and I need him without us asking. Michael has a meekness about him that is indescribable. He sets the bar for what they should be praying for in a husband. He taught me that love isn't conditional or something you should have to earn. That it is unconditional and everyone is worthy of finding it despite their path. That you are worthy of a love that parallels the love God has for you. The echoes of my past have been caught and answered, revealing the darkest parts of me. But I am happy to say that I let them transpire into the air, knowing I will never have a cloud of darkness hovering over me again.

October of 2076

It has been one year without Michael. One year of figuring out what went wrong, trying to piece together what happened. And all I could think about was how I can't change anything. There was no going back or do-overs. This has become my new reality. It was a Saturday just like any other, and Michael was driving home from the mall. He had bought me a ring with all of our birthstones. On the way back, he stopped at a red light; and out of nowhere, two semitrucks hit him at the same time. I tried to get the imagery out of my mind, but all I could think about was getting a phone call, and when I arrived, Michael was lying in a body bag. I couldn't remember anything at that moment. I don't even remember locking the door or putting in shoes. I just ran to the car. When I arrived, an officer brought me to Michael. I could hardly recognize him. But through all the blood, I smelled his cologne. They didn't even attempt CPR or call an ambulance. He was gone. The medic had given me his wedding band and the ring he had bought me that day.

The girls had moved away. Isla was in Los Angeles, Lucy lived in Dallas, and Elle was closer and in Miami. I was alone as they took away the love of my life. He was the person who let me know love was out there, that it existed. I didn't get to say goodbye or tell him I loved him. Even though we both knew. Our daughters and grandchildren didn't get to hug their father or grandfather. He was so far gone that there wasn't a body to bury. Just a casket with his ashes in a wooden box. The box was from our first trip to Europe. It was a darker wood with our initials on the front along with the date we first met. I couldn't think of anything else I would want to go with him even though nothing could erase the memories we made those short weeks that led to a lifetime of happiness. Nothing could replace the time we had together.

The days were long, but at night, it was unbearable. I couldn't sleep. I had nightmares replaying every second of that day. The last words we ever said were "I love you." We had planned to take the boat out and ride around as the sun set, just like we did every night. But I couldn't bring myself to even walk out there. I had left all of his belongings where they were. I left his clothes hanging in the closet, his toothbrush in the holder next to mine. I couldn't find it in me to throw it away or bag it up, because in a way, he is still here. I know, and I believe.

———————————— ⬝ ⬝ ————————————

One stormy evening, I decided to reminisce about Michael's and my journey by digging up the time capsule we had buried. I sifted through the postcards, Polaroids, and miscellaneous items that brought me back to life as I had flashbacks of everywhere we had traveled to. And at the bottom was the scrapbook that he placed but wouldn't let me open. I remember picking it all out at the craft store and buying the stickers for it. It was a brown leather material with our initials carved on the front. I flipped through the pages as they beamed at me with fondness from the past as if it was just yesterday. There were pictures, postcards, stamps, old receipts, and even matching bracelets we made in Italy. At the end, there was a hard drive with a note that said, "Everything I wished I had told you."

I recognized the paper. It was the vintage paper I had picked out one day when we were in town. It was an off-white color with edges that looked like they were lightly burned. We used it to write our love letters. It was the paper he used the day we got engaged, what we used for our vows, and every other monumental moment. I unfolded it, and my mouth dropped the more I read.

Adaire,

I hope you're reading this far in the future and maybe I'll be gone. But all I have to say is I'm sorry. I wish I had told you. I wish I had done things differently but I didn't and now I'm here writing this letter as I am lost for words myself. But there is something you should know. I knew who you were. I knew the whole time. I knew your aunt. I knew she had two daughters. I knew. She reached out to me to protect you. To keep you safe. She wanted you to be okay. But when I saw you, everything I thought I knew evaporated into thin air. You gave my world color and life. You make me excited to be alive. I wanted to tell you but didn't want to run or think I loved you because I was told to. I didn't want you to think my intentions were malicious. But everything about me is true. And if you know one thing, know that if it wasn't for you, I would be lost. You found me and brought me back to life. You are my everything.

You are the sun in my life. Not the sunrise or sunset but the sun. You rise every day but when the world goes to sleep, you transform into the stars. Your light is brighter than the sky. And your love runs deeper than the ocean. How could I not fall in love with you?

I hope you find it in your God-given soul to forgive me. I know you will. But just know, my love for you has only grown. It is authentic and real. I know you must be slightly angry at me but I didn't want there to be a chance you would run. Because I know I would have. If I'm there when you read this, please talk to me. And if I'm not, I'll see you again one day. You & Me, Always & Forever.

All my love,
Michael

After reading the letter, it was like time froze, and I felt like my life was based on a lie. But in a way, Michael was my guardian angel and led me to the truth. I felt that my mother sent him and that she knew I needed him. When I caught my breath, I walked over to my desk and plugged the drive into my computer, only to find a video of Michael from fifty years ago. I remembered his young eyes and charming smile that made my heart pound. The video revealed that he was hired by my aunt Sonia to find and protect me. He went into detail about how she found him. Sonia had done research about doctors since they would be moving to the States and stumbled upon Michael. So when he heard about the crash, he reached out to Robin to work on it with her. Robin never knew the truth. He also claimed that once he met me, he could never tell me. And he didn't. He knew who my aunt was; he knew about Lucy and Isla. And he knew where to take me to find out the truth. This whole time, he knew. I felt hurt, betrayed, and manipulated. But at the same time, he was the love of my life and the man who helped me come out of a dark place. I was caught in a cross fire. I felt like I was being pulled in two directions leading to the same destination.

I stood there with my world spinning as if it was going to all crash down at once. Every memory of Michael that came to me raced through my brain, trying to escape. A montage with music played in my head—the first time we met, our first date, our first kiss, the shooting, our first trip to Disney World, walking through the streets of Europe, the day we got engaged, the adoption, the day we got married and read our vows, the day I found out I was pregnant, the day each of our children graduated from high school and college, and our retirement. I remembered how he smiled with his eyes or how we used to dance in the kitchen. It was all coming to me and fusing together. I fell to my knees and held my chest as my soul left my body. The lights flashed, and when I opened my eyes, Michael was standing in the doorway.